The Good Activist

THE GOOD ACTIVIST

BRONAGH CURRAN

Merdog Books

Merdog Books
The Exchange, Castle Avenue, Buncrana, Co. Donegal, Ireland
Web: merdogbooks.com
Email: info@merdogbooks.com

First published 2022

2 4 6 8 10 9 7 5 3 1

ISBN 978-1-915318-00-8 Paperback
ISBN 978-1-915318-01-5 Ebook

Typeset in Ireland by Merdog Books
Printed and bound in Great Britain by Clays Ltd, Elcograf S.p.A.

To my best friend Deborah,
Thank you for always being the activist of good in my life.

Blood is warmer than I realised. I suppose I've never really given it that much thought before. But now, it is all I can think of as it gushes through my clasped hands, oozing like lava from the source of intense, unfathomable heat. Its warmth contrasts the bitter damp air that's circling around us and through the watching trees and it is almost pleasant. Somewhere back there, in my rational mind, I know that's not the response I should be having to this situation. I know I should be screaming, calling for help, fighting to save the life I've been complicit in taking. It is so dark up here on the mountain, the blanket of city lights are too far away from our site to offer any assistance in illumination. Our fire is dying. I know that the ashes are grey, the soil is brown and the blood is red. But colour does not exist without the light to see it. They all mix together at my feet, creating a new substance, a new reality. Maybe this is how it was all supposed to end. Maybe this is my silent, irrevocable revolution. Yes. Because what are words without actions? What is light without shade? What is life without death?

Chapter 1

When I dreamed about my new life, this is not what I had in mind.

The house is in a cul-de-sac, within a cul-de-sac. Grainne literally couldn't have found anywhere more claustrophobic and contained for me to stay. I'm in Dublin to be free. There's no way I'm spending my first year in college here.

'Oh hello, you found us.' An enthusiastic blonde woman with two blonde kids in tow awaits us at the door of her semi-detached house.

'Hi Sandra, I hope we're not too late.' Grainne apologises for no reason as she gets out of the car. We didn't even give a time of arrival, so why is she saying sorry for missing it.

'Not at all we're just excited to meet Maeve, aren't we guys?' She encourages the children to speak. They just glare at me. The boy sticks out his tongue.

'I don't want her living here,' the girl says from behind her mother's legs. 'She's a stranger.'

'Now Leah, I explained to you that Maeve is not a stranger, she's a nice girl.' She looks at me and grimaces. 'Sorry, we are teaching her about stranger danger you know.'

I shake my head. 'It's fine.'

'Who's she?' Leah points to Grainne.

'Oh that's Maeve's big sister Grainne. She's just dropping her up.'

As Sandra continues to explain the situation to her daughter, I can see Grainne trying to catch my eye. She's pissed off because I've done it again.

'Actually Sandra, I'm her mam.' Grainne sets the record straight, making Sandra blush with embarrassment.

'Oh ... sorry ... yes, you did say that in your email. I must have gotten confused when I read Maeve's text, I thought she said her sister was bringing her up.' There's an awkward moment of silence before Sandra makes it even worse. 'I have to say, you look fabulous for having a daughter of that age.'

'Thanks.' Grainne ends the topic of conversation.

'So ... do you want to bring in your stuff now or after we have a cup of tea?' Sandra steps aside granting us access to the hallway.

'If it's okay with you Sandra, I'll just leave Maeve to it now, I have my own pair of toddlers at home.' Grainne's already turning away. Her duty done for today.

'Oh that's absolutely fine, sure I know how mad it is. Give me a shout if you're worried about anything. Come on so guys, let's get the cake ready for Maeve.' Sandra leads the now screaming kids inside, leaving us alone on the driveway.

'Why did you tell Sandra I was your sister?' Grainne asks as she opens the boot.

'What's the big deal, like make up your mind Grainne, you told me to call you that for the first ten years of my life.' I know it hurts her when I do it, maybe that's why I did it. There's still a part of me that wants to punish her. And she knows it. But I've already waited too long for the eagerly anticipated maternal bonds to bind us. It's too late now Grainne, you had eighteen years to make this work, a crash course in parenting on my car ride up to college just isn't going to cut it.

'When are you going to forgive me for being a stupid kid who got taken advantage of Maeve? I had hoped that being one yourself would help you understand a little better.' She lands my suitcase on the tarmac with a little more force than is necessary.

She'd better not be trying to compare what I did to what she did. Talking to someone online is hardly comparable to having sex in a Honda civic with a married 35 year old father of four during your school lunch hour. 'I only talked to him.' I mutter under my breath as I stare intently at my phone. 'And it was five years ago.'

'I don't want to fight about this again, not today. And put down your phone, can you not give whatever this week's cause is a rest just for a couple of hours? I'd like to actually have a conversation with you before you leave.' Grainne closes her eyes and inhales before opening her arms to initiate a hug. I step into them. She holds me tight and kisses my cheek.

'Love you, mind yourself.'

'Ok,' I mumble into her thick dark hair. I breathe in her scent of fresh cotton. She always smells clean, newly washed, unblemished.

'Grainne,' I say after a moment's silence.

'Hmm?'

'You know in a few months' time, when I'm settled and make new friends and that ...'

'Yeah?'

'Do you think I could get my own place to live, like a house-share?'

'I don't know Maeve.'

'But why not? If I find somewhere that's the same rent as Sandra and Michael's?'

'It's not just the money Maeve, Daddy has said he's happy to pay whatever it takes to get your education.'

'Well what then?'

'It's other things, safety, knowing who it is you're living with, that sort of thing.'

It's about control, that's what it is. They want me to live the exact same life I've lived on that farm in Ballycastle for 18 years but with a different Eircode. How am I meant to ever learn anything about life or myself if I don't get to experience new things?

I want to see things, feel things, taste and touch and transform. I want to evolve and I can't do that if I'm tethered to the inertia of my life so far.

'It's just that living with two small kids, I'm worried it will be hard to study.' I try that tack, hit her with the study stick.

'Sure that won't bother you, didn't you study for your Leaving Cert in my house with the boys.'

I didn't actually study at all on the weekends I lived with my real mother and her new family. My half brothers made sure of that, you can't really negotiate quiet time with a feral two year old and a new born. Their father, my step-father I guess, wasn't much help either. To be fair I think Declan forgot I was there most of the time, holed up in my box room, happy to use the impending exam as an excuse to spend as little time with them as possible. It had been a compromise when she married him. She wanted us all to live together as a family. But I didn't and I know he didn't either. The fifteen-year-old kid that your new wife had when she was a fifteen-year-old kid is not exactly top of most newlywed husbands' wish list. Anyway, my grandparents Paudie and Maureen are my parents as far as I'm concerned. They were there all the nights she wasn't. I couldn't just flick a switch and start calling her Mam, not just because she was finally ready to be it. And now she's landed me with the county Dublin version of herself. A perfect little family unit of mother, father and two kids under five. And here I was thinking I was getting to start a brand new life.

'Let's just see how things go okay? Call me regularly and Mam too, she's going to find it very lonely without you. Will you try to come home at least once a month? I don't want you losing touch with Aisling either, she's been a good friend to you through everything. She was always the one sticking up for you in school.' She extends me at arms' length to make her appeal.

'I'll try.' I smile, hiding my lie.

'Good girl … and give them a chance.' She nods in the direction of the open threshold before opening her driver door.

I wave her out of the driveway, taking one last mental photograph of my mother, uncertain as to when I'll see her again. I have no intention of rushing home to Ballycastle anytime soon. I'm finally out of that town where everyone knows about me but no one actually knows me.

The truth is I don't know who I am, but I know what I'm not. I'm not one of them, a parochial placeholder who only views the world through a microscope. I want to see it through a telescope, I want to see and feel everything there is out there and let it fill me up until there is nothing left of this Maeve Daly. Until there's someone new, someone better in her place.

Chapter 2

It's different in the movies. My expectations of the first week of college were formed mostly from films where the new sacrifices are indoctrinated into clubs and societies – the knowing students who will form their identity for the duration of third level education. It's not like that here, not at The Dublin School of Media. Fresher's Week, your opportunity to ease into college life, get to know your fellow first years, enjoy yourself before the work starts, get pissed, get laid, relax, don't take life so seriously. I've heard that last one a lot. Don't take life so seriously Maeve, you're only young Maeve, why do you have to worry so much. Smile. Calm Down. It will all be alright in the end. In the end? When the earth finally gives up on us and implodes in a molten pool of human soup? My grandfather had laughed and patted my head at that response, before slipping into his wellies and returning back to the yard after his 11 o'clock cup of tea. I bit my tongue then and every other time he and Nana shrugged off the catastrophic state of our planet or the injustice of minorities or the inhumanity of war and the ineffectiveness of government. All of it or none of it, they just don't get it. But I do and I know I can make a difference. And this is where I intend to start. Finally among my tribe. Passionate, like-minded people who will become the voices of the revolution, using all forms of media for the betterment of the planet. It's only been four days, I'm still waiting for the political activists, climate change protestors, refugee rights, free Palestine, feminists, LGBTQ and ethnic minorities societies to appear. I know I'm neither of the last two but that doesn't mean I can't support them or speak up for them. For now all I have to show for my initiation into the liberation of my potential is a biodegradable goodie bag containing a reusable water bottle, a book of money-off vouchers for local clubs and fast food places, a mobile phone portable charger and a condom. One lone condom. And it's not even a brand that uses sustainably sourced latex.

I tuck the bag under my seat in the lecture hall and sit back, watching the others enter from behind the shield of my phone. Two girls take the seats in front of me. I recognise them from the Introduction to Ethics lecture on Tuesday. I lean forward and place my face between them. I need to start making some friends.

'Hi, you guys were in Ethics on Tuesday right?' I say to the void between their shoulders.

'Sorry?' One of the girls turns to look at me.

'The lecture, what did you think of it?'

'Oh yeah, that,' the second girl says while scrolling on her phone. 'Awful boring wasn't it?'

'Oh no, I didn't think so.' Maybe I can help them to see it the way I do. 'I just think the entire concept is a moot point, truth, accuracy and fairness – it's the complete opposite of what's really happening in media today, isn't it?

'What do you mean?' the first girl replies.

'Well you know like Instagram accounts, it's all filters and engineered hashtag good times isn't it?'

'Yeah well that's social media, that's different to actual media,' the second girl says.

'I just think social media should be used as a platform for the truth, you know, to make the world a better place.' I stay true to my instinct even if I feel my audience is waning.

'It's not lies, it's enhanced, that's what you've got to do to make it as a blogger or an influencer,' the second girl says with increased conviction.

'Oh right, yeah I suppose.' I sigh, leaning back. Don't get

off on the wrong foot with these girls Maeve. This can't be like school, you will fit in here, these are your people. They have to be.

'Yeah, this is the Introduction to Social Media as a Marketing Tool lecture, like hello.' She's laughing at me now.

The lecturer commands their attention away from me, he scans the room without speaking before taking a fluorescent marker in hand and writing in large neon pink print on the white board.

I am a camera with its shutter open, quite passive, recording not thinking.

Someday all this will have to be developed, carefully printed, fixed.

He turns and rests his backside along the edge of his desk, steadying himself with one hand while the other gently caresses his manicured hipster beard.

'Does anyone know this quote?' He asks in a high pitched Northern Irish accent.

I look around for an elevated hand. There aren't any. Crap. Why don't I know this one, my mind is full of useful quotes I regularly pull out to support my arguments. In my Leaving Cert English I supposed my entire essay around the quote from Reverend Martin Luther King, **'Our lives begin to end the day we become silent about things that matter.'** Why couldn't he have written that on the board, I could stand and teach the class on that one.

'No one?' His voice rises even higher. 'It's from a writer called Christopher Isherwood from his 1939 novel *Goodbye to Berlin*. What do you think it means, someone shout up an answer.'

'That everything we do is being watched by someone, so try to only do good?' I get in there first.

He nods his head a little but doesn't give me the enthusiastic finger point I was expecting.

'Anyone else?'

'That we are sponges,' a guy behind me says and I wish I had said that. 'We soak up everything we see whether we realise it or not and someday in the future, all of that will come out in one way or another.'

He gets the finger point.

'Pretty much, yeah that's it.' The lecturer has now written his name on the board as Conleth or Mr. O'Mealoid if we insist on formality. 'And what do you think that quote, written 80 years ago, says about modern culture, in particular the reason we are all sat in his dark lecture hall instead of being out enjoying this exceptionally warm day here in Dublin?'

That would be the global warming Conleth.

'That we can use social media to influence people,' one of the girls in front of me says.

'Well yes, I think that goes without saying. But people aren't stupid, they know when they are being manipulated or cajoled into buying something - you have to be smarter than that now. You have to in essence, sell to them without them even realising it, without even showing them a product sometimes. Sell them the dream as opposed to the drug that puts them to sleep in the first place. Show them the idyllic family dinner instead of the frozen turkey, the feet in golden sand and not the budget airline seat sale.'

He follows his well-rehearsed speech with videos of what he deems to be near perfect marketing examples. All commercial enterprises, consumerist bullshit, convincing people they need more crap until they are buried in it. But hey, show them the grave as opposed to the shovel.

When they end I raise my hand and await his attention.

'Yep.' He points at me.

'So, is this whole module going to be an exercise in consumerism?'

He grins and I feel patronised.

'Making a profit is certainly an essential part of marketing, yes, but there are other ways it can be beneficial.'

'Like how?' I really hope I haven't made a mistake picking this course. I want to change the system, not promote it.

'The exchange of ideas, the forming of a common goal, a community, revolutions - all present on social media platforms. But even still - the bigger these ideas become the more pressing the need for corporate sponsorship. It doesn't matter if you are saving the Amazon rainforests or selling coffee made from the beans in that rainforest - everyone has a target market. And over the next nine months I'll be showing you guys just how to tap into that.' He spins on his red converse and wipes the board clean with one long stroke.

There's a missed call from Nana when I check my phone after the lecture and of course the obligatory voicemail. I must have about a dozen now all unheard since Sunday alone. I've told her a million times not to leave them, it's always just background noise of her flapping about in the kitchen or a formal verbal description of the information my phone is designed to tell me. Maeve your grandmother called, at 11.30am on Thursday. Call me back. Okay bye love, It's Nana.'

'You really balled him out of it in there, didn't ya,' someone says behind me as I'm deleting my voicemails outside the lecture hall. I look up to see the guy who got the finger point. 'But you raised an interesting question.' He's tall and broad faced, there's a country look off him.

'Yeah, you think so?' It would have been nice if he said that in there and showed a little solidarity.

'I just don't agree with you when it comes to the big bad capitalist monsters.' He laughs.

'Well it just annoys me that everything we do as human beings has to boil down to whether or not it generated a profit.'

'I can tell you one thing for certain, I'm far from generating a profit in this place for the past week, Dublin is mad expensive isn't it.'

I start to move away as he speaks and he just follows.

'I'm Shane by the way, from Galway. Where you from yourself eh …?' He lets his question linger, no doubt expecting me to jump in with my name.

'Maeve – Cavan.'

'Ah I thought I suspected another culchie in my midst, you living up here or commuting?'

We approach an external door and Shane steps his large frame in front of me to perform the chivalrous act he has been led to believe through centuries of male subjugation of women that we actually want, need or indeed desire doors to be opened for us.

'I can get that, thanks.' I make the point of pushing the door even further open.

'Oh right yeah sorry.' Shane looks to the ground but his slight embarrassment is not enough to deter him from continuing to engage with me.

'I'm in digs in Citywest, it's bloody miles out but it was all we could afford and it's close to the M4 for getting home at the weekends. I've got a bar job at home in my local to help fund me up here, what about yourself?'

He asks a lot of questions, which is par for the course I guess for a media student. 'Donabate. I'm living in Donabate and it's an absolute hell.'

'Want to get a coffee and hang for a bit, I'm not really in a rush to head off on the Luas, my treat.' Shane gestures to a coffee dock on the campus grounds. I nod and we walk in that direction.

'What you having?' Shane asks when we get to the kiosk.

'Flat white please.'

'Real milk or one of the others?'

'Real.' I say quietly, noting the queue behind us, which was pointless because Shane bellows the order in his booming west coast accent.

I let him know I'm going to grab us a seat on one of the benches dotted around the yard and leave him to it. When my flat white appears hovering in my eye line, it disturbs my You-Tube search. The seat bounces when Shane plants himself next to me.

'What ya looking at?'

'I dunno, something I can use against O'Mealoid at his next lecture.'

'Why have you got it in for him?' He tips his extra large cup into his mouth.

'I don't, I just have to prove my point that marketing doesn't have to be about money, not all the time.'

'You could show him any video of a political protest, the 8th Amendment, Same Sex Marriage, Climate Action, they're all examples of marketing being used for a common good. The organisers need to get the word out don't they, so they use social media to market the event. I bet if you search the event listings for Dublin right now you'll find some planned protests.'

I'm Googling as he speaks.

'Yeah, look this Saturday on O'Connell Street, there's a group called The Clan holding a public gathering on Climate Action.' I follow the link for more details.

'Show me.' Shane edges in to look at my phone. 'Oh I think I've heard of them, there was this massive protest in Salthill last summer about importing fracked gas, I think they were the ones organising it. I remember one fella chained himself to a lorry. I don't think he was in charge though, there was a woman leading the chants.'

'Is that her?' I hold my phone to his face to show him Ferdia Cusack, the leader of The Clan. Her face is contorted in mid chant but I can still see that she's beautiful. She is angular but not severe, pretty but not weak, her features framed by short undyed hair that is a natural blend of her once blond and now graduating silver.

'Yeah that's her, she was screaming all sorts.'

'I'm going – you coming?'

'On Saturday?'

'Yeah.'

'Can't – I've the job at home remember.'

'Oh right, yeah.' I hadn't.

'But maybe another time we can …?'

'Hmm.' I enter Ferdia's name into the search box in YouTube and watch as the feed floods with images of her.

'… Do something.' He continues to speak.

'Yeah, sure.' I stand up and drain what's left of my flat white. 'Thanks for this.' I say as I shake the empty disposable cup and throw my bag on my back.

'You heading off now?' He half stands off the bench and I gesture him to sit back down.

'Yeah, got to catch the train, see you tomorrow?' I wave and make my way to the front gates of the college, my pace fuelled not just by the three shots of caffeine but the incentive of a 30 minute train journey with quality WiFi to watch YouTube videos.

Chapter 3

Platform 7 in Connolly Station is fast becoming my least favourite place on earth. Even now, when it's so sunny that I can't take off my sunglasses, it's a strip of shaded gloom. The grey metal seats separating it from platform 6 are cold against my bare legs, the overhead canopy having starved them of any of the day's warmth. I suppose I should be grateful I have a seat. On Monday and Tuesday I made the mistake of hanging around the city after college and put myself right in the middle of commuter rush hour. I had thought all trains in Dublin were the DART, the fast and frequent service that services the city from coast to coast. But no, I'm living so far out the DART doesn't go there. Instead I'm on the Drogheda train, teetering on the edges of the border of Dublin and Louth. Once an hour on weekdays it leaves this platform and chugs along the rail, getting further and further from civilisation. At least I've learned my lesson not to attempt my journey between the hours of 5pm and 7pm. It's just gone 2pm now and its quiet here, just a few mothers with buggies and retired older people heading home to the place that retired older people are supposed to live. Not me, not someone who wants to immerse themselves in the lifeblood of the capital, mould myself into its structures and contribute to its national grid of energy and ideas.

I stay seated when the green and blue train comes to a stop and releases the doors, letting the mothers and pensioners get on first. I know there'll be seats anyway. I take one by the window and put my ear buds in before opening my saved videos in

YouTube. The WiFi automatically connects and her voice travels up through the wires and into my brain.

'Be the change you want to see in the world.' She stands over a sea of heads in a city street.

'People will try to convince you that you can't make a difference, that one person can't possibly make a difference. But when I look out here today, at all of you who have come out to fight, I don't see just one person, I see hundreds. And hundreds of people can make a difference. So you know what I say to those people who try to tell me that we - you and me - can't make a difference?' She awaits the anticipation of the audience before answering, their energy rumbles below the platform.

'I tell them … maybe you haven't met my friends.'

The chants of the crowd are so loud the volume rings in my ears. Her face changes from anger to joy, lighting up from the response to her words. Arms hold up painted signs over their heads and voices begin to chant. 'We are your friends.'

The footage shakes, no doubt recorded with a smartphone by a now singing and swaying member of the crowd. Ferdia holds up her own sign high above her head. It says FRACK OFF! in bold black paint, a silhouette of a hand giving the middle finger next to it. The video ends then in a blur. I let it roll onto the next one.

Grainne's face appears at the top of my screen, blocking out the banner hung behind Ferdia's head as she faces the camera. My WhatsApp messages come through now that I have WiFi, the only benefit of Sandra and Michael's coverage being so patchy is that she can't keep track of me all the time.

Ring Mam back. You know she worries when you don't answer your phone.

Busy. At college. I text her back

It's the first week, I doubt that. Ring her.

I mute her messages and return to the video of Ferdia being

interviewed for a news segment. She's standing in what looks like a building site, scaffolding all around her, the only colour visible among the grey is her orange and red sign that reads BUILD HOMES NOT HOUSES.

The interviewer asks her what that means and she tries to explain it to him.

'The government no longer build homes, they build houses, commodities to be bought and sold, a product, a price tag, a chain around a person's neck strangling them in debt until they slowly die.'

Not quite understanding her reason for protesting at the site, the reporter asks what she hopes to achieve exactly.

'I hope to achieve humanity Brian. Isn't that something we should all be hoping for?'

He doesn't get it but I do. My signal goes as the train passes under the bridge into Malahide station and I look out the window for the only pleasant part of the journey, crossing the viaduct to Donabate.

My attention is back on my phone when I reach my stop and I keep my eyes down as I walk from the platform up the concrete steps and over the bridge into the village. In the supermarket I pick up some instant noodles and pasta. Sandra will place a meal in front of me tonight at 7.30pm as per the €90 a week arrangement, but if the past three nights are any indicator, it will be inedible. I use the self-check out and throw the food into my free biodegradable bag.

The estate is still, void of life until the workers get released. Dutiful dogs and suspicious cats sit on window sills and on the back of couches, watching me as I pass on my way to the end of the cul-de-sac. The alarm beeps as soon as I open the door and I panic for a moment that I've forgotten the code. I haven't. It's the girl's birthday. I wonder if that means she's the favourite. Her pink plastic toys block my path to the kitchen so I push them to one side. The kitchen is the only room in the house where the

WiFi coverage is consistent. I prop my phone on the counter and set up another video as my chicken noodles start to simmer in the saucepan. This clip is a less official one, just Ferdia and some other members of the group sitting in a garden, talking about climate change and what lifestyle changes they are making to reduce their carbon footprint. They are all smart and well able to put their point of view across without getting upset and frustrated. I always get upset and frustrated.

'I've stopped throwing away clothes just because something's got a hole in it or it's not in fashion at that particular moment in society's perception.' A guy with thick shoulder length, golden red hair says as he places one of his slim legs on top of the other, exposing his pale white knee through the slit in his jeans. He squints in the sun as it catches him in its spotlight, glowing him up like when we used to put buttercups under our chins as kids, casting a yellow reflection onto our bemused, innocent faces. A loud beep makes me jump a little and dribble some of the watery chicken broth down my white t-shirt.

A message from Aisling.

Hey missus, how's college life up there in the big smoke? When are you home in The BC? Wanna FaceTime?

I put my phone down for a second, not really sure of my response. Do I? Don't be that girl that moves to Dublin and ditches her old school friend who stayed at home, even if you will never understand their choice. I select the little camera icon and await Aisling's smiling face to appear.

'Aaarrrrggghhh.' She squeals and her shaking head blurs on my screen.

I laugh and catch sight of myself in the bottom left hand corner. My hair looks shit. Maybe I should cut it, short.

'I miss you!' Her round face settles on the screen, her pink cheeks indicating she's been exerting herself.

'Yeah, I miss you too. What are you doing?'

'Like right now?'

'Yeah, where are you?'

She turns the camera around and I see the place I'm trying to forget.

'Oh you're up town.'

'Yeah, I have to get stuff for my lunch tomorrow, we're going on an observation to a calving. Can you believe that, on the first week they're going to shove us face to face with a cow's vagina?'

'Well, I did warn you but oh no, you were certain veterinary nursing at Cavan College was for you, so enjoy the moo moo's foo foo.'

'Oh, I might say that tomorrow to Elaine, she's our agri lecturer, she's gas craic. What are your crowd like up there, c'mon tell me all about the media, is it all fake news and dopes posing with products on Insta?'

'I'm trying hard not to judge it too soon, but, yeah it might be.'

'Ah come on Maeve, I'm only saying that coz it sounds like something you'd say. Remember why you put this course at the top of your CAO form, to make a difference, to use your voice. Stick it out and you'll love it in a couple of weeks, trust me. Oh fuck, there's Cian Hanly.' Her attention is pulled and she holds the phone further away to share the scene with me.

'Hiya Cian.' She shouts.

'Ais,' he mumbles.

'Did you see that?' She turns back to me.

'See what?'

'The look he gave me.'

'No, I couldn't see detail or anything Aisling.'

'Thank God he didn't leave the town, at least getting to look at him every now and again softens the blow of you abandoning me. Are you home on Friday? We could have a Netflix night at mine, catch up properly.'

'Eh, no sorry I have something on up here in Dublin.'

'Ah big shot now are ya?'

'It's kind of related to a college module research.'

'I'm only messing, sure maybe next weekend?' She pauses and it takes me a second to realise she's actually expecting an answer.

'Yeah, yeah maybe next weekend. Sorry Ais, I have to go, Nana is trying to call me.'

'No bother bud, say hi to Maureen for me. Mind yourself up there.'

'I will. Enjoy your date with the cow tomorrow.'

'Oh Jesus.' She laughs. 'Okay bye, bye … bye.' The screen goes green.

I put my bowl and saucepan in the dishwasher, leave the kitchen as I found it and head upstairs to my room.

My solitude is disturbed by the bang of the front door, followed by the rapid tapping of small feet on faux wooden floorboards, then the screams. I cover my head with a pillow, already knowing how useless it is to combat the lung capacity of Leighton and Leah. She's crying now and Sandra is shouting at Leighton for doing whatever he's done to his little sister. He shouts back and something hits a wall.

'Michael,' Sandra calls for her husband's backup. 'He's after throwing his tablet against the wall.'

'What do you want me to do about it?' Michael's voice is further away. He's probably trying to hide in the downstairs toilet.

'Put him on the naughty step, he won't do it for me and I'm trying to get the dinner started, I can't do everything.'

'Leighton, buddy, you can't be doing that, that tablet cost Santy a lot of money last Christmas.' Michael's at the bottom of the stairs now, just below my room.

'I don't want it, I want one like Leah's.' Leighton squeals through his tears.

'Well I want a lot of things too but sure look, we're stuck with what we're stuck with in this life.'

'Huh.' The five year old stops crying.

'Tell you what buddy, if you sit here for five whole minutes, I'll give you a biscuit before your dinner, just don't tell Mammy.'

'Will Leah get a biscuit?' Leighton's voice is chipper now.

'No, just you, so don't say anything okay?'

'Okay.'

'Good man.' Michael's footsteps travel in the direction of the kitchen to retrieve the promised bribe I assume. He returns with the biscuit and Leighton is silent until his mother comes to release him after his sentence has elapsed.

'Are you going to be a good boy now?'

'Yeah.'

'Are you going to say you're sorry?'

'Yeah.'

'And be nice to your sister?'

'Yeah. Sorry Mammy,' he whimpers.

'Okay, go on in and watch telly with Leah. Maeve – are you home?'

The unexpected calling of my name jolts me and I sit upright in my bed.

'Yeah, I'm up here.' My voice sounds weird in the cocoon of my room.

'We're having chicken kievs for tea, they'll be ready in about half an hour. That okay with you?' She shouts up to me, even if there really is no need. I can hear her from every room in this paper walled house.

'Yeah, that's grand, thanks Sandra. I'll be down then.' Can't wait.

The mirror in the bathroom is lit by a stark fluorescent strip that I don't usually turn on. Why would anyone want to see their pores up close? But today I'm finding it useful. I tilt my head from side to side, up and down, searching for a flicker of silver that I am certain to be there. Separating sections through my fingers I take a picture of my parting. Maybe if I can apply the right filter my natural greys will show up from wherever they are hiding in my long boring brown. I know I'm attractive. I'm not oblivious to how the world sees me physically. But it means nothing to me, unless I can weaponize it. No one ever changed the world looking like a reject from a dry shampoo ad. Ferdia's beauty is not for the male gaze. It's more a celebration of nature, like a colourful bird or a majestic glacier. As if she just sprung up like a February flower, but the kind that breaks through the concrete of the footpath to find the light. That's the kind of beauty I want.

Chapter 4

My heart quickens as I navigate my way through the zombiefied Saturday morning shoppers on Talbot Street. I'm too early, it's only 11.40am and the protest isn't due to kick off until noon. I can't be the first person there, I don't even have a sign. I didn't prepare one for fear of writing the wrong thing. I need to hear Ferdia's speech before I can decide on my opinion on the issue. The information on the event guide was sparse, just time and place and general climate action vibe but that could be a thousand different things. I've brought some A3 sheets of paper and large felt tip markers to make just the right statement at the right moment. The Spire reflects the strength of the September midday sun like a lighthouse flashing its beacon, calling all ships to shore. Guess that makes us the ships, me and all the others who are giving up their Saturday morning to try to do something meaningful to save the planet, to undo all of the mess our parents' generation have made.

I pass the statue of James Joyce where a man has set up a speaker and box platform so he can preach the second coming of Jesus Christ. Shoppers stop momentarily as he shouts at them, promising hell and damnation if they do not repent, or go back to mass, or stop fornicating or exercising bodily autonomy or whatever panacea he's peddling. No one pays much attention to him and they are right. His sermon isn't going to help them now, not when the world is literally burning beneath our feet. What fear does his threats of hell hold when it's already happening all around us, insidiously boiling everything and everybody like the ignorant frogs in a pot we are.

I take a left on O'Connell Street and enter the Starbucks. The queue stretches the length of the shop and I'm glad of it, it will help kill some time. Drinks here aren't cheap but holding one of their cups with my name on it and walking through the city kind of feels like a membership card. I was a Hicksville bogger that thought a takeaway coffee meant fill your own from the machine in the local petrol station shop. Now I'm a student in a diverse multicultural European capital city. I know what all these different coffee types mean and I know which ones I like. Asking for an Americano just sounds better than a black coffee, even if I do add quite a bit of milk. I take a picture of my cup with my name spelled correctly, positioning it on the wooden self at the window, making sure to capture The Spire in the background.

#CityLife #BestCoffee #FuelForTheRevolution

Aisling likes it straight away. She must be online right now, probably stalking Cian Hanly. She needs to get some more important interests in her life. I perch on a stool and watch as a few people start to gather on the large traffic island, forming an awkward alliance. Too soon to join. There are two middle aged women with rain jackets tied around their waists stopping, are they there for the protest? Not exactly what I expected. Oh that's more like it. A group of three guys and four girls cross the street and join them. They all look like students, just maybe a bit older than me, and like a promotional ad for Irish diversity, each one representing a different ethnicity and culture. All are carrying boxes which they set down on the island in the middle of the city's main street. As they put together their sound system more bodies join them. A few older people but mostly students like me. I should get out there before Ferdia comes, I don't want to miss anything she has to say. My coffee is still half full and hot so I take it with me across the street.

The green man finally beckons me over and I nervously plant myself next to a girl that looks like she's in control, assembling flags and signs. She has a perfectly shaped shaved head and flaw-less dark skin. Graduating silver loops travel along both of her ear lobes. She clocks me and turns back to her flags.

'Sorry, are you one of the organisers?' I try to sound like I belong here.

She stays hunched but turns her head back towards me. 'Yes, are you here to take part? Her voice is a melodic blend of central Africa and inner city Dublin.

'Yes, if that's okay?'

'Of course, everyone is welcome here.' She smiles.

'Great.' I shake my bag off my back and try to look as busy as her. 'What do you want me to write on my sign?'

'Whatever it is you want to say about our wasteful consum-erist culture.'

'Okay, thanks.' I take a sip of my coffee.

Her eyes narrow at me as if she's trying to focus. 'You might want to get rid of the disposable paper cup from the coffee con-glomerate first though.'

I stiffen as I look down at my hand. The shame flushes my cheeks. Before I have time to mumble some sort of futile apol-ogy, she returns her attention to the preparations and the other protestors. All the other people who didn't just make a complete show of themselves. Shit. Shit. Shit. The nearest bin is across the street so I dodge the No. 13 bus and cyclists to save time. When I turn back I see they have formed a tighter circle, all focusing in the one direction. She's here.

The wall of people around her is holding firm and I can't find a way in. Above their heads I see her rise, elevated on a platform in the centre. Her head and shoulders seem so slight, like her body is not big enough for the energy it contains, somehow. Her thin bare arms are toned and tanned and she lifts them rhyth-mically to raise her crowd in a rousing clap. Her mouth con-trols a smile and instead expands to produce a roar. I don't think it's something I've seen a person do before. Kids screaming, yes plenty. Lads shouting, drunk or from the side-lines of the Gaelic pitch. Girls squealing for all reasons and none. But an actual roar, wild and guttural and visceral. That I've not seen before. Then the rumbling starts, a vibration that lifts me and stuns me stiff. The sound is almost beyond hearing, the collective roar of those gathered at her feet. I must be the only one of the 100 or so of us here that is too slow or too inexperienced to respond.

'You are all looking at me.' Her voice is clear and sharp. 'Because I am the one up here on a wooden box, holding a microphone. Did you all just come here to look up?'

We all continue to do just that, no one offers an answer to her question.

'You are focusing your attention in the wrong direction. Look around you.' The mic echoes. The heads move.

'What do you see? Is this all so normal now that we have become incapable to see the absurdity of what we have become? The cyclical scurrying to get more, buy more, consume more - when will it be enough? When will we stop taking and start giving?' She pauses as if to give us time to fully observe our surroundings. 'The constant ebb and flow of people carrying paper bags full of their purchases, rushing to the next shop and the next shop to get just that one more thing. These are the things we need to live.' She recaptures our attention. 'Air, water, food, shelter, love. How have we relegated these in preference of fashion, technology and greed. How can we happily watch images of our homeless, starving, dying brothers and sisters on our €800 smartphones. Have we lost our humanity? Can we not see the real price we are all paying for this insatiable need to consume more? The buck stops here.' She raises her arms skywards and our eyes follow their direction.

'All around us. In the air, the water, the food - in all the things we actually need to survive. The price is being paid here, by the planet. It cannot cope with the demands of our lifestyles, our corrupt, unnatural greed. We are killing it. All for our Saturday morning shopping sprees here in our fair Dublin city.'

'Shut the fuck up you crusty cunt.' An angry male Dublin accent cuts through her speech. Our heads turn in search of its source and disembodied voices shout out in retaliation and defence of her.

'Don't, don't give it oxygen. That is something we cannot spare. I am more than prepared and willing to take whatever abuse comes my way. No one likes to be told that their way of life is wrong. But you have to be strong enough to continue to say it.'

We cheer and this time I am ready.

'When it all comes down to it, you have to ask yourselves what are you?' The rumblings of traffic and the conversations of people passing fill the void of her silence. 'Are you a citizen of the society, or are you a citizen of the planet?'

Our arms and voices rise in solidarity with her and then a chant begins, led by the beautiful shaved head girl of the coffee cup incident.

'YOU CAN'T BUY ANOTHER PLANET!' She calls out in a staccato rhythm. We repeat it, louder and with more intensity. Signs are raised now, bobbing overhead. Crude paintings of Earth dripping in red paint, another in a ball of orange and yellow flames. Enlarged images of cities being flooded, polar bears balancing on a tiny iceberg, scorched, arid ground and a burnt out rainforest. I watch Ferdia's eyes as they scan each one, her heart shaped face reflecting her satisfaction with the efforts of her followers. I am completely invisible, hanging on the periphery, sign less, purpose less, pointless. The chant evolves into a foot stomp and a hand clap. All of the extra motion pushes me further and further from the circle. My feet lose their purchase on the island and I slip onto the street. A taxi speeds by and I push myself back up. Cars slow to a stop as the red light demands it, allowing a stream of bodies to cross over to Henry Street, the city's busiest shopping street. No one here would even notice if I slipped away with them, joined the uninformed masses in their mass consumption. I have to make them notice me. Otherwise what is the point of me even being here? How am I different to those people heading off mindlessly to the shops aside from the fact that I don't actually have any money to spend in them? A car horn blows in my ear and the crowd hollers in response, taking it as a sign on unity and endorsement. I need to get the traffic to make more noise.

Crouching down on the edge of the kerb, I unroll the sheet of hard A3 paper from my bag and select just one of my markers, red. In large letters that stretch from one side to the other, I write the word STOP. There is a natural lull in the oncoming traffic and people wander across the street in crisscross patterns, not bothering to use the pedestrian crossings. I join them and walk into the centre of the street, stopping to face O'Connell Bridge, the GPO on my right side. A few passing faces turn in my direction as I come to a dead stop, but no one in the assembly has noticed, they are still focused on Ferdia as she leads a new chant of CLIMATE ACTION NOW!

A bus is approaching on the inside lane, a taxi is coming up behind it on the Luas tracks. They seem much further away than I initially thought when I raised my arms high over my head and held up my stop sign. The piercing sounds of their horns carry on the wind. I close my eyes and allow my feet to take root, rigid with fear on the concrete. The taxi swerves around me, the driver looks out the window calling me all sorts of names. The bus being a lot less agile, is forced to come to a stop as the driver leans on his horn. More cars pass me by on the left lane as I hold my ground in the centre.

'Get out of the road.' The bus driver shouts out his window.

I keep my gaze fixed in the distance. The horn sounds again

in a long, persistent bellow. The bus driver continues to shout and curse at me as he looks behind, planning his manoeuvre. The passing cars ignore his request for an opening in the lane as they focus on getting past me themselves. I shut my eyes. My heart is pounding and it's only now, at this moment that I think maybe I could actually die doing this. This could be my final moment. Please don't let it all be for nothing. Trembling, I open my eyes to the looks of frustration and contempt towards me. Still holding my sign firmly, I turn my head back towards them, my heart pounds again. This time in elation. All eyes are on me. All bodies turned in my direction, watching, waiting for what I will do next. Even her. I have her attention. It's worked. I have to hold on to it. I drop my sign to my chest, just as the bus manages to overtake me, the faces of the annoyed passengers blurring into one big ball of fury. Another lull but I see the Luas coming over the bridge. I have more time. I lower myself to my knees, placing one hand out to rest it on the concrete tiles. I allow the rest of my body to follow it and lie perfectly flat across the tracks. Voices are all around me but I can see only sky. It is clear and blue, only the slightest scattering of cloud. A bird enters my vision and exits it.

'What are you doing, you'll be killed.' A man says as he walks by.

'I'm protesting,' I shout in response.

'You mad bitch.' His voice moves further from me.

The wheels are getting closer and I can hear the loud beeping of the tram has already begun. I close my eyes and hold up my sign, willing it to work as my only means of self-defence.

'Come on, there's a Garda coming,' a clear voice says close to my ear. She's next to me, hunched down at my head. She stands and extends her hand to assist me up. I reach out to take it and let her guide me back to the safety of the island. The traffic speeds by us.

'That was quite the test of commitment, you okay?' Her eyes

are so light blue they are almost grey and the edges crease when she smiles at me.

I nod my head and pat down the back of my dirty leggings.

'I'm Ferdia' She offers her hand again, this time for me to shake it.

'Maeve.'

'You out here often Maeve? I've not seen you at one of our demonstrations before.'

'No, I've just moved to Dublin, so not very, you know, familiar with everything.'

She takes a black tin water bottle out of her canvas bag and offers it to me. 'Here, you must be a bit worse for wear after that.'

'Thanks,' I say as I take the water, realising only now how dry my throat is. Fear can bring on a thirst.

'Hey, Zamara, come meet Maeve.' Ferdia draws the attention of the beautiful shaven headed girl. She walks towards us.

'Yes, we met.' Her face remains unchanged as she acknowledges me and swiftly returns to the rest of the group.

'Oh good, so now that you already know two of the Clan, you only have another four to meet.' Ferdia smiles.

I look around at the gathering of over a hundred strong, still chanting and holding up signs and handing out leaflets to the public.

'But aren't they all your followers?' I shift awkwardly under the weight of her focus. Not sure what to do with my hands, I clasp them and hold them loosely as if in relaxed prayer.

'I don't like to think of anyone as "my followers" Maeve. These amazing, awesome people came out here today because they believe in the message, not the messenger. I mean, that's why you're here right, to be part of the solution, to fight for what's right, not to listen to just one middle aged woman shouting in the middle of O'Connell Street. That's just the method, not the aim.' She keeps her eyes set on mine as she speaks and

I notice she's also holding her hands in silent dedication. Good, that means I don't look stupid.

'Hardly middle aged.' I say before realising that's probably the least important part of what she just said.

Ferdia laughs and lays a soft touch on my shoulder.

'Well, I'm approaching 40 Maeve so yes, quite middle aged if you consider the average life expectancy of an Irish woman. But thank you. And if we continue to destroy the planet at the rate we are, what will our age matter anyway, right?'

'Right.' I'm not sure if I should laugh, was she making a joke? I can't risk it.

'So you'll come then Maeve, yes?' Both hands rest on my shoulders now, pulling me in closer to her. I can smell lemongrass.

'Where?'

'To meet the rest of the Clan.'

'They aren't all here?'

'No, we tend to divide and conquer. The guys are staging other demos all over the country today.'

'Oh and then you all get together at your meeting to make plans and that?' Insightful Maeve.

'Oh no.' Ferdia shakes her head and her asymmetrically longer strand of hair on the left side of her face falls from behind her ear. 'We live together. So we can do that all the time.' She looks behind her.

'Hey Zam,' she calls out. 'Do you know if everyone is going to be around on Monday night?'

'Yes, Aide and Eimear will be back from Cork late tomorrow so we should have a full house on Monday, why?'

'Great, Maeve is going to come by and say hi, aren't you Maeve.' She turns back to me.

'Eh, yes, yes I'd love to.'

'Wonderful, give me your number and I'll send you the address. The house is in Donnybrook, you know it?'

I don't. 'Sure, just let me know what bus or train I need to get and I'll find it.'

Ferdia smiles and looks at me like she's waiting for me to continue speaking. 'Oh sorry, I thought you were joking. Sorry. You can walk to Donnybrook from here Maeve, it's only about 30 minutes. I'm sure you don't use a carbon footprint when you can use your own do you.' It's a statement, not a question.

'Of course.' I nod and smile broadly.

'Here, put your number in.' She hands me her phone.

'Hey Ferdia.' Zamara reappears at her side. 'The Garda wants to talk to the person in charge.' I can feel her eyes on me as she speaks, causing me to fumble with my number.

'Okay, on my way. So, Monday Maeve yes?' She holds out her hand and I place her phone into it.

'Yes.' I say before I watch her return to the centre of the circle where a beleaguered looking man in a navy suit and a high viz jacket is waiting for her.

Chapter 5

The study hall is almost empty at 5pm on the second Monday of term. It's just me and one other guy who has huge headphones on and is annoyingly tapping his fingers on the desk in rhythm to whatever awful music he's listening to. Even Shane passed up my invitation to spend the hour with me researching activism videos to dissect their effectiveness in messaging and engagement. He had seemed interested in hanging out with me again when I suggested it after our Audio Production class but then suddenly remembered some important thing he had to do when I filled him in on the details. It doesn't matter anyway. I only have to kill another half an hour here with tapping boy. Then I can start making my way to Donnybrook. When I put the address Ferdia had sent me into Google Maps, it said it was a 52 minute walk from the campus. I don't want to look like a loser and turn up too early, but it would be even worse if I were late. So best to give myself plenty of time. I text Sandra to tell her not to keep dinner for me. An added bonus of my visit. I'll splash out on a burrito on my way home. I wonder how long they'll keep me there and what will they think of me. I know already that I'll like them. If Ferdia likes them then so will I. The finger tapping has escalated to tuneless humming so I gather my things into my bag and loudly bang my chair against the desk as I get up.

I take the route along the Grand Canal. It's still sunny and the scenic way will slow my pace. God this is so much nicer than having to traipse to Connolly station to board the soul crusher express to the hinterlands. The trees rustle in the soft breeze above me and the ducks and swans sail by my side. I pass couples sitting on benches, their bodies almost fused together they sit so tightly to one another. Cyclists and people on scooters use the bike lane alongside me. We all move along so easily, like blood cells along an artery of the city. Along the edges I can make out collapsed canvas tents, half hidden behind bushes. Tonight they will provide whatever safety and security they can to their homeless owners. A girl just like me is sitting on a bench and I suspect she's one of them. She has that look, like she's perpetually cold or in pain, her back arched. Her hands are in her pockets and her long red hair falls over her thin face, shielding her from my gaze. I only realise that I must be staring when her eyes are alerted and focus into mine. I'm uncomfortably close to her, as if I've approached to give money. But I don't have any.

'Sorry,' I mumble awkwardly as I quicken my pace away from her and take the right turn Google Maps instructs me to. I can hear her respond in my wake so I don't slow down to make out the words. Tomorrow I'll find her and give her some change so she won't think I'm one of them, the establishment. The kind of people who live in these huge stones houses that I'm passing that I can't imagine are home to just one family. They must all be apartments. The houses continue like this all the way to Donnybrook village. My directions lead me through the main street of posh food shops and cafes and onto Belmont Crescent, a pretty street of red brick terraced houses. You have reached your destination.

I'm still ten minutes early, should I walk around the village again and come back at 6.30pm on the dot? Yes, I think that would look better. I turn away from the black metal gate with the intention of retreating down the path. My awkward movement is compounded by another set of feet coming towards me, slowing to a stop. I lift my head to follow the feet to legs and body and face. I feel a flicker of recognition.

'Oh sorry.' He smiles as he shifts from one side to the other.

'Are you going in?' He opens the gate and gestures my entry before his.

Well now I have to. 'Yes, thank you. I just wasn't sure this was the right house.'

'Who are you looking for?' He takes a small bunch of keys from his tight black jeans pocket and walks the three concrete steps up to the white wooden door.

'Ferdia, I'm here to see Ferdia.' I sound shrill in my head. He takes off his sunglasses and tucks a wing onto the opening of his black shirt. The sun causes his icy blue eyes to squint as he looks at me. He extends a slender, elegant hand. The kind of hand you could picture playing a piano.

'Oh great, you must be Maeve. I'm Aide, well Aiden but everyone calls me Aide. Come in.'

He looks different than in the video I saw of him in the garden. He has a beard now that is a slightly darker shade of red to his hair, which is tied back off his face in a bun, exposing the shaved underside. I can see where the late summer sun has been colouring his delicate skin on the nape of his neck.

'Maeve.' My name rings out in the thickly carpeted hallway, drawing my attention from Aide and towards her as she glides down the stairs. She is wearing a long white dress with yellow flowers on it that continues for three steps after her. Her arms outstretch to greet me and before I speak she has enveloped me in an embrace. Her lemongrass scent strengthens the warmth of her welcome.

'I see you've already met Aide.' Her left arm extends to grab him by his wrist, halting his departure. 'He's a spectacular person Maeve. The things this young man has taught me.' She looks at him as she moves her hand around his until they are intertwined.

'Don't listen to her Maeve.' He breaks her gaze to look at me. 'We're all just trying to match up to this woman here.' His eyes return to her. 'I just have to go upstairs for a bit, then I'll come down for the gathering, okay?'

'Of course,' Ferdia says, raising her hand to cup his bearded jaw gently. He moves away from us and up the stairs, pausing on the second step to look back at me. Ferdia's attention is fully on me now, both hands clasped on my upper arms as she speaks, words of welcome and gratitude. I try to focus on what they are but my concentration is pulled to the image behind her head. The graceful turn of his toned back, tight beneath his shirt, his shoulders in my direction. I can't be sure if he's smiling but I know he is looking. He is looking at me. And there is disappointment when he stops and continues up the stairs.

Now that he is out of sight I can take in the rest of my surroundings. A large dark wooden cabinet sits to my left, topped with candles, picture frames and what my grandmother would have called knick knacks. The walls are a deep orange, like the colour of autumn leaves just before they fully give in to their winter fate. The carpet is patterned red and blue and leads all the way upstairs on the left and down to a lower floor on the right. Ferdia steps to her right and ushers me into the first room along the hall.

'Thank you so much for coming Maeve. I hope you found us okay.' She presents a red plush armchair for me to sit on. There are lots of chairs in here, a large green floral sofa with colourful blankets draped across it, a smaller cream one with large yellow velvet cushions, a brown leather recliner chair and a huge black bean bag with a sunken centre that looks like it could swallow a person whole. They are surrounding a low wooden coffee table that is almost entirely covered in papers. When I sit, the dust mites that are displaced dance in the sunlight that's streaming in through the large bay window looking out on the street.

'Yes, it was easy, this place is so close to town, you're so lucky,' I say nervously as Ferdia opts for the brown recliner opposite me.

'I am lucky, this house was my grandmother's. She lived here alone for the last forty years of her life. I always thought it was such a waste, you know, when so many people could enjoy the same benefits she did.'

'So you rent out your spare rooms?'

'Rent?' She shakes her head slowly. 'No, we share a home, that is all. I have no albatross of a mortgage around my neck so why should I impose the shackle of rent on them.'

I nod, starting to understand that these people are living here for free. In walking distance of town, in this massive house. I wonder if they all have their own rooms.

'That's very kind of you,' I say trying not to break her eye contact and give in to my urge to look around the room at all the posters, paintings and objects sitting on various pieces of antique furniture.

'It's not kindness Maeve, it's instinct. It's the natural way of things, the distribution of wealth … Ah Zamara, come in and sit down.' Ferdia looks to the door behind me, her eyes widened by the appearance of the girl from the protest.

'Hello again.' She offers her hand to me and I'm relieved to see a sincere smile on her face. Don't overthink the coffee cup issue Maeve, there is no reason for her not to like you.

'Hi, nice to see you again.' I stand and sit again almost instantaneously. She takes a seat on the big green couch.

'Seb and Posey are on their way,' she says to Ferdia who responds with a knowing nod.

'Great, well let's wait for everyone to arrive before we start getting to know Maeve.'

'Would you like a drink Maeve?' Zamara asks. 'Or something to eat?'

I'm starving but there's no way I'm making a nuisance of myself asking for food so I settle for a tea.

'Milk and sugar?' Zamara asks as she passes me heading for the door.

'Just milk please.'

'Tea, Aide?' I hear her from the hallway.

'If you're making some of that rooibos I'll go in for a cup, thanks Zam,' His voice gets louder as he approaches the sitting room. I sit up straighter when he enters.

'Sorry about that guys, just had to change my shirt, I spilled fabric stiffener all over myself in college.' He rolls up the sleeves of his clean cream linen shirt as he sits on the sofa, revealing tapestries of colourful tattoos on both arms. Ferdia doesn't speak so I fill the silence.

'What do you study Aide?'

'Fashion - at the Institute, special interest in sustainability and eco manufacturing. What about you Maeve?'

'Oh, just media. I'm a first year at DSM, so not sure if it's what I really want to do.'

'Don't worry, you'll figure it out. I'm in my final year now but it took me a while to get there, I took a few years to explore myself and the world.' He runs a hand down his beard to the point under his chin, his eyes travel to the wall as if in reflection.

'And that's why you are the person you are today Aide,' Ferdia offers, causing him to blush. The soft pink in his cheeks offset the maturity of his dark auburn beard, making him an intriguing blend of boy and man.

'Tea.' A cup appears floating in my line of sight.

'Yes, thank you Zamara.' I take the hot cup in my hands, there's no handle. I try not to show that this confuses me. The tea is darker in colour than I usually like it. Cautiously I take a sip. It's boiling hot and slightly sweet.

'Oh, I think I might have gotten one with sugar,' I helpfully suggest to Zamara as she presents Aide with his cup.

'No, just soy milk, as requested.' She affirms.

'Oh, yes - my mistake.' Shut up and drink it Maeve.

The front door opens and I hear the sounds of two people,

one male, one female. They bound into the room still in full conversation. He has an American accent, hers is Irish but with a hint of something Eastern European maybe.

'Hey clan.' The short girl with long straight blonde hair and brown eyes greets us as she lays her bag on the floor. 'Oh, we have a new one.' She waves at me and I reciprocate, looking like an idiot no doubt.

'Maeve, this is Posey and Seb, two more valuable members of our clan,' Ferdia says. 'Guys, this is Maeve, the girl who lay in front of the Luas for climate action on Saturday.'

I'm bolstered by her introduction and suddenly don't feel so self-conscious here among them. Posey shakes my hand enthusiastically before Seb, who is over six foot and broad shouldered with wavy jet black hair and thick rimmed glasses, follows her.

'Oh, we have heard so much about you Maeve,' he says in what my limited knowledge would indicate is a west coast US accent. They take the cream couch and I wonder if they are a couple. Zamara has placed herself next to Aide, does that mean they are a couple?'

'Sorry I'm late everyone.' A low voice fights to be heard amongst the rising chatter of the collected clan. All eyes turn towards the door.

'Eimear, you're home. Great, now we can get started.' Ferdia stands to greet the newest member of the party, who also happens to be the least intimidating to me. She looks like me or at least a version of me, country bred and country fed.

'Sit down next to Zamara.' She guides Eimear to her seat. 'Now.' She sits down and places both hands out flat on the armrests. 'Maeve, why don't you tell us all about yourself.'

I take another sip of my sweet tea, the cup acting as a momentary barrier between my face and all the expectant eyes that are on it.

'Well,' I begin, resting the cup on my lap. 'I'm Maeve, Maeve

Daly. I'm 18, 1st year media student.' I glance at Aide because he already knows this about me. I'm from a town in Cavan called Ballycastle, my friend Aisling and I call it The BC, she thinks it's because it sounds gentrified but really it's because it's prehistoric.' I laugh a little allowing them the space to join me. They don't, so I continue. 'Eh, what else. I have a ...'

Ferdia raises a hand and I stop speaking. 'How about you tell the guys about Saturday and what motivated you to do what you did.'

'Yeah, of course, sorry.' I can feel my face redden. 'Well, all I did was stand in the middle of O'Connell Street, then I laid down for a bit before you came over and got me.' I nod to Ferdia and she sits forward, cupping her hands together and resting them on her knees.

'Yes - but Maeve - what was it that I said that sparked such a reaction in you? Or was it me at all, was it something else that fuelled you?'

I can feel the look of uncertainty hitting me from the direction of where Zamara is sitting.

'Your speech was so important and it just made me angry that people were ignoring it, just carrying on with their mindless shopping. I had to do something to make them listen.'

'You don't believe that if you talk long enough and loud enough that people will listen?' Zamara asks.

'Yes.' Aide adds. 'If you apply enough pressure over enough time, eventually you will achieve what you set out to do, no?'

'But what if we don't have the luxury of time?' I respond. 'What then?'

'Then you do something else, right Maeve.' Ferdia backs me up.

'Right, I mean, there's a time for words and a time for action and I just felt at that moment, it was a time for action.'

'Well I think it was fucking awesome,' Seb contributes

to the collective.

'Weren't you scared though Maeve?' Eimear asks, her accent is flat, most likely lower midlands. 'I'd have been shitting myself, some of those taxi drivers would run you over standing up let alone lying down.'

'I was a bit scared, yeah,' I confess to her and she gives me an encouraging smile.

'Of course you were.' Posey reaches across the divide of the cream sofa and my armchair so she can rest her hand on my knee. 'That's why you were so amazing, it's not brave unless you're scared. Right guys.' She looks around the circle. 'Remember that time I broke into the mink farm, I was terrified, that guard dog took strips off me.'

'Show her your leg Po.' Seb nudges her.

She lifts the fabric of her wide legged trousers to expose the flesh on her calf, a distorted red half-moon of scar tissue clearly visible on her pale skin.

'You're so committed,' I say, touching her battle wound reverently.

'They all are,' Ferdia says proudly.

'We learn from you,' Posey defers.

'Thank you Posey but I just support the power for good that's already in each of you. So, what do you think Maeve?'

I look at their beautiful, interesting, alive faces and feel the better for being reflected by them.

'I'm just so happy to finally meet some people who give a shit about the state of the world as much as I do. I'm blue in the face lecturing people back home about climate change and social injustices and the tightening grip of capitalism on our socialist state. I had thought I'd find some like-minded people in college but it's full of vapid robots and the next generation of promo models.'

'Oh, promo models aren't all bad.' Aide gives me a quizzical look. 'Not if they're endorsing sustainable products.'

'Eh, yeah, I suppose. ' I back track, I don't want to disagree with him.

'Aide, stop teasing our guest,' Ferdia says while keeping her eyes on me. 'Maeve, how would you like to help us out with something?'

I don't need to ask her for any further details.

'Yes, yes of course. I'd love to.'

Chapter 6

I'm in such a good mood this morning that I'm making an extra effort to be nice to my classmates and embrace my college course.

'Hey, what are you eating?' I lean over Shane's shoulder after I take the seat behind him in our Writing for Print and Digital Media class.

He jumps a little, not expecting an intrusion into his breakfast.

'Sausage and black pudding roll with red sauce,' he replies without a hint of embarrassment. 'You want some?' He thrusts the bread and flesh combo up to my nose.

'Eh, no thanks, it's disgusting. Do you have any idea of the carbon footprint of that sandwich?'

'Carbon footprint - is that like how many footsteps I'll have to take to walk it off or something?' He turns to give me a bemused look. I can't tell if he's taking the piss.

'I'm serious, you should swap it for something more environmentally sustainable like free range eggs and avocado.'

'Avocado?' He says in a high pitch. 'Oh you mean the avocados that grow out in Blanchardstown, freshly picked this morning?'

'Well, it's better than meat products.'

'Is it though Maeve, is it really worse than the air miles clocked up to deliver your avocados from Mexico?'

'I don't have the exact figures on me.' I look around for something to shift the conversation into a more favourable light for me. At first they are just a shiny distraction, then their usefulness becomes clear.

'Are they car keys?' I try to sound casual about the over accessorised bunch sitting between his iPhone and his large takeaway coffee cup.

'Huh?' His eyes leave mine to look at the desk in front of him. 'Yeah, why?'

'That's very handy for you, what with you going up and down to Galway at weekends.'

'Yeah, I wouldn't be able to do it otherwise. I don't use it much up here though, it's cheaper and easier to get the Luas.'

'Oh, why are you driving today then?'

'I'm signing out a camera from the AV lab, so didn't want to chance carrying it on the Red Line.' He turns his torso fully around in the seat to commit to the conversation.

'Probably a wise decision.' I give him an agreeable smile. I can't be sure but I think he likes me. He's fine, there's nothing awful or disgusting about him. He's just not the type of guy I'm looking for. But there may be benefits to his friendship. His transport being a very present and pertinent one at this moment.

I take my time packing up after class, giving Shane an opportunity to walk down the stairs before me.

'Hey, are you planning on going to that libel talk in the library later?' I ask as I step slowly behind him.

He stops to wait for me. 'Well yeah, it might come in handy for a journalist to have some sort of handle on libel laws, don't you think?'

I scrunch up my nose. 'I just think it's a bit soon to worry about it. We're only two weeks into the first term and libel laws change all the time, it's pretty uncharted territory what with social media and GDPR and God knows what other factors will be in play by the time we actually graduate.' I can see I'm making sense to him.

'So, do you have a better suggestion of what we should do with our afternoon then?'

'I do actually.' I hold open the door to the lecture hall and wait for him to exit.

'Oh yeah, what's that then?' He grins.

'How about we go for a drive, make the most of having your car in today. I don't know about you but I'd kind of like to see a bit more of this capital city of ours apart from the railway line to Donabate.

'I've not seen that myself but I can pretty much guarantee you it's better than the Luas from Citywest.'

'That's sorted so.' I slap his broad country shoulder. 'Go get your camera signed out and meet me at the main gate in fifteen.'

It's been over twenty minutes already and I'm wondering if he's chickened out and went to the lecture. He strikes me as a bit of a lick arse. My detour to the art supply room only took me a couple of minutes. They didn't make me sign out the pair of craft scissors and tin of red spray paint. I just told the guy it was for a marketing project and that's not really a lie.

'About bloody time.' I shout as I see him lugging a camera bag up the footpath.

'Sorry, I couldn't find the charger.' He looks contrite as he nears me. 'I'm parked just around here.'

I follow him all the way to his silver three door hatchback parked on a tree lined street.

'How do you actually fit in this car?' I try to take in his frame and that of the vehicle.

'Go on take the piss all you want, she's reliable and easy on fuel so I couldn't give a damn about what she looks like.'

I feel an instant hit of shame. Of course I shouldn't judge his car by how it looks. I should judge it on its fuel economy and CO2 emissions.

I ask just that as I sit into the passenger seat.

'I haven't a balls notion Maeve.' He says as he starts the quiet, tinny engine. 'Are you really obsessed with all of that or are you just trying to be cool?'

'Trying to be cool? I'm trying to save the planet.' I click my seat belt and roll my eyes at his assessment of me.

'Well thank God we have you is all I can say. Can you take a break from saving the planet to have a look on Google Maps there and tell me where it is you want to go.'

'Can I use your phone? My battery is almost dead.'

'Only if we can do a quick selfie to mark our first day out exploring Dublin.' He snaps it before I have time to oppose. 'I'll tag you on Instagram.' He says before passing his phone to me.

I place my own phone on my lap and open the message Ferdia sent me last night. A name and address. I type it into the search box on Google Maps. It's not far from here, just a fifteen minute drive, so I think a detour is called for before we fulfil the mission.

'Let's head for the city centre and then down the Quays and towards the coast. There's a nice village called Sandymount near the beach.'

'A walk on the beach?' Shane takes his eyes off the road and glances over at me.

'It's just a suggestion.' Jesus don't be getting romantic ideas, that is not on my agenda. Not today anyway.

'No, no, I like the plan.' He turns on the radio and presses buttons until he finds something he likes.

'Right, well take the next left then.'

We follow the slow moving traffic through Leeson Street all the way to St. Stephen's Green. Shane asks me if I want to stop to have a walk around it but I can't really be bothered. Not today. I direct us down Kildare Street and past the government buildings of Leinster House, Gardaí in their fluorescent vests surveying the people coming in and out of the gates.

'That's where you'll be in a few years Maeve.' Shane says.

'Hardly, they are all corrupt idiots in there.'

'Well even more reason for you to be in there, someone who is passionate about what they believe in and is willing to stand up and be heard.'

I take his compliment now that I know it is one. Actually it's probably the best one I've ever received. Does he really see me? Well in about thirty minutes he's going to witness just how right he is.

'Oh I think that's Trinity College in there.' He points to a high wall straight ahead.

'Google Maps confirms.' I say.

'Want to stop and have a look around in there, see where we really should have gotten in?'

'Hmm, not really, let's keep going.'

'So is there anywhere in the city you actually want to get out and see?'

'Sure I can do that any day when I have no choice but to walk. I want to enjoy the rare luxury of being driven around.'

'That's grand so, I'll just be your sexy chauffeur for the afternoon.' He attempts and fails an alluring wink.

'You can be my unpaid taxi driver, take a left here and we'll go down the Quays.'

Shane is talking a lot. That much I know. His voice is sucking all the oxygen out of the cramped car cabin. I feel like I can't breathe. I open the window and let the rushing air hit me. The noise it brings also makes it harder to hear Shane's rambling. He just turns up his volume. I reach my hand into my bag that's resting on my lap, fingering the tin and scissors, reassuring myself that they are still there, that I am still going to do this, that Ferdia will be pleased when I tell her it has been done.

'Maeve,' he shouts.

'What?'

'What turn? Quick!'

'Eh … right.'

'Fuck, I missed it. Ah well let's just keep going straight and see where it takes us.'

'No,' I say a little louder than necessary, 'I want to go to

Sandymount, this is rerouting - it says take the next right.'

'Jesus this Sandymount better be the Salthill of the East, that's all I can say.' He laughs and I pretend to be also amused. We're just five minutes away.

We pass beautiful houses on narrow tree lined avenues where elderly people walk slowly along the paths on their way to or from the village. It opens up before us, a picturesque square with a park in the centre. A supermarket, cafes, chemist, a pub, a corner shop and then there it is, the name and address that has led us here. Sionnach Boutique.

'So I think we need to take a left to get to the beach.' Shane pokes his large head into my eye line to look out the passenger window.

'Yeah, can you stop here for a minute. I just want to get something in the shop.'

'Sound, will do.' He indicates to pull up alongside the path.

'You can keep the car running, I won't be long,' I say before getting out and slamming the door behind me.

The shop looks expensive, the kind of place I would never set foot in. The kind of place my grandmother has probably never even seen in her life. Thick wool coats, silk dresses, sparkling shoes, bags and jewellery all screaming excess from the front window. And there nestled among all the supposed beauty lays the chemically treated pelt of murdered animals. The lifeless carcasses of God knows how many mink were skinned to stitch that monstrosity together. And what kind of monstrosity could wear it?

Two of such people are already in the shop when I enter. Running their heavily fake tanned hands over the garments on display. I'm glad for them, they are keeping the retail assistant busy, asking inane questions about shades of purple and designer labels. She doesn't ask me if I need any help. She probably thinks I'll take one look at a price tag and bolt. I'm not exactly her usual clientele I'd imagine. The coats are hanging on a rail to my left. White and grey, thick and durable, the protection that Mother Nature intended mutated into some barbaric statement of complete and utter contempt for life. I unzip my bag and take out the scissors, keeping my eyes across the shop floor. The assistant still has her back to me. With one swift snip, I remove a chunk of one of the sleeves and shove it into my bag, taking the can of spray paint out in its place. I have to be quick, the second I press the release, the noise and smell will have all eyes on me. I take a step back from the rail and closer to the door. My heart is thumping. I can't believe I'm actually doing this. The can shakes in my hands they're trembling so much and I worry they will hear it, but their attention remains on each other. Just do it Maeve, do it now. I press the nozzle. Chemicals sting my nostrils, red paint fills the air in microscopic dots like blood splatter at a crime scene. They land onto the once living fur of hundreds of tortured mink. I make my best possible attempt to form a C shape across the coat.

'Oh my God, what are you doing?' The sales assistant shouts as I run out of the shop and across the street, not looking for traffic. I hear a car beep and voices coming after me. High pitched howls of anger. The noise attracts Shane's attention. He looks up from his lap and gives me a startled look as I plunge into his car.

'DRIVE.' I scream at him.

'What the fuck.' He fumbles with the ignition.

'Now … GO … just fucking go!'

He slams his foot on the accelerator and the tiny car screeches its way out of the village, almost hitting the furious sales assistant as she reaches us in time to bang an open hand on the bonnet. I'm breathing so heavily I can't hear anything else, just the sound of my lungs and heart operating at their full capacity. Shane speeds towards the coast road, he breaks a red light and cars beep. A woman with a push chair jumps back in fright.

'What the hell did you just do Maeve?' he says slowly and in a tone I've not heard him use before.

'I just righted a wrong, that's all you need to know.' My voice sounds disembodied to me.

'Did you steal something in there?' He starts to slow down a bit and takes a right turn off the main road.

'Well if you consider this theft.' I pull out the piece of fur sleeve from my bag.

'What is that?' He looks at it and me in confusion.

'It's the pelt of animals that they are selling as fashion, don't tell me they aren't the criminal ones here Shane. I'm just letting them know we won't stand for it.'

'Well you might have let me know you intended to use me as a getaway driver in a fucking crime,' he raises his voice and it shakes me a little.

'I didn't want to get you involved, this was my mission from The Clan.'

'Not get me involved?' He repeats my words. 'Are you mental? How much more involved could I be now?' He stops the car abruptly. 'Get out.'

'What, here? I don't know where I am.'

'Get the fuck out of my car … now.'

'I don't know why you're being such a fascist about this Shane. Do you agree with fur farming … is that it?'

'You're a headcase.' He looks straight ahead, done with the conversation.

'Shane, wait,' I call out over the revving engine.

He turns his head reluctantly. 'What?'

'Can I just use your phone to check Google Maps?' I smile.

He turns back to the road and drives off, leaving me some-where in the Southside of the city.

Jesus what an overreaction, it's not like I asked him to come in and distract the shop assistant or do any actual damage. Off he goes now to Citywest, fuelled by his righteousness and fury. The privileged white man directing his anger at the woman who is just trying to scoop the rising water out of this rotting wooden boat.

'Excuse me.' I stop a woman as she jogs past me. 'Am I close to Donnybrook at all?'

'Yeah, just go straight down to the end of this road and onto Ailesbury, then the village is just there.' She places her ear buds back in after barely coming to a complete stop.

I thank her and keep going. Each step closer intensifies my anxiety. What if I had picked Ferdia up wrong when she told me about the shop and what they were selling. After Posey had told me about her mission to free the mink, they began discussing this awful boutique in Sandymount that had just put a real mink fur coat in its window display. Posey had broken down in tears when she cycled past it the other day. Retelling the story brought out some more tears. Ferdia had rushed to her side and cradled her head in her hands, then she looked directly at me and said, 'Someone should do something about that shop, don't you think so Maeve? Someone needs to show them that the Clan will not allow for the torture of animals.'

I had nodded along, of course. Then when I was at home in bed in Donabate her text had arrived.

'Sionnach Boutique – Sandymount Green. Leave a mark from us.'

That part gave me cause for celebration. Am I already part of the 'us'? Well if I wasn't last night, I sure as hell hope I am now.

I find the house from the village, even though I've come in the opposite direction. My stomach knots and my pulse quickens as I lift the heavy brass knocker and wait. Nervously I fumble around in my bag, clutching my trophy.

'Maeve – what a nice surprise.' Her thin grin widens as she begins to understand what she's seeing.

Outstretched on my offering hand, I present her with my trophy, my spoil of war; the piece of liberated animal fur.

Chapter 7

Ferdia pulls me closer to her, simultaneously embracing me and dragging me into the hallway.

'Come with me,' she says quietly as she floats down the steps, leading me to a basement extension on the original house. She opens a glass panelled door to reveal three people sitting around a small round table. The room is painted a burnt orange on the bottom half of the wall, a discoloured aged white on top. There's a disused tiled fireplace with candles in various stages of demise in the grate. Books are stacked on the open shelves and on the desk to my left where a PC and various technical equipment cover every inch. The heads turn and I recognise Posey, Eimear and Seb. They are drinking matcha tea and sewing something long, all working on the one piece. They put their needles down when we enter.

'Guys,' Ferdia says. 'Maeve has something to show you.' She gives me an encouraging nod and I do as she suggests, placing the fur in the centre of the table.

Posey releases a sound, like a tyre letting out air. She holds her hand to her mouth and pushes her chair away from the table. I've disgusted her, she's horrified by my presentation of a dead animal, like a cat dragging its kill into the kitchen in an attempt to impress its owner.

'I'm sorry.' I look to Ferdia for my next move. She shakes her head. I do nothing.

'From that awful place?' Posey asks from behind her hands. I confirm.

'Sit down Maeve, tell us what you did.' Eimear gets up to pull a fourth chair from across the room. I take it. Ferdia continues to stand.

'Well after I cut this off, I sprayed the rest of the coat with a huge red C,' I inform my audience.

'Holy shit.' Seb slams an enthusiastic fist on the dark wood table with foldable sides. 'You didn't get caught?'

'No, not exactly, almost I mean. The sales assistant made it to the car after me and gave it a good bang.'

'You drove?' Eimear asks.

'No, my friend, a guy from college, drove me.'

'Oh my God what a legend, he is so evolved to help you. What a true friend of the planet.' Posey finds the reserves to speak now.

I smile and elect to allow her misconception of Shane to remain intact.

'Tea?' Seb offers and I accept. He walks into what appears to be a tiny kitchen at the other end of the dining room. He returns with a cup. I sip the strange green liquid and will myself to look like I'm enjoying it.

'So how did it feel, your first mission?' His expression is open and warm and I feel instantly at home around this table.

'At first, on the way there, just anxious that I would find the place and actually have my shit together to do it, then when I was in there I just felt numb, like I was watching someone else holding the scissors. And when it was happening, I don't know how to explain it – like alive.'

Ferdia's hand squeezes my shoulder from above and the three heads nod in unison.

'I'm sure I don't have to explain that to you guys, you must feel that all the time.'

'Yes,' Ferdia adds. 'But the first time is always special.'

The others mumble words of agreement. Posey reaches her hand across the table, resting it gently on the fur. She strokes it and begins to cry, quietly. Moving from my side to hers, Ferdia lays a reassuring hand on her shoulder.

'We couldn't save these creatures, but we will save the next, have faith Posey.'

Her blonde hair falls in front of her face, obscuring her tears. 'Can we have a ceremony?' She asks through her veil.

'What a lovely idea.' Ferdia's voice rises. 'Seb get the spade from the shed. Eimear will you get the sage from the cabinet and met us in the garden. Come with us Maeve.'

I stand along with the rest of them and wait until they pass me on route to the back door. I complete the procession of what I can only presume is a burial.

Without discussion, Ferdia and Posey stop at a centre point in the long rectangular garden. I follow them along the paving slabs and step onto the slightly overgrown grass. A concrete wall separates them from their neighbours, a suspicious ginger cat stops on her journey along it to survey us. Clothes of muted hues hang behind us on a line that stretches the length of the garden, an eclectic selection of chairs and wooden crates surround us.

'Maeve, here.' Ferdia reverently hands me the piece of fur. 'It is only right that you commit the mortal remains of these animals existence to the earth.'

I hold it as I would a wafer of Holy Communion at Sunday morning mass. Seb appears at my side and strikes the earth beneath us with a sharp blow of the spade. Ferdia and Posey keep their heads bowed and their eyes closed. So I do the same. A warming, comforting smoke fills the air around me. I breathe it in deep. Its presence is followed by Eimear's voice.

'With this cleansing sage I banish all negative forces that met these souls on their journey. In this new clear path of their spiritual awakening, may they be surrounded by only love, light and everlasting peace.'

I instinctively whisper Amen as she stops speaking and my cheeks flush with embarrassment when I realise I'm the only one who does. The others respond in a low, throaty humming, it's almost a sound that has to be felt instead of heard.

'Maeve.' Ferdia places a hand on my lower back. I take it as an instruction to put the fur into the hole Seb has just dug. I look to her for further instruction and she urges me to speak.

'Mmm, I'd just like to say I'm glad I did something to stand up for your rights to dignity in both life and death. And that I'm sorry I wasn't there to save you when it really mattered.'

I cast my eyes to my left to gauge her reaction. It's good, she's smiling. Seb loads some soil onto the spade as Posey begins to add words to the humming. Something slow and lamenting in what I assume is Polish. I make an attempt to join in the humming. When the final pat of the spade is made, I'm gathered into a group hug. As much as I'm enjoying the scent of lemongrass and the warmth of Ferdia and Eimear's bodies either side of me, I feel the natural moment to release pass by. I can't be the one to break the circle so I commit to it, for however long it takes. A shadow casts at my feet and I can sense a body behind me. Before I have time to react, another hand wraps around my waist, it's firm and confident. There is a brush of hair against my shoulder, tingling and sending little shocks down my back. I create just enough space to look at who has just taken the place of Ferdia at my side. It's Aide. He brings a scent of firewood to the mix, as if he's been infused with smoke and oak. I inhale him deeply.

'What are we doing?' He whispers into the gathered bodies.

'A ceremony for the mink.' Posey explains.

'And for Maeve,' Ferdia adds, releasing her arms from Aide and Seb, breaking up the bond. 'I'm glad you're home, we have something to discuss as the Clan. Maeve, you understand?'

'Oh of course.' I register her dismissal. 'Should I go?' I point to the back door and take a retreating step.

'No, please - just take a seat in the living room. We will come find you when the time is right. Can someone get Zam on Face-

Time,' Ferdia asks the others as she walks and takes a seat at the top of the garden. They all follow her as I stay still for a moment. Aide looks back as he walks and smiles at me. His hair is loose and brushing his shoulders. He runs a long slender hand through it. He shines in the sun. They take their seats around her. I go to find mine, alone in the house, to wait for whatever it is they are planning for me.

It's so quiet in the large front room on my own. In the silence my ears are focused on a gold carriage clock, ticking from the mantelpiece. I sit down on the same red chair I had sat in the night before from the same perspective. My curiosity to see it from the other positions brings me to the cream sofa which is a little hard and unyielding. I move to the green one opposite, placing myself where Aide had been, imagining how I might have looked to him across the low coffee table. Next to me, the brown leather chair entices. I stand and will myself to sit down into the groove she has made, but something stops me. Fear or respect, I don't know, but I remain standing. How long will I be waiting here for them to join me? For something to pass the time, I investigate the things on top of the sideboard, a huge heavy piece that takes up almost all the back wall. Lifting candles to my nose and intricately detailed crafts to my eyes. I try to soak up as much of their lives as I can. A wooden statue of an African tribal warrior loses his spear as I disturb it from its location on the surface. The narrow spear rolls along the polished wood and slides into the waiting crack of the drawer underneath. My heart stops briefly when I think I'll have to scramble on my hands and knees to relocate it in the thick pile carpet. I place my hands under the slightly open drawer and drag it out slowly, trying to control the noise of heavy wood on wood. Inside is neat and organised, not at all like the drawers at home that are jam packed with bits of crap that my grandfather insists we'll be glad of some day. The tiny spear is resting on the distinctive maroon vinyl cover of a passport. When I carefully retrieve it, I notice it's not just one passport but a stack, tied together with a rubber band. I wonder if Aide's is in this pile, I could find out his age. I know he's been in and out of college so he's a bit older than me but not too old. I still myself so I can listen out for activity in the hallway. It's silent. I release the band and check the first passport. It's Ferdia's, she's 38. I hope I am as cool and beautiful as she is when I'm that age. The next one is Zamara Bangura, she's 25. Then Posey, whose real name is Przemysława Sajdak, she's 22. Sebastian Gutierrez's is blue, American Citizen, 23. Then his, Aiden Dunleavy, 23, his face is clean shaven and his hair is short, he looks so much younger. I prefer him now, he looks like he's seen and done some interesting things. There are two more in the bundle. Eimear Walshe, 20 and another girl who I've not heard of, Hannah Fox, 19.

The sound of a door opening and closing at the other end of the house prompts me to return the passports to their positions with the rubber band and the drawer. I close it as quietly as I can and slip myself onto the nearest seat, the cream sofa. I take my phone out of my pocket and try to look engrossed in it.

'Maeve.' Ferdia enters first. 'Thank you for waiting so patiently.'

'Oh no problem, I barely noticed the time.'

They all take their seats around me, Ferdia in her chair of course, Aide next to me, his leg is touching mine. The small couch causes both our bodies to dip towards the gravitational pull of the centre.

'Sorry,' he mouths as pressure increases against our legs.

I try to say don't be, but I don't think words come out, just a combination of head shakes and mumbles.

'So Maeve,' Ferdia says once all the Clan, except Zamara, are seated. 'We would like to talk to you about joining us, how do you feel about that?'

'Me?' I say like an idiot. 'You want me to join the Clan?'

'Well, yes of course, why else do you think we gave you a mission?' Ferdia smiles.

'I just thought maybe you asked everyone you meet to do things for the planet or animals or whatever social injustices you're concerned about.'

'We kind of do.' Aide nudges my side and looks at me from the corner of his eye. 'But just the special ones actually do them.'

'We think you're fantastic Maeve.' Seb sits forward enthusiastically, his long legs knocking into the coffee table. 'You've got what it takes to really make a difference.'

Posey and Eimear makes sounds of agreement.

'I do?' I mean, I've always felt that I had, but I still want to hear them say it.

'You're fearless Maeve, you know what's right and you're not afraid to fight for it,' Eimear adds.

'Thank you, really, this is just such an honour - that you all want me to be part of your group.'

'We took a vote and it was a majority that you join us - if you want to of course.' Ferdia holds my gaze, awaiting my response.

The word sticks in my mind and repeats. Majority. Not everyone wants me. Who doesn't want me? It could even be two people that voted against me. I try to read their faces, they seem genuine in their pleasure of the proposal. It could only be Zamara. She's still hung up on my disposable coffee cup. I will have to work extra hard to impress her.

'So what do you say Maeve - are you going to become an official member of the Clan?' Ferdia stands and walks towards me, extending her arms.

'Yes, yes of course.' I stand and her slight frame envelopes me in an embrace.

'Wonderful.' She holds me away from her by my shoulders. 'We are so happy to have you here. Come with me and I'll show you the rest of the house and where you'll be sleeping.'

'Sleeping?' I say, not having thought that far ahead.

'Yes, you'll be moving in of course.' Ferdia leads me into the hallway.

'You'll be sharing with me.' Eimear appears beside me and links onto my arm. 'It's going to be so much fun having someone else in the room again, welcome home roomie.'

Chapter 8

Sandra looks up from her reality TV show to give her full attention to what I'm telling her.

'You're moving out?' she asks, seemingly incredulous.

'Yeah, sorry I know it's not ideal.' I perch on the edge of the armchair of her three piece leather suite. Michael stares at me, his face completely unreadable.

'Well no Maeve, it's not. You're not even here a fortnight.' She continues, putting her tea cup down on the glass and chrome coffee table.

'I know but I've found a place to move into with some friends and it's walking distance to college, so you know, I can't pass it up.'

She lets out a loud sigh and looks over at her husband, who is now flicking through the TV channels.

'Michael.' She gets his attention. 'What do we do about the contract and everything?'

Michael shifts slightly towards his wife. 'I'll give Grainne a call and sort out the money, she'll lose the deposit and the rest of this month.'

'No.' I interrupt him. 'That's fine, I mean. I completely accept I'll lose the money already paid, no need to call Grainne.' Last thing I need is her getting involved.

'Right, well, that's that then.' Sandra folds her arms and gives me what I think is some sort of pout.

'Okay, thanks and sorry again,' I say making my exit.

'When will you be out Maeve?' Michael asks as I'm out the door, I hold it and look back to answer.

'Tomorrow, when you're both at work my friends are coming to help me move.'

'You won't even get to say goodbye to Leah and Leighton?' Sandra whines. 'They'll be devastated, they were getting so used to having you around.'

I never spoke more than two words to the terrible two but I give her a perfunctory sad face so she'll think I like her kids.

'Okay, well night.' I wave and leave them.

Luckily there isn't much to pack in my room, most of it will fit back into the one suitcase I brought up. Sandra bought the duvet and pillows, they're really comfy, I wonder if she'll mind if I take them. She's getting my deposit so that's the least she could sacrifice. I snuggle into them, content for the first time in this room now knowing it's my last night in it. Tomorrow I will be where I belong, with people who get me and who I want to learn from. It's like my life is finally starting. One thing that's definitely a first for me is sharing a room. I've always had my own. I have no idea what it will be like, how do you decide when to turn off the light or window open or closed and what if Eimear snores or talks in her sleep or sleep walks? Guess I'll find out soon enough.

I sometimes think my grandmother is a witch of some sort. One of these white wiccans that dance and chant around megalithic tombs during a full moon. I know that kind of thing goes on up on Loughcrew Carins just over the Meath border from our farm. But then I tell myself she couldn't possibly be that non Catholic and put her innate ability to sense when I'm trying to keep something from her down to her motherly instinct. I answer her call just after 9am, from my warm bed.

'Hi Nana.'

'Oh Maeve, I was just going to leave a message on your machine again.'

'Well no need now.'

'Are you in school, am I keeping you from your studies?'

'No I'm just sitting in the hall waiting for the lecturer to arrive.'

'Oh, very good, what are you learning about today?'

'Ethics,' I lie, ironically.

'That's lovely, very useful I'd say. Aisling was here helping to birth a calf yesterday. She asked Paudie if she could come over to watch him with the yearlings and sure next thing she was elbow deep, not a bother to her, she's a great young one so she is.'

'Is there something you want Nana, it's just that my lecture is about to start.' I feel a slight pang of guilt, but just slight.

'Oh yes, sorry love. Your grandfather was asking about your rent.'

'What about it?' Bloody Michael must have called Grainne.

'Does he need to pay it into the bank for Sandra and Michael for October or just give you the cash to give them? He said Grainne said something about them being worried about tax.'

Grainne had paid the first month and the deposit, but Paudie had insisted he would take care of the rest of the year.

'Cash,' I say empathically.

'Right, I'll tell him, you sure now?'

'Yes, they don't want a bank record of the payment because then they'd have to pay tax as landlords. Just give me the cash and I'll pay them.'

'Grand love. I'll tell Paudie to have the cash for you when you're home again. When will that be? Aisling is mad to see you, she says you're very busy up there and she hasn't been talking to you much. Don't be getting too stressed with college now, you have to have time to enjoy yourself too.'

'Yeah, I won't. I'll be home the end of the month, okay?'

'It's not the same here, house is awful quiet now.' Her voice lowers.

'Well maybe now is a good time for you to get involved in

something, like volunteering – what about the Tidy Towns?'

'Oh God, I've enough tidying to do in my own house never mind the rest of Ballycastle.'

'Right well there's always Grainne and Declan and the kids if you're bored.'

'Oh they're very good, Declan is driving us to the removal later. You heard who died?'

Jesus, I wondered how long before this game started. 'No, I didn't.'

'Frank Joyce.'

'Who?'

'Frank Joyce, you know him.'

'I don't.'

'You do, he was a county councillor, ran the Co-Op for years, your grandfather was very great with him.'

'Right, was he old then?'

'Only 87, awful tragedy.'

'Not a tragedy Nana.'

'Don't be so heartless Maeve, his children are devastated.'

'His children are probably in their 50s.'

'That doesn't make a difference. God, I dread to think what you'll be like when your grandfather and I take our leave, like taking out the bins, you won't care unless someone puts us in the regular bin and not the brown compost one.'

'I'm just saying there are actual tragedies happening all around us, the decimation of the rainforests, the melting of the ice caps, the extinction of animal species, the genocide of ethnic minorities, the displacement and homelessness of thousands of people – not the natural death of a 90 year old man.'

'87.'

'I'm sorry Nana, I've really got to go now.'

'Okay love, sorry for delaying you before class. Call me when you can and we'll have a proper chat about how you're getting on up there. Love you pet.'

'Yeah, bye, love you.' I press the red button and get up to start packing up my room. Aide and Eimear will be here in about two hours.

I'm stuffing some forgotten socks into the side pocket of my wheelie case when I hear a car come to a quiet stop outside my window. The blind is half down so I use it as a shield to watch them. The car is an electric, of course, light blue, Japanese. Its environmental benefits overshadow its apparent unattractiveness. The driver more than makes up for that anyway. From my vantage point I can just make out his long fingers on the steering wheel and the tops of their heads. They unclick their seat belts and turn off the engine. I let the blind fall back into place, expecting the doorbell to ring any second now. But it doesn't. I check my phone to see if they have text me. They haven't. Returning to the window I see they are still in the car, their faces in view now. Eimear is beaming, a smile stretching across her face. Aide's arm reaches across the divide between them but the dash obstructs my view of where his hand lands. Then in slow motion, their faces get closer and closer until the inevitable happens. Fuck. He's kissing Eimear. I hadn't even considered her as a possibility. Zamara, Posey, even Ferdia at her age maybe. But Eimear just seems so ordinary. I didn't think girls like her could get boys like him.

The doorbells rings. Shake it off Maeve. Better to find out now before you tried it on with him, be grateful you saved yourself a world of embarrassment. Happy face on and get the hell out of this shit hole.

I open the door with my suit case at my side.

'Wow, you all set to go already?' Aide wipes his feet on the welcome mat. There's no need, he's not coming in.

'Yes, that's everything.' I step out of the house, hastening our exit.

'Amazing,' he says lifting the heavy case effortlessly and taking it to the boot.

'Let's go,' I mutter through Sandra's 15 tog duvet, handing it over to Eimear's awaiting arms.

'We're all so excited to have you move in Maeve, especially me.' Eimear peers in at me on the back seat, smug in her position at Aide's side up front. Stop it Maeve, be nice. Get over it. Maybe Seb is single and straight. He's not bad, a bit Clark Kentish but not untouchable by any means. And he's enlightened which is all that really matters anyway.

'Oh me too. I'm so grateful to you all for voting me in.' I hope they have.

'We're going to stop at the refill store to get some supplies for your welcome party tonight.' She smiles and twists back in her seat.

We each take empty bottles and plastic containers from the boot of the car and bring them into the shop. I've heard of these places, where all the produce is loose and you have to buy by weight, but I've not been in one yet. Can't let them notice that though so I confidently place one of my containers under a raw peanut dispenser and turn the valve.

'Oh Maeve,' Eimear calls from the counter.' We just need to weigh our containers first.'

'Oh, yes of course, sorry.' I try to appear forgetful as opposed to stupid when placing the container of three peanuts on the counter.

'We'll pay for those,' Eimear assures the cashier.

'Hey Maeve,' Aide beckons me from the fruit and veg. I leave Eimear to the scales. 'Are you any good at picking out avocados? I always seem to get them too hard, hold out your hands.'

I do as he asks and he places an avocado in each hand.

'Just squeeze your fingers a tiny bit.' He asks, his icy blue eyes boosted by the light coming through the shop window. 'What do you think – too firm?'

'Mmm maybe. I'm not really sure.'

He places his hands beneath mine, cupping them so his fingers reach all the way around, applying twice the pressure on the fruit.

'I think there's a little give in these, don't you?' He seems to have stepped closer to me, but I can't be sure, maybe I have.

'Yeah, yeah these are good.'

'They just needed the right touch to reveal their potential.' He smiles at me before tossing the avocados up in the air in a two handed juggle. 'Thanks Maeve.'

'Sure no problem,' I say, rooted to the spot as he makes his way to the chilled section.

'Oh great, you're making your famous guacamole,' Eimear says as she joins him at the fridge. 'Wait until you try it Maeve, it's honestly the best I ever had.'

I'm sure it is Eimear.

'Oh yeah, can't wait to try it out so.'

'No pressure so, I hope I don't disappoint,' he says mock humbly. 'Maeve, can you grab the cream.'

It takes me a second to register his request, which is odd as he's just as close to the cartons of sour cream as I am. But I do as he asks and hand him one. He looks at me blankly. The silence attracts Eimear's attention. She lets out a disingenuous little laugh. What am I missing here?

'Is this not the right one?' I study the carton closely. Sour cream, that's what you use in guacamole right?

'Yeah if you support animal abuse.' Eimear's laugh intensifies to manic and I realise my fuck up. I echo the forced laughter.

'Just messing with ye.' I put the carton back and scan the shelves to convince them that I know what I'm looking for.

'The creamed coconut is just there to your left,' Aide directs me.

'Great, love this stuff,' I say a little too loudly before they walk away towards the till. Guess this means I'm vegan now.

We park the car further up the street as the spaces outside the house are full. Aide wheels my case down the uneven, narrow footpath while Eimear and I carry pillows, duvet and shopping bags. There is no one else at home so after we put away the food, Eimear and I bring my stuff up to our room. It's at the top of the house, up three short flights of stairs. The first floor has three rooms, two bedrooms and a bathroom, the second floor is just one large room that overlooks the front street. Our floor comprises of our big bedroom, another smaller single and a bathroom. Ferdia had explained the layout to me but I hadn't seen inside or found out who sleeps where, except for myself of course. I have a small single bed along the window, Eimear's relatively huge double bed being the focus of the attic room.

'Welcome to your new home.' She ushers me in like a butler. 'We have the best room because there's no one walking around above us but Ferdia can hear us below so you know, shoes off upstairs.'

'So that big room is Ferdia's?'

'Yeah, she's got an ensuite so the bathroom here is just for us and Posey – she's in the next room.'

So that leaves Aide, Seb and Zamara on the first floor.

'Ok, great and do the others have their own rooms or …?' I ask, knowing it to be a physical impossibility.

'No, Aide and Seb share, Zam does. She's been here the longest, about six years I think.' Eimear sits crossed legged on her massive bed and pats it for me to join her.

'And how about you, how long are you here?'

'Oh just over a year, I came up to Dublin for uni and met the guys at an affordable housing protest, they've been so amazing.'

'Where are you from?'

'Laois.'

'You go home much?' I'm hoping she says yes so that I might have the room to myself sometimes.

'No, I've not been home since I dropped out, my parents aren't exactly supportive.'

'You dropped out of uni – why?'

'I was studying politics but when my eyes were opened here I realised I was wasting my time. Nothing I was ever going to learn there was going to help people or the planet. I had to act now, fight the system instead of becoming the next generation of the political puppetry.'

'So what do you do instead? Do you have a job?'

'Yeah I work in a coffee shop in the village, but I mostly volunteer, that's the great thing about living here, Ferdia doesn't charge us any rent, she just wants to help us to become the best people we can possibly be.'

'That's all I want,' I say, making myself more comfortable in my unnatural yoga-like pose opposite her.

'You will be, trust me. This is where you belong. There is nowhere else you should be.' She smiles broadly and reaches out to gently touch my forehead. 'All you have to do is open up here.' Her hand moves to my left breast, her fingertips applying the slightest of pressure. 'And open up here.'

I return her smile now, understanding the intent of her touch. But her hand continues to travel down until it rests between my open legs. I'm wearing leggings so I'm not completely exposed but I still feel like I am, especially when she presses her open palm firmly against my crotch.

'And here.' She says softly, her eyes locked onto mine. I stare back, open mouthed, not sure of how to respond. I let out a nervous giggle. She does the same. A noise from downstairs cuts through the awkwardness.

'Oh great, they're home, come on Maeve.' She gets off the bed and grabs my hand. 'It's time for your official welcome party.'

Chapter 9

There's music coming into the house from the open back door, low base and slow tempo. It's punctuated by the sound of voices in cheerful conversation, an occasional giggle or exclamation of excitement.

'Come on, they're all outside.' Eimear takes my hand once again to lead me down the five steps to the basement floor and out to the garden.

'Maeve.' A body comes at me instantly, enveloping me in a tight embrace. 'I'm so sorry I wasn't here to officially invite you into the Clan, I'm so pleased you have agreed to join us.' Zamara beams a warm smile at me and despite my instincts to the contrary I choose to believe it.

'Here, try some of my homemade gin, it's pretty strong though so sip it.' She hands me the glass she has been drinking from. I put it to my lips, the alcohol fumes reach my senses before the liquid has a chance to touch my mouth.

'It's really good, thank you Zamara.'

'We are family now, what's mine is yours.' She greets Eimear with a kiss and a hug before linking us both further down the garden.

'Hey Maeve, how are your DIY skills?' Seb asks as I near him amid what looks like a dismantled gazebo.

'I'm not bad actually, I help my grandad with stuff like this all the time.' Summers spent mending barbed wire fences and broken boards in the slatted units have formed quite the handy-woman.

'Oh thank God.' He places both hands in his messy black

hair. 'I'm currently the go to guy in the house for this sort of thing and I suck big time, help me out?'

'Sure.' I take two pieces of the wooden frame and hold them in place. 'Just hand me the hammer.'

While Seb and I assemble the gazebo, Zamara, Eimear and Aide bring out food and drink and arrange them on a large picnic table. I sip the elderflower gin as I work and watch how they interact with each other, seamlessly, like dancers moving in rehearsed choreography. But maybe it's just Aide that makes their movement appear so graceful, he doesn't just walk, he glides, he doesn't put things down, he places, he arranges. When he passes Eimear and Zamara, he lays a fingertip touch on their backs or their arms, acknowledges their presence, presenting his own. Yes Maeve and as you are now aware, he is most probably also presenting Eimear with his penis on the regular so try to focus your attention elsewhere.

'So, where are you from in the States Seb?'

'Spokane, Washington, you know it?'

'No, I've not been to American at all yet, my friend Aisling is talking about us going over on a J1 next summer to Florida or California but I dunno.' I bet that sounds lame to an actual American, it was out of my mouth before I had time to analyse it.

'Oh stay away from Florida, it's just swamps, theme parks and ageing republicans. Northern California is nice though.'

'Yeah, I'd love to go but maybe for something more important, like volunteer work or something.' Yes, that sounds better, now divert. 'So what brought you to Dublin?'

'Tech job, I came over in a big recruitment drive about two years ago.'

'Seb is kind of a genius.' Aide's face appears at my side.

'Only people like Aide who are completely technically illiterate think that.' Seb dismisses his housemate's endorsement.

'So you do all the online stuff for the Clan.' I assume.

'Yeah but I'm glad to have you help out with that now, being a media student you're bound to have some great ideas.'

'Well I hope I'm better at that than building, how is this looking?' I push the gazebo to test its sturdiness.

'Oh wow that looks amazing.' Posey walks toward us, carrying a paper bag. Ferdia is standing at the back door on her phone. 'You did that Maeve?'

'Yeah well, we did.'

'Oh Seb honey you got some help didn't you.' Posey laughs before kissing him full on the mouth. Well there goes any chance of the ride with Seb.

'I've got something extra special for all of us.' Ferdia calls the others to join us under the gazebo before revealing what's in Posey's bag.

'This stuff is premium so pace yourselves guys. Maeve if you are not a regular smoker, maybe don't inhale okay.' She sets down the bag of weed on the table and lays cigarette papers on her lap. As she assembles the joint, we all take a seat around her. Ferdia greets us all with a kiss on the cheek before taking the finished product from Posey and lighting it.

'Here's to the newest member of our weird and wonderful little family. May she teach us all to be better inhabitants of this planet and may we in turn help her to grow into her destiny. To Maeve.'

'To Maeve,' everyone but me responds.

She takes a drag and passes it back to Posey. I await my turn, anxious that I'll remember how to do it. I've smoked hash before, just once with Aisling. I bought it off the older brother of a guy in my year. We smoked it in her mother's car down by the lake. She had freaked out, insisting she could see the future and know what I was going to say before I said it. I just remember laughing a lot, which was much nicer than being drunk. And now I get to experience that feeling among my people. I hold the roach between my fingers and inhale as deeply as I can, holding it for a second before releasing the burning smoke. I pass it to Seb, silently congratulating myself for not coughing and spluttering like an amateur.

'Shit you weren't kidding Po.' Aide holds back the choking smoke and winces at the strength.

'Oh come on, you've had worse.' Eimear shoots him a mocking glance.

'I personally think Zam's gin is more potent,' Seb deadpans.

'Cheers.' Zamara lifts her glass before draining what's left in it.

'As long as we don't have a repeat of Budapest,' Ferdia adds with a smile.

'What happened in Budapest?' I ask and watch as everyone begins to snigger.

'Let's just say I had a very good trip.' Aide's pale cheeks flush with colour.

'Yeah, you weren't the only one,' Seb says under his breath.

'I don't think the local police particularly enjoyed the experience though.' Zamara laughs as she searches through her phone before handing it to me to reveal a picture of Aide, astride a grand bronze statue of a horse in an old town square.

'Oh my God, how did you get up there?'

'A combination of class B drugs and sheer confidence.' He smiles coyly.

'He got charged with public nuisance, we had to spend all our money to cover his fine.' Eimear shakes her head and rolls her eyes.

'Yeah well at least I took the opportunity to call for gender equality while I was up there.'

'Sorry buddy but I don't think anyone was listening to your political proclamation once you whipped your cock out,' Seb says causing me to almost choke on my drag of the joint.

'Sorry Maeve.' Posey pats my knee. 'We don't have a picture

of that.'

I make an over compensating shrug of not being interested. I bet that looked cool and convincing. They are laughing now, sharing more war stories about protests in London and Paris, weekend trips to Amsterdam and Berlin. I've only ever been to Gran Canaria on a package holiday with Aisling after the Leaving Cert. I got pissed on piña colada, let a guy from Doncaster stick his hand up my skirt in the middle of the dance floor, puked up the piña colada and fell asleep on the steps outside my budget apartment. I'm not sharing that travel story.

'Sorry Maeve, you must think we are completely mental, usually we are a pretty civilised bunch,' Ferdia assures me.

'Oh please, don't worry. I'm used to knuckle draggers and cow shit so this is definitely a step up.' I wave a dismissive hand, feeling nice and pleasantly light headed.

'Cow shit?' Zamara repeats.

'Yeah, you know that brown stuff that tends to come out of cows?' I laugh at myself.

'Your cows?' Eimear asks.

'Huh?' I focus on her fuzzy, floating face. 'Yeah, my cows, well my grandad's cows, fat smelly fuckers. Believe me this is paradise compared to the smell of cow shit when you open your bedroom window.'

'Your grandfather's a beef farmer?' Aide sits up straighter and leans into the circle.

I copy his movement so I am close to his face. 'I'll have you know that Paudie Daly is the largest purveyor of moo moos this side of the border as was his father and his father before him.' I perform my best Cavan accent for them, enjoying the attention. I wait for the laughter, the admiration for my wit. But silence follows, for a lot longer than it should. I can feel the air has shifted. It's not fun anymore. Their eyes on me aren't generating love and warmth. They're crawling on me. I want to scratch my skin.

'Maeve.' Ferdia breaks the unbearable silence that has filled the gazebo. 'Are you telling us that your family breed cattle, the third biggest source of pollution in this country, which they then sell to be butchered to feed the barbaric masses of meat consumers? You are from this industry that propagates the abuse and slaughtering of animals that serve no other life purpose than to produce levels of methane gas that is slowly but surely destroying the planet, is that what you are telling us?'

The joint is burned out. The sun is hiding behind a cloud above her head. I try to focus on her steely grey eyes as they bore into me, but I struggle to match her strength. My head feels like it's bobbing all over the place as I try to still myself and absorb the seriousness of what she's saying. I perform a definite nod of my head.

'Yes.' I feel the weight of all of their disapproval. 'I'm sorry.'

'Okay.' Ferdia sits back in her chair and presses her hands together, extending her fingers. 'So what do you propose to do about it?'

I stare at her blankly, my thoughts not clear enough to conceive the reply I think she wants.

'Not eat beef,' I say almost as a question.

Seb laughs and it cuts through the tension. I look at him and join in. Ferdia's hand rises and he stops, so then I do too.

'Tell me Maeve,' she pauses before continuing. 'Do you believe it's possible for someone to affect change if they are a willing participant of the inherent system that requires changing?'

No one is eating or drinking, all their heads are bowed, eyes focused on the grass at their feet. I'm on my own here.

'Eh, no I suppose not.'

'You have spent your entire life living in a death factory and never thought to do anything to stop it?'

'Well, I was a kid.' I look around for some back up but I don't find it. 'I got out as soon as I could.'

'And now?'

'I'm here now.'

'Yes - you are aren't you. Why?'

'Because I believe in what you all do. I want to be part of something great.'

'Yes, they are nice words Maeve.' She sighs heavily before standing up and leaving the circle.

No one speaks as she walks towards the house.

'Guys, please.' I force their focus on me. 'What do I do?'

'Go after her,' Eimear says as loud as she can while still whispering.

'No leave her, she needs her space when she's upset,' Zamara offers.

I weigh up both suggestions and basing my choice on who has provided the greatest support to me so far, I go with Eimear.

Even though I am aware that I've upset or annoyed her, I can't stop giggling on my way back to the house. I call her name once I'm through the back door. There's no response. I check the dining room and the small kitchen, she's not there. The front room and the room in between that is used for storage are both empty. I take the stairs, calling for her again. The bedroom doors are ajar, I peek into the one I know to be Aide and Seb's, it's neat for two guys. Their beds are made, no dirty jocks or socks on the floor, no posters of porn stars on the walls, instead there's a polar bear perched on a diminishing iceberg, a world scratch map with lots of coloured countries and an array of hand written schedules and charts that have been well amended. A sound above my head alerts me to her whereabouts. I ease out the door, leaving it as open as I found it and slowly take the next flight of steps to the large main bedroom. I knock on the door.

'Yes?' Her voice is shallow on the other side.

'It's Maeve, can we talk?'

'Come in,' she says without an indication of what my

reception will be like.

I turn the brass knob and step into the room that's flooded by the natural light of two almost floor to ceiling windows. Straight ahead there's a salmon pink velvet arm chair, a desk and a chair, old and ornate, like everything else in this house. The walls are covered with an intricate floral flock wallpaper of mustards and greens, the curtains are discoloured beige, to my left there's a four poster bed with carved mahogany posts, it's so big it almost touches the walls, leaving just enough space for her to get in and out. The internal wall of her added ensuite stripping the room of some of its original width. She's sitting in front of the far window, writing in a hard backed notebook, she doesn't look around when she eventually speaks.

'Do you like this house Maeve?'

I shuffle from foot to foot not sure whether I should sit on the armchair at my side.

'Yes, it's a beautiful house, I'm very happy to be here, I'm sorry about what happened down there, I didn't mean to...'

'My grandmother left it to me in her will.' She cuts me off. 'Did I tell you that?'

I shake my head.

'Please, sit.' She points to the armchair and I do as she says. 'She wanted to make sure I would be okay, my grandmother, she knew they wouldn't.'

'They?'

'My parents – her son in particular. She knew what kind of monster he was.'

I know this is a serious story she's telling me but I'm as high as fuck right now and I really just want to lie down on her thread-bare rug and stare at the plaster on the ceiling. Focus Maeve. Ferdia walks around her bed so she is sitting along the bottom of it, facing me.

'I understand what it feels like when you grow up to realise your parents are monsters.'

'Well, I wouldn't say that.'

'Destroyers of the planet are our enemies Maeve, whether or not they are our blood, it doesn't matter.'

'It's just a small farm, he's downsized a lot since he turned 60.'

'Yes and my father tried to tell me that his one little factory dumping their waste into Dublin Bay was not going to make that much of a difference to the eco system.'

'I know, parents can be shit but at least we, the next generation know better, we can do better, there isn't really anything we can do about them is there?' I don't know if it's the drugs or my stupidity but I'm still not grasping what she wants from me.

'That disappoints me to hear you say that Maeve.' She walks over to the window and looks out at the street.

'What do you want me to do? What did you do?'

'I burned his factory down.' She says bluntly, her focus still on the outside world. I can't hold back the nervous laughter, it erupts.

'Maybe you're not cut out for this, I acted in haste, at least you're not fully moved in so no harm done.' She walks to her door, I think I'm being ushered out.

'No, sorry … no – did you seriously do that?'

'Yes. No one was hurt. His factory was destroyed, the polluting stopped, his insurance money covered his losses and my mother got her golfing partner back for three days a week. All in all I'd say it was one of my most successful missions.' She smiles a tight smile and perches back on the edge of her bed.

'Did you not get in trouble for arson?'

She shakes her head. 'No, my father accepted liability, there was no criminal case. It was the least he could do after what he did.'

'So he forgave you?'

'Forgave me?' She asks puzzled. 'Why would he do that? He

doesn't understand enough of my reasons in order to be able to forgive. No, we don't speak.'

'Oh, I'm sorry.'

'Don't be, I'm not. I did the right thing.'

'I admire your commitment, really I do.'

'Do you not feel that you possess that same commitment?' She kneels down in front of me and takes my hand in hers, her grey eyes lighten in the late evening sun. Because I feel that you do.'

'You do?'

'You wouldn't be here if I didn't.'

I know that my security here in this house, in this group, in this world that I've been searching for is dependent on the next words out of my mouth. I know that once I say them, I have to stick to them, there's no take back. No matter what the consequences.

'Tell me what to do Ferdia and I'll do it.'

Chapter 10

The bus to Cavan is full, which makes the lack of air conditioning even more uncomfortable. I had thought getting a Saturday morning bus as opposed to a Friday evening would make a difference but no, turns out the city is full of country expats only too eager to bring home their bag of crusted underwear and sweat sodden socks to Mammy. Maybe that means you're a big boy now, look what I made in college, a bag of dirty clothes for you to wash. I can smell them from the overhead shelf. Why they couldn't put the bags in the storage underneath I don't know, separation anxiety from their separates. I pride myself on not being among that cliché. My bag contains fresh clothing only, having done my washing in Ferdia's yesterday. I know I've only been there a couple of days but it instantly felt like home. So much so in fact, that I'm not sure I'd be making this journey to Cavan at all if it wasn't for her request. It will probably be the last trip home for a while after this I should imagine.

I see him sitting in his old forest green Jeep as the bus pulls into the depot. It's caked in so much cow shit that the license plate is unreadable and parked two wheels up on the footpath. So many traffic violations in one man. He honks the horn as I exit the station, should I happen to miss him. How I would do that I don't know.

'There's the scholar home now, we weren't expecting ya for weeks yet.' He bellows from the window, his smile wide within his yellowing grey beard.

'Well,' I greet him as I throw my bag onto the back seat.

'You're looking well anyway, not starving yourself up there.'

'I've only been gone for three weeks.'

'Tell that to your grandmother, driving me mad so she is, talking to me all the time. I haven't got time for that shite, with 30 yearlings out in the paddock and with Declan busy with his own animals, he's after getting a llama, a fucking llama mind you. Gobshite.' He leans over to emphasise his outrage.

'Mind the road grandad.' I grab onto the door handle as he narrowly misses an oncoming people carrier.

'You heard Frank Joyce died,' he says quietly after a brief reprieve.

'Yeah Nana told me.'

'Course she did, never off the fecking phone. Aisling was asking after you as well, she was helping me out on the farm, great young lassie so she is.'

'Yeah she is.'

'You'll be seeing her this evening no doubt, heading into McEvoy's for a few cocktails or pink gins or whatever you college girls are into now.'

'I dunno, I haven't really planned anything with her, I've been busy.'

'Sure you have to see your friend Maeve, you won't find any like Aisling Monaghan up there in the big smoke. Notions up there the lot of them. I suppose you've met all sorts already?'

'Yeah, I have actually. I've met some really interesting people with different views and ways of life, exactly the kind of thing you'd expect when you go to college, you know?'

'Just mind yourself now and don't get into any trouble. Grainne got you a good place up there with decent people.'

Here's my opening.

'Oh yeah, that reminds me. Sandra wants to know if you can pay in cash from now on, she doesn't want my rent going into her bank account because then she'll have to pay tax on it as a landlord.'

'Your grandmother was going on about that earlier in the week alright. I'll let her sort it out with you, I just earn the money, I don't get a say in the spending of it.' He taps the steering wheel with his thick, dirty fingers.

I unlock my phone. Suppose I had better let Aisling know that I'm home. I send her a text. She replies instantly confirming our catch up later complete with an array of gifs of dancing girls and anthropomorphic alcoholic drinks clinking #girlsnight. How can we have only been apart for just over a fortnight. It feels like a chasm has already developed between us.

Being away from the smell has only made it all the more pungent when I get out of the Jeep. Breathe in the faecal infused air. My grandmother is on her knees on the kitchen flagstones and looks up upon our entrance.

'Did you get the cheese?' she asks my grandfather.

'What?' he says, hanging his cap on the hook inside the back door.

'The smelly cheese Maeve likes, I asked you to get it in town. For God's sake Paudie, I'm up to my elbows here in ice and meat and I was looking forward to having that for lunch with Maeve.'

'I don't know why you're even bothering to defrost the freezer now Maureen, I have all the beef cuts in the chest freezer out in the shed.'

'Yes, well I don't want to be traipsing out there during the winter and I need to clear some space for Christmas.' She attacks an ice shelf with her carving knife. 'How are you Maeve? You look pale.'

'I'm grand Nana, do you need a hand?' I leave my bag by in the hall and return to her at the fridge.

'Oh just grab that top joint there and put it on a plate to defrost, we'll have that tomorrow for dinner.'

'Is there anything else I can eat?' I say while doing as she asked.

'What do you mean? You love a Sunday roast.'

'No Nana, I don't eat meat anymore, remember.'

'Since when?' She stills her blade and looks at me.

'Since ages ago.'

'First I've heard of it. Paudie, did you hear this?' She shouts to my grandfather in the adjoining sitting room. 'Maeve's gone vegetarian now.'

'Hah?' he bellows back, not actually wanting or expecting a response.

She mumbles into the icy void.

'Well actually I'm vegan.' I may as well pull off the plaster completely.

'Don't be ridiculous Maeve, you'll get malnourished.'

'I don't expect you to understand my choices but I expect you to respect them.'

'Right well, isn't it better so that your grandfather forgot the cheese, I suppose you don't eat that now either. Make yourself a cup of black tea there and sit down and tell me all about college. Grainne says she'll be over later to see you too.'

'What time will she be over?' I click on the kettle.

'She didn't say, you know yourself, it will depend on the kids and getting everything organised, she never stops God love her. Why?'

'Oh just that I'm meeting Aisling later so I might not be here when she comes.' Aisling is definitely the lesser of two evils in this situation. I can stomach an evening of interpreting Cian Hanly's eye movements and monotone salutations over Grainne and her questions. Last thing I need is her getting involved in the conversation of me living at Sandra's and the cash only rent.

Upstairs in my bedroom, I can see the paddock from my window, the yearling calves like black and white checkers on a playing board. How have I watched them grow year after year right there under my nose, fully complicit in the savagery of their murder. A life only lived for the sole purpose of ending it. It's barbaric and my grandfather needs to know that it's not okay. Not anymore. We, the generation that will change the world, will not stand by silently. My own role in the revolution will have to wait until nightfall. The few glasses of Dutch courage with Aisling will come in handy.

I can't walk to Ballycastle from the farm but Aisling lives just a few minutes outside the town. Paudie drops me outside McEvoy's Bar and I agree to get a taxi home later because I won't be staying at Aisling's this time. He'll be long asleep when I get in. Hopefully. Aisling is not here yet. Why is it always the person who lives closest is the latest to arrive? I text her.

Get here quick. I'm standing outside like a turd.

Sorry on my way – heels! She replies complete with a grimace emoji.

She's wearing heels? Aisling Monaghan wore heels one time in the 13 years I've known her and that was our Debs. She had taken them off after the starter and even chucked them in the bin in the ladies toilets as punishment for the torture they had inflicted on her toes. This has something to do with Cian Hanly no doubt. I can hear her tottering up the road before I see her, the strappy black block heels struggling to maintain their equilibrium.

'Aaarrrggghhh,' she squeals as she nears me. 'You're home!' Her arms grab onto me and I suspect it's more for support than affection.

'Jesus Ais it's been a few weeks.' I refuse to join in this forced reunification crap.

'Yeah but everyone else was home last weekend and you were the only one missed.' She steadies herself on her feet.

'I'm sure you were the only one who missed me.'

'Don't start.' She points a bright pink fingernailed finger at me. 'We're going to have a good night, no giving out.'

Her attempt at authority makes me smile and remember why

I like her. There's an innocence and absence of cynicism in her that I've always admired. Envied even.

'Right, come on Keyser Söze, let's get you off the street before you do any damage to yourself or others.' I pull her inside the pub as she laughs hysterically and I start to believe a good night is actually possible.

I was wrong. I swear to Christ if I hear one more thing about Cian Hanly's sexy crooked smile I'm going to smash my fish bowl gin glass and slash my ears off with the shards just to make it stop.

'What do you think though Maeve? I need you to tell me the truth because you always do.'

I sigh heavily. 'I don't know Ais, like have you actually had a conversation with him since we finished school?'

'Well not a conversation exactly.' She takes a large sip from her glass. 'But we see each other nearly every second day around the town and he always says hello and gives me the look, you know that look he used to give Saoirse O'Donnell and it would send me spiralling into insanity?'

I do remember him giving her genital warts too, if the rumours are to be believed.

'Just grow some balls Aisling, if you like him and you think he likes you do something about it. Don't be the pathetic woman that sits around waiting to be noticed or sexually validated. You are more than capable of setting out your intentions and saying what you want. You do realise that women are equal right?'

'I know, I know but this isn't one of your political debates Maeve, what if he tells me to fuck off? I'll be mortified and I'll have to face him every day.'

'Every second day,' I point out. She gives me a disparaging look.

'Oh I don't know what to do.' She dramatically holds her head.

'Well I suggest you figure it out pretty soon because he's just walked in.'

'Oh shit, oh shit, how's my hair? Is my makeup messed up?'

'You look beautiful and if he doesn't see that, let him off.'

'Laugh,' she says.

'What?'

'Quick, he's coming over, laugh like I've said something hilarious.'

That old chestnut. I die a little inside as I fulfil her request.

'Hey Ais – Maeve.' Cian purrs as he saunters past our table. He's even more confident now than he was in his school uniform. Where he gets it from I'll never know.

'Oh hey Cian, how's it going?' Aisling's voice is squeaky.

'All good – I'm just going to get a round in for the lads but I'll catch up with you later, yeah?' He winks.

'Cool, cool, chat later, we'll be here whenever.' Aisling may as well bow. I pinch her thigh under the table.

'What?' she whispers once he's turned around to the bar.

'Don't be so available to him.'

'You just said to do something about it. Anyway I don't want to have worn these shoes for nothing.' She rubs one of her swollen feet. 'What about you?' She turns in her seat to face me but I can see her eyes still set on the bar.

'I wouldn't wear those if Germaine Greer herself told me they were the last bastion of feminist liberation.'

'What?' She looks at me blankly. 'No, you – any boys you like in college? Come on, tell me.'

I shake my head and answer honestly, 'No.'

'None at all? I find that hard to believe.'

'The people in college are proving to be a let-down generally actually.'

'And what about where you live? Donabate isn't it, any nice locals?'

'The last thing I want to do in Dublin is meet locals Aisling, it's a multicultural European city, not Ballycastle only further south.'

'Have you not met anyone interesting at all?' She looks concerned or maybe surprised.

'Of course I have, actually I've met six of them.'

'Oh – how many are boys?'

'Just two.'

'How many of the two do you wanna bone?' She squeezes my arm and stares into my eyes.

'Just the one – but he's with one of the other girls.'

'Shit.' She sits back deflated. 'Are they in your course at college?'

'No, I know them from somewhere else.'

'Stop being so bloody mysterious Maeve.' She pushes me.

'Right – if I tell you do you promise not to tell Paudie and Maureen, I know how much you love hanging out and having tea with them.'

She crosses her chest. 'Come on Maeve, friends before parents always.'

'I'm living with them – I moved out of the place Grainne got for me, it was a kip.'

'Oh that's cool, a house share! Sure why would Maureen and Paudie mind that, why aren't you telling them?'

'It's not just a house share, it's a way of life, they wouldn't understand.'

'Are they into the same stuff as you, like the environment and that?'

'They're one of the best activism groups in Ireland, I'm really lucky to be welcomed into their family.'

'Oh well that's good, as long as you're happy there and you know, you can trust that they are who they say they are.' She gives me that look she always gives me when she wants to remind me of mistakes I've made. I think it's intended to be caring and cautionary, but really it's patronising as fuck. She flips it into a smile. 'It doesn't hurt that the ride is living down the hallway, you just have to get rid of the girlfriend.'

Two fresh fishbowl glasses of gin and tonic appear on our table, followed by the grin of Cian Hanly and his idiot sidekick Cathal Power.

'Mind if we join ye ladies?' Cian says as Aisling struggles to use her words.

I scoot over on the leather bench and let Cathal in next to me. Great, my punishment for the rest of the night.

The gins descend into shots of Jägermeister and soon the night becomes like all the others I've spent in McEvoy's bar. Aisling is slurring her words and literally throwing herself on Cian, like full body slams into him. Cathal is shouting about some fella who looked at him funny from across the bar, his voice only ever found in the bottom of a glass. I'm completely bored. Looking around for someone interesting to talk to is pointless. It's the same old faces, the resident alcoholics propping up the bar, the underage fifth and sixth years desperately trying to assert their maturity by being even louder than the other punters and then there's the rest of the college diaspora, home for Saturday night in the local. Nothing like college to broaden the mind, but just in case it gets a bit too broad, come home to your bog town every weekend to keep yourself grounded. Don't want to be getting those notions Paudie is so afraid of. I'd leave right now if I could be sure he's asleep, but it's just gone 11pm and I know he'll be napping in his armchair and prone to being startled by an errant light or noise on his farm. Best to wait until he's tucked up in bed and dead to the world, which will be midnight, he never stays up to see the new day, he thinks it's bad luck. He makes an exception for New Year's Eve when he rings in the change until 12.30am.

Oh great, Cian has just stuck his tongue into Aisling's mouth. I can feel the weight of Cathal's inebriated gaze on me.

'You're looking well Maeve.' He leans in closer to me, his breath reeking of liquorice.

'Thanks.' I move away from him, pushing a little harder into Aisling than I intended. She takes a break from face sucking to look at me.

'I always thought you were a bit of a ride,' he continues. 'Is it true though that you're one of Mark Hennessey's? You look a bit like the younger one who runs the shop.'

The sound of my biological father's name lingers in the silence that follows.

'Hi … is it?' He persists 'I'm only asking cos that's your brother over there if it is' He points to the bar where my one of my half brothers is perched. It's not unusual for me to be confronted with a sibling in this town. Even if none of them acknowledge the fact.

'I don't know Cathal, sure your guess is as good as mine.' I use the method that usually gets me out of this conversation. Everyone knows it's true, that Mark Hennessy, the owner of the local supermarket and undertakers, has a penchant for school girls. His extra martial activities are a socially acceptable form of statutory rape in this town. And I'm the by-product.

'Jesus, if I were you I'd find out, sure he's loaded, you'd be entitled to some of that you know. Mind you the other four wouldn't like it.'

'What a great idea. I'll look into it.' I say, taking my phone out to text the one and only taxi driver in Ballycastle. Johnny replies that it will be at least twenty minutes. I don't tell Cathal that, or Aisling, not that she cares at this moment.

'I'm off, taxi's outside,' I say, squeezing by a languid Cathal.

'What? Wait, Maeve, it's so early,' Aisling says through her numb, bruised lips.

'Night's over for me Ais, you enjoy, see ya Cian.'

He salutes me, no doubt glad to see the back of Aisling's chaperone.

'Oh well text me when you get home and call me tomorrow, okay?' She manages to get the words out before her mouth is occupied again.

I hide in a toilet cubicle until Johnny the taxi man rings me and I sneak out of the bar unnoticed. It's after 12 when we pull up outside the house, the headlights shining into the bedrooms. I keep the chat brief in the hope that he'll leave and not disturb my parents any further. After he leaves I walk to the paddock, quietly and in darkness. It's mild and I don't feel a chill in spite of the lack of a jacket. Maybe I'm fuelled on the inside by fear or excitement. I don't know exactly, but I feel alive, that I'm doing something that matters, that will make a difference. I can hear them mooing as I near them, their hooves pad along the soft mud on their way to the gate. They are babies, fully reliant and trusting of their human caretaker. And the sick thing is my grandfather truly believes that he loves them, that he takes good care of them. The whites of their eyes glisten in the moonlight, looking at me for food, not knowing of any other reason for my presence. The light is not strong enough to illuminate the scene, I need to use the torch on my phone. The synthetic blue light casts them in a spotlight. I hold the phone up until they are in frame and press record, their innocent faces staring back at me. With my free hand I pull the heavy bolt bar out of the hold, releasing the gate. I step aside, expecting them to flee instinctively, but they remain still, the camera recording. I need them to run out of the paddock, to embrace this life saving freedom I am giving them. I can't give voice commands in case it identifies me in the video. I bang on the gate and the first calf walks through. Then another follows. It's working. I see a stick in the mud at my feet and stoop for it, banging it against the metal gate, loud enough to encourage their exodus but not enough to rouse Paudie. I follow them with the camera as they wander freely down the yard and even out of the front gate. I wait until the last calf is free before switching off the camera. I tiptoe back to the house, creep up the stairs and lie wide awake in my bed, the adrenaline coursing through me like wildfire. They say charity begins at home, so maybe it's the same for activism. Ferdia will be proud. I send her the video. I will make her proud.

Chapter 11

The tinny ringing of the house phone wakes me when it's barely had time to get light outside. I turn over and bury my face into my familiar duck down duvet. For a moment I'm satisfied that a return to oblivion is imminent but then my grandfather shouts up the stairs for my grandmother.

'Get up Maureen, quick.'

'What is it, is it one of the kids, who's dead?' My grandmother's instantly at full panic mode.

'No one's dead, not yet anyway. The fecking calves got out. Get up, I'll need you at the gate.'

It's not that I had forgotten what I had done about four hours ago, it's just that I hadn't really thought about this part of the plan. The fallout. The cover up.

'You up Maeve?' My grandmother appears at my door, her dressing gown barely covering her.

'Yes, I'm coming.'

'Good girl. He's going to give himself a heart attack over those stupid cows.'

I pull on my yoga pants and runners, throwing a fleece over my bed t-shirt. Right, time to be a good little farmer's granddaughter and go recapture the abused merchandise.

My grandfather is on the phone when I join them in the kitchen.

'I did not leave the gate open.' He blows at whoever's on the other end. 'I am not forgetting things … right … well, when you can. Mattie Willis … says he saw one at Lamb's Cross. Right so, good lad.' He hangs up.

'That little prick Declan telling me I'm forgetting to lock my own gate. Thinks he's an expert now he's got a fucking llama in the field.' He mumbles as he digs his feet into his wellies at the back door.

'Calm down Paudie, you're to have a cup of tea or something before you head out there.' My grandmother fills the kettle.

'Tea? Tea Maureen? There's 30 calves out there, roaming the roads, that's at least €40,000 of our money out there wandering around like gobshites, falling in ditches and getting hit by cars. And do you know what will happen if some drunk yahoo coming home from town hits one of them, do ya?' He looks at me for the first time this morning. I shake my head, giving him the opportunity to resume his rant.

'They'd trace it back to me and sue the shite out of us, we'd lose the house.'

'We're not going to lose the house.' My grandmother sighs. 'Maeve, will you go out with him, he's going to have an aneurysm, I'll stay and guard the gate.'

I nod at her request and stand by the door, waiting for him.

'I'll bring the mobile Maureen, don't be on to Grainne or anyone else now because I'll be ringing you to come out.' He slaps on his cap, ushers me out the door and releases a string of obscenities once he's out of my grandmother's earshot.

'I told you about the gate,' my stepfather shouts from the bottom of the drive as he gets out of his car.

'Don't annoy me.' My grandfather swats him away. 'There's nothing wrong with that gate.'

'So it's you then?' Declan sits into the driver side of the Jeep.

'It was not me, someone must have opened it.'

'Right, who would do that now Paudie?' Declan rolls his eyes at me. 'Alright Maeve, how's college going?'

'Great, yeah thanks.' I smile innocently and take my place in the back.

'Head to Lamb's Cross.' Paudie orders.

'Yes I know.'

'That Mattie Willis, ringing me at cock's crow, delighted with himself the little bollix. You'd swear his calves never got out before. Found one of the feckers looking in my kitchen window one morning. But did I ring demanding he come fetch it, no I did not. I did the decent, neighbourly thing, farmer to farmer. I put the dying looking yoke into a trailer and dropped it back to him. A cow fucking taxi, that's what I am.'

'Is that one there?' Declan points across my grandfather at a dark mass in the hedgerow.

'It is in all. Maeve, you get out and watch the road for traffic.'

Declan pulls up and they cajole the first of the escapees into the trailer as I pretend to care if there's a car coming on the deserted road. I check my phone. There's no reply from Ferdia. Maybe she didn't get the video through WhatsApp, the connection can be hit and miss up here. She mustn't have, she would have replied by now. She must be asleep. Of course, that has to be the reason. I enable my data and refresh the feeds of my social media accounts just to make sure my connection is up to date. It takes a second or two to load and when it does a familiar sight appears. My hand on a gate, my grandfather's paddock, the trusting eyes of his calves glistening in the moonlight, staring at the camera, at me, their emancipator. The video is live. She got it, she uploaded it on the Clan's official channels. I check them all, it's there, it's getting views, likes, comments, shares. It's working. It was worth it.

'Maeve, get back in the sodding car,' Paudie shouts from the passenger seat.

I return my phone to my waist band and resume my façade of familial fidelity.

'Well that's one of the fugitives, just another 29 to find,' Declan says as he starts the engine. Paudie huffs. I smile in the secrecy of my back seat, cosseted in the security of a successful result. My old family will get over it, they'll get their cows and cash back. But my new family will benefit, they'll get more followers and support for their vegan, animal rights agenda. My actions will ultimately save lives. I know that, I just have to remember it and not allow any guilt to cloud my mind. I did what I had to do. They will never understand my reasons. And that doesn't matter. They don't need to.

Hey are you free and fit to drive today?
I text Aisling after the socially acceptable time of 12 noon.
Oh my God Maeve. Best night of my life.
Yes great Ais, I'm thrilled for you but answer my question.
Tell me all about it on the way to Cavan bus station?
Oh yeah, course, what time you want a lift?
ASAP. Reached my Daly family quota about an hour ago.
Cool. I'm still in bed so give me an hour to delouse myself.
I send back a thumbs up emoji.

'Sorry Nana, I can't stay for dinner. Aisling is heading into Cavan in an hour so I'm going to get a lift in with her,' I inform my grandmother as soon as she returns from one of her many trips to the paddock this morning.

'Don't be silly, your grandfather or Declan will drop you in later, no need to miss your dinner.'

'No, he's too busy getting the calves back, I don't want to bother him, it's grand honestly.'

'You're very good pet, but he has 22 of them back already and a few others have been seen in Hennessy's field so won't be long now until they are all back safe and sound.'

That's an odd way of describing captivity and certain death.

'If it's okay with you, I'd rather just head in now, it takes so long to get back to Donabate and I have an assignment due tomorrow I want to work on.' What's another couple of lies added to my karmic debt.

'You won't even have time to call up to your mam then?' She'll be sorry to miss you love.'

'No, not this time, next weekend I'm home.'

'Well here.' She takes a €50 note from her handbag and gives it to me. 'Ring me if you get short up there, I know how expensive Dublin is and I want you to enjoy yourself as well, it's not all about study.'

'Thanks Nana.' I kiss her and head upstairs to pack and wait for Aisling.

She arrives bang on an hour, beeping the horn of her mother's Fiat.

'Well,' I say while adjusting the passenger seat for legs longer than most of the Monaghans.

'Alright missus, I hear you had a bit of drama this morning?'

'What?' I look at her blankly.

'The calves, it's all around the town, it's like a treasure hunt.' She laughs as she pulls out of our driveway.

'Ah that. Well they managed to get them all back so, more's the pity.'

'Sure that's a good thing isn't it?'

'Yeah, if you agree with that sort of thing.'

'What – farming?' She laughs.

'Well, yeah.'

'And you don't now I suppose?'

'No, I don't actually.'

'But you're a farmer Maeve.'

'I am not, I'm not responsible for the sins of my grandfather.'

'Settle down Maeve.' She sighs. 'Jesus, anyone would think you'd let them out.'

Silence. I focus on the passing trees.

'Maeve.'

'So tell me about last night then, how was Cian, everything

you have ever dreamed about?' Distract her.

'Eh, we'll get to him.' She turns off the radio. 'Did you let your grandad's calves out?'

'What if I did. It's wrong, setting them free is the right thing to do, whoever did it.'

'Jesus Christ Maeve, why would you do that?'

'You wouldn't understand.'

'It's dangerous for the animals, they could have been killed.'

'Oh come on Aisling, they're dying anyway.'

'Yeah but ... people could have been hurt too.'

'Oh people ... people can look after themselves, who looks after the animals? I thought you loved all creatures great and small.'

'I do, but there's ways of doing things.'

'Yeah well sometimes it takes someone to change those ways.'

'Like who – you?'

'Someday me, with the right help.'

'From those people you're living with I suppose.'

'The Clan,' I affirm proudly.

'This the sort of shite they get up to so?'

'Oh Aisling, please – let's just not go there. We've very different ideas of what constitutes shite.'

'Maeve, I'm worried about you, is it happening again?'

'Don't start.' I rest my head against the glass.

'That guy had you ready to run away with him, and you hadn't even met him in real life. What are these people going to make you do?'

'I was a kid back then.' It's not as if I was the only thirteen year old who made a friend online who turned out to be a little older than they said they were. 'I wish everyone would stop throwing it in my face, especially you, you're meant to be my friend.'

'That's exactly what I'm trying to be Maeve.' She focuses on the road for a while.

'Are you going to tell me about last night or not?' I encourage her tales of romance with the vapid Mr Hanly and it fills the air space for the remainder of the journey. I don't kiss or hug her when we stop, just say thanks and shut the door firmly and promptly behind me. She shouts 'text me later' at the glass but I ignore it and walk into the station.

Still no communication from the Clan. I thought maybe one of them would call and let me know the video is okay, that's it's useful to them. But my phone is silent. My anxiety grows the nearer I get to Donnybrook. What if they are displeased with me? I haven't even considered that. My key turns in the lock and I enter cautiously.

'Hello, anyone home?' My voice sounds shaky and pathetic.

'She's here.' Eimear's disembodied voice rings out and then they appear, all of them, one by one from the kitchen, the living room, down the stairs, rushing to greet me. Hugs, kisses, acceptance, respect, adulation.

'Maeve.' Ferdia holds my shoulders. 'You are a true friend and warrior of the weak and wounded. It's an honour to have you serve with us.'

'It was nothing, really.' I blush.

'Come on.' Eimear grabs my hand and drags me towards the stairs. 'We're having a party in your honour tonight so we have to figure out what to wear.'

'I don't have anything fancy.' I protest, mentally scanning my collection of leggings and t-shirts.

'It doesn't matter what you wear.' Aide stares at me as I pass. 'You'll be beautiful in whatever it is.'

I grunt an awkward acknowledgement of his compliment and float upstairs.

That feeling continues, right through trying on Eimear's clothes, selecting a pretty black floral dress that makes my body look better than I thought it could, then through the group screening of the video, the readings of all the positive, encouraging comments. My natural high is only supplemented by the passing weed and wine. It lulls me into a warm, comfortable space, here in this darkened, candle lit living room, with people who get me, who like me. I close my eyes and give in to the music, a slow rhythmic pulse travels through me until I release it through my fingers. I raise them up, my feet stretch to follow them and for a second I'm weightless until a searing pain shoots me and I'm hopping, grabbing onto my wounded, elevated foot.

'Fuck, fuck,' I say instinctively and wish I had stopped myself. It's not enlightened to be unable to control your suffering.

'You okay Maeve?' Aide stops dancing, leaves his drink on the mantelpiece and comes to where I'm hiding in the corner of the room.

'It's nothing, I think I just put a candle out with my foot, my own fault for dancing barefoot with my eyes closed.'

'Oh come on, sure that's the best way to do it.' He smiles and I like his attention on me. 'Can I have a look?' He points to the limb being squeezed between my hands as the wall provides my balance.

I nod in agreement and slowly release my hands.

'I can't really see anything in here, come on.' He takes hold of my arm and moves towards the door. 'We have an aloe vera plant in the kitchen.'

I pretend to be less able than I am as he guides me down the hallway, taking extra care on the steps. I allow my body to rely on his more than it needs to. Why not make some lemonade out of this burnt lemon.

The kitchen is half lit by the moonlight coming through the one large window straight ahead, revealing our reflections. Aide flicks on the light switch and shuts the half glass panelled door behind us. The Aloe Vera plant has taken over the others on the sill, its spidery tentacles claiming all the space and sunlight it can. Aide snaps off a piece of the thick, viscous leaf and lays it on the draining board.

'You wanna hop up there?' He nods towards the counter top and I shake my head.

'No, I'd never get up there, it's okay, I can just lift my foot.' I reach for the piece of the healing plant.

'Oh whoa there.' He raises a halting hand before placing both of them on my sides and lifting me up in one swift, confident move until my ass is perched on the fake marble counter.

'Comfy?' he says quietly as he reaches for the tap.

I am absolutely anything but comfy right now. What the hell is happening? He runs a cloth under the stream, rings it and turns to me. He kneels and takes my foot in one hand, wiping it gently with the cool cloth.

'You have to wash it first Maeve.' He looks up at me and I am so aware of the fact that I'm wearing a dress and the only thing between him and the most intimate part of me is a strip of cheap polycotton blend underwear that is getting damper with each stroke of his hand. The gel oozes out of the leaf and onto my hot skin providing sweet relief, for my burn at least.

'There, that feel better?' His voice sounds deeper than I've heard it and for a second it distracts me from the feeling of his hand still caressing my foot, my ankle, long fingers travelling further up my leg. I can't speak, afraid I'll say something completely unsexy and break the intensity of this, whatever it is. I don't want anything to stop him. Please don't any of you out there desperately require a glass of water anytime soon, especially Eimear. Oh, Eimear, shit. I feel bad. I do. But I choose not to care about that right now.

'Maybe I should kiss it better?' I can't be sure if he actually says this or I imagine it because it's happening before I can process it. His lips touch the sensitive, red swollen skin on my foot and I pull away. Reflexes, not reasoning. He locks his eyes onto mine and I notice how much darker they are now, the blackness of his pupils overwhelming the blue. My mouth is open but no words come out. I steady myself on the counter, digging my hands into the edge for support. I open my legs, granting him access. He kisses the soft white flesh of my calves as his hands move further, over my knees and under the black floral cloth of my dress. The touch of his fingers on my thighs cause me to make a sound. He likes it, it encourages him and I make another, louder, longer. Come on. I want this. I open wider for him. He moves in closer, forcefully edging me off the counter so my legs are supported on his shoulders, his head is between my thighs, he sucks at the flesh. I release my grip on the ledge and grab fistfuls of his thick, soft hair. I pull it lightly. Does he like that? He groans, his sound reverberates through me. I pull it tighter. His face is against me, I can feel the warmth of his breath through the wet fabric of my knickers. He applies pressure with his mouth and I fold onto him. Fuck. This is not like anything I've ever experienced before. A dry, abrasive finger bang in the back seat of Fintan Scanlon's car, a 45 second devirginising with Sam Redmond the night we finished the exams. What the fuck was that? Not this, nothing like this. A low guttural noise leaves my throat, I can't control it. He responds to it by taking away the barrier, sliding my black knickers down my legs, discarding them on the cold tiled floor. And then he's inside me, his tongue firm and then soft, exploring all of me, reacting to my sounds, my body guiding his mouth. He moans and I could fucking die right now. How can he be enjoying this as much as I am, he can't be ... oh God ... oh holy fuck, I'm going to come. I pull his head closer, letting him know I need more pressure. My body contracts, he knows what to do, what I need. For the first time in my life another human being is making me orgasm. I really thought that shit was just for the movies and that masturbation was the only true climatic guarantee in this life.

'I'm coming.' I whisper because I think it's sexy. I want him to know that he's making me come. I would want to know if I was making him come. Is he hard? I have no idea, he must be, what if he's not? Someone's coming. Someone is actually coming, there are voices outside the kitchen door, I can see the pixelated outline of a body through the patterned glass. No, no, no, please don't come in. I can't stop now. The voices fade away until all I can hear is our breathing again. He looks at me, my hands tangled in his hair. He watches me climax until there's nothing left to give. If he took away his physical support, I'd fall to the floor.

'Better now?' he says as he removes himself from between my legs.

I pant some sort of reply, still not confident of my voice. I steady myself against the counter and reach for him, pulling him towards me, expecting his mouth on mine. Still hungry for him. But he stops me, demonstrating his strength over mine, restricting me. I watch his mouth move further away, the edges curving into a smile, his hand reaches up to it, a long lone finger extends across it.

'Sshh.' he hisses before opening the door and leaving me standing there, alone in the kitchen, completely spent yet not completely satisfied. I pick up my knickers and put them back on, they irritate the tenderness. I flick off the light and fix my hair in my reflection in the window. I have no idea if this meant something, is this just what people do now at parties, a progression from kissing in dark corners. Is this college? Is this just Aide? I don't care. I want more. I need more.

Chapter 12

Words jumble on my screen to form a pixelated soup of marketing jargon. I can't concentrate on anything, walking across the street, brushing my teeth, pouring hot water in my green tea this morning in the kitchen. That kitchen.

'Maeve.' My name echoes in my ears. Did I imagine it? 'Maeve.' No, there it is again. I focus on the face of Irene our tutor.

'Can you tell me the seven tenets of marketing?'

They all start with P. That much I know 'Em, price, packaging, promotion and …' Come on that's only three and I'm struggling. '… people.'

'Anyone else actually paying attention?' She scans the heads around me. 'Yes, Shane.'

Of course he knows.

'As well as the four Maeve mentioned, there's product, place and positioning.'

I look behind me to see his smug face as Irene carries on with her lecture. When I catch his eye he looks away sharply. Still pissed with me then I take it. Maybe I should consider apologising, it might be beneficial to be friendly with the smartest person on the course. I'll write something contrite and vaguely flirtatious later, that should appeal to him. I look at him again and this time I catch him looking at me. Yes, that will work. My phone vibrates in my pocket. Aisling.

What the actual fuck Maeve? Captions my calf liberation video.

You can't stop change I reply.

You also can't stop this getting around the town, everyone is talking about it.

Good, that's the point. The Clan needs the exposure.

What if your grandparents see it and link it back to you?

Yeah coz Maureen and Paudie are well up on social media.

Just be careful, I'm worried about you up there with those people.

Those people are MY people Ais. You'd understand that if you actually left Ballycastle and saw a bit of the real world.

Maybe that was a bit harsh. But it's sent now. No reply. I watch the screen as her speech bubbles appear and disappear. That's the end of that conversation. She needs to know where the line is and not to cross it. And to think if she was a real friend who I could trust, I could be telling her about the most mind blowing experience of my life last night. Instead I get this shit from my supposed best friend. I really want to talk about it, I need advice on what to do next, do I hold back or push forward? It's not as if I can ask my new roommate.

I had tried last night to get some information out of her, tried to gauge just how serious she and Aide are, because if their seemingly platonic interactions and his having just gone down on me in the kitchen are anything to go by, then not exactly life commitment stage.

'So, who's coupled up in the house?' I dropped seamlessly into our early morning roommate chat about souls and the afterlife. I know Eimear was speaking on a more existential plane but I was very much grounded on a baser level.

'What, like boyfriends and girlfriends?' She almost laughed at the absurdity of my very basic question.

'Yeah.'

'We don't use terms like that Maeve, we don't believe that anyone can belong with or to another person.'

'But you do, like, get with each other?' I knew this as a very visceral fact.

'It's not like your programmed understanding of societal coupling of sexual interaction, boyfriends, girlfriends, husband, wife, they are not our natural state of being,'

I wasn't going to get a straight answer from her.

'So, you're not with anyone?'

'Yes, I am.'

Fuck.

'I'm with everyone and no one. I'm with you.' She had reached out to gently stroke my face.

I took this as my cue to cut the conversation.

'Ah, cool, that's so cool.' I edged off her bed then and made my way to my own, promptly pretending to pass out once I got under my stolen duvet. I replayed every second of it in my head, wishing I had the privacy to physically recreate the pleasure.

I leave college early, it's beyond boring and useless and I can't take anything in anyway. I can't pretend that I'm not also motivated by the prospect of finding Aide at home. When I joined them all again in the living room last night, he had just given me a knowing look, but otherwise it was business as usual, no public display of our obvious attraction, no giving away of what had just happened between us. So I had mirrored that, played it cool. I want to be able to continue like that, but I'm not so sure it's my modus operandi. The least I can do is research his connection to any other girls and judging by my conversation with Eimear it's not that strong.

The house is quiet when I enter. I make some noise just to alert anyone who might be here. The ceiling creaks above me. Ferdia's room, she must be home. I don't want to disturb her so I take the stairs lightly, tiptoeing by her door. Before I take the turn to the next flight of stairs, the door opens and I'm stuck in that awkward decision mode of do I turn around and speak or keep shuffling on my way. I opt for the former, it's less weird. The face I'm expecting to see doesn't materialise, instead I'm looking into the face that was only hours ago, looking up at me from between my legs.

'Oh hi.' I can feel the flames in my face.

'Maeve,' he says cheerfully, shutting Ferdia's bedroom door behind him. 'Great to see you.'

What the hell. 'Yeah, you too.'

'Did you enjoy the party last night?'

I can't tell if he's flirting or literally making polite conversation. 'Mm yes – I did. Did you?' I try my best to apply weight and meaning to my innocuous question.

'Oh yeah, it was great. I really feel like you're part of the family now – don't you feel the same way?'

Is that a declaration of interest? 'Yes, of course I do. Everyone here has made me feel so welcome, especially you and Eimear.' I take the risk and say her name, watching for the reaction on his face, any guilt? There's no change.

'Ah thanks so much, yeah Eimear is super buzzed not to be the new girl anymore so she's extra keen to keep you around.'

We stand there outside Ferdia's door, awkwardly trying to fill the silence.

'Is Ferdia home or …?' Are you just hanging out in her room when she's not home?

'She is actually, maybe now that you're here …' He stops to think before continuing his sentence. 'Yeah, come on, there's something we'd like to talk to you about.' He raps his knuckles on the door and awaits her permission to enter, ushering me in ahead.

She's lying in bed, sheets covering her from the waist, a delicate cream silk night gown falling off her shoulders as she rises a little to greet us.

'Maeve, how lovely to see you, please come sit.' She pats her bed and I take a seat. Aide sits on the other side of her.

'I'd like Maeve to lead the protest this weekend with me, what do you think?' he says to her and I know that whatever he wants me to do, I'm in.

'Do you think you make a good team?' Ferdia smiles at me and I look away. She can't know, he can't have told her.

'I do,' he looks at me as he answers her question.

'Well then,' She reaches out a hand to rest on both of us. 'I give you my full blessing and support. Aide, you will have to hire a people carrier, I know it's not ideal environmentally but make sure it's an electric. The train will just not work, we need to arrive without attention.'

He nods in agreement. 'Maeve, want to get started on the arrangements?'

'Yes.' I hop off the bed. 'Lead the way, I'm all yours.'

A huge fashion retailer that already has three branches in Dublin is opening their largest ever megastore in Belfast, Aide explains to me as he waits for his laptop to start. We are sitting on the cream sofa, two seater, legs touching. Could something else happen? I watch his mouth as he speaks, noticing the glisten on his bottom lip, how he sucks on his top one when he's thinking. I care about what he's telling me, I do. I care about the sweat shops in India exploiting underage and underpaid workers, polluting the local drinking water with the chemical run off from their cheap, must have, throw away fashion. But the more impassioned he gets, the more I want to pull him on top of me.

'So what do you think?' He sets down the laptop on the coffee table and twists to face me.

'Oh it's awful, truly shocking.' I gaze intently at the screen displaying images of thick toxic streams and chemically scarred factory workers.

'Yeah, but – about the plan – what do you think? Not awful I hope.' He smiles.

'Oh God no.' I grab his arm to emphasise my misunderstanding. Also it's an excuse to break this unbearable physical barrier. 'I think it's genius, Ferdia will be so proud of you.'

'Thanks Maeve, but it's not just about that, pleasing Ferdia you know.'

Fuck. I've said the wrong thing.

'Oh no, I didn't mean it like that, just that you are so committed to what you believe in, I know how much this means to you.' Did I save this?

'I really do, this is my thing.' He shifts his leg so it is bent and resting between us. 'This is why I'm studying fashion, I want to create a clothing brand that is cool and fashion forward but 100% sustainable. I hate this whole culture of €10 pairs of jeans, do you have any idea of the energy and water required to produce just one pair?'

'No, tell me.' Tell me anything.

'1,800 gallons – for one pair. 1.3 billion gallons a year for dyeing fabrics alone. And then people wear them five times before chucking them in a landfill.' His voice rises and I like the passion in him. 'Sorry, I get a little carried away sometimes.'

'No, it's fine, I get it.' Is now a good time to mention the last time he got carried away? 'Eh, speaking of that …' I hold his gaze. 'Last night.'

He blushes and I like having that power. 'It was pretty intense.' He smiles.

'For me anyway.' I try to give him an alluring look. 'I mean, it was good … I like you.'

He places a hand on my knee. 'I like you too Maeve.'

Thank God for that. 'So, do you want to like, go out sometime or …' That's what you're meant to do before you do any of the other stuff.

'Sure, we can go out, in fact, let's go out right now.' He gets up quickly.

I follow, a little more reservedly. 'Okay, where to?'

'I want to show you how to shop for clothes responsibly. Trust me, after today you'll never set foot in a high street shop again, unless it's to spray paint some furs.' He laughs as he opens the front door.

I guess this means we're going on a date. Is this a date? Is he my boyfriend now?

We walk to the nearby village of Rathmines, chatting the whole way about the Belfast job and the evils of the fashion industry. He's the opposite of every other guy I've known, intelligent, passionate, responsible. I fight the urge to reach for his hand as mine grazes it each time we are forced to move closer on the narrow path. Take it slowly Maeve, no need to force things, you don't want him to think you're needy or immature. You're a strong independent woman who doesn't need to be validated by a man. He enthusiastically heralds our arrival at a vintage second hand clothes shop, the smells of old leather and industrially laundered linens hit me as he opens the door.

'Prepare to have your mind blown.' He extends his arms dramatically.

'Hey Aide.' A heavily tattooed girl with pink shaved hair shouts from among the fabrics.

'What's up Roisin – I've brought a new victim for you.'

'Oh fantastic – I've just got some amazing 80's dresses in that I need to model on someone – you look like the right size.' She looks me up and down.

'I'm not really a vintage kind of person.' I scan the rails of sequined gowns and puffy taffeta.

'Oh please girl, you just haven't had the right stylist, isn't that right Aide?' She leads us to the back of the shop.

'Roisin is the best vintage collector and stylist in Dublin, trust her Maeve.' He winks at me as she shoves me into a dressing room, pulling the curtain.

'Strip off and I'll pull some items for you.' Roisin shouts. 'Oh

Aide, I have the most incredible jacket for you – suede fringe – come with me.'

Their voices are further away as I take off my clothes and wait there in my tragically unsexy underwear, having no other option but to stare at myself in the full length mirror. I've never really thought about my body before, like, if it was a good or bad one. It was functional, fit for purpose. I was never one of those pathetic girls who counted calories or worried if their tits were big enough, their asses small enough. I was above that, evolved. Or at least I wanted to be. I knew it was pathetic to feel that way. But now, here in this cubicle, the sound of his voice filling the space around me, I can think of nothing else other than what he would think of it, of me. If he thinks I'm sexy, does that mean I'm sexy? If he thinks I'm beautiful, does that mean I'm beautiful? Knowing that he has the power to decree such truths terrifies me.

'Here hun, try these.' Roisin's tattooed arm reaches through the curtain, presenting three dresses.

I try the first one on, white floral with high shoulders and a synched in waist. It makes my body look like an hourglass, shit, she is good. I pull back the curtain to find them both waiting expectantly.

'Wow,' Aide says quietly and I drink it in, his approval.

Chapter 13

I get shotgun. An indication of my importance to today's mission and perhaps even a reflection of my status as the driver's significant other. It's not like the words have literally been spoken between us, they don't need to be. We don't need labels, I can tell all I need to know about how he feels when he looks at me, like he's doing right now. Seb's large head breaks our connection when it bobs in between us.

'Did one of you remember to pack the First Aid kit?' He leans in from the middle seat of the people carrier.

'Yeah, it's in the boot with the blankets,' I assure him.

'Good, because we don't want a repeat of the Cork incident.'

'Oh give it up Seb, I've apologised a million times for that, you'd think you're the only person who has ever needed stitches,' Posey shouts from the back seat.

'Well I wouldn't have needed them Po if you had remembered to pack the paper stitches.'

'Can someone give Seb some CBD or something, his energy is really vibing me out.' She says, quieter this time.

'Guys, stop it.' Eimear takes on the role of peace maker in the absence of both Ferdia and Zamara. 'We need to be a cohesive unit if today is going to work.'

'Yes, thank you Eimear,' Aide adds while keeping his eyes on the road.

'Besides, it wasn't even my job to pack the kit that day, it was Hannah's if you remember correctly.' Po just can't let it go.

No one else speaks, a tumbleweed silence passes through the car. It takes my brain a couple of seconds to register where I know that name from. Hannah, it's familiar but I can't remember meeting her at one of the protests or parties. No, I've not met her, I've only seen her face in a passport photo. Hannah Fox. So she was a member of the Clan, but this is the first time I've heard them mention her. And why is her passport still in the house, surely that's something you would think of taking with you when you leave, no matter what the circumstances were surrounding it.

'Let's go over the plan one more time,' Aide says in his most authoritative voice. 'Maeve, why don't you take us through it.'

I gladly oblige and demand the attention of the passengers as the car crosses over the border into Northern Ireland.

The shop is on a pedestrianized street so we park as close as possible, avoiding multi stories. We may need to get away quickly. After we take what we need from the boot, Aide extends his arms and beckons us towards him. I latch on to his left side, Eimear to his right, Seb and Posey completing the circle.

'I just want to say it's an honour to lead you here today to follow in the footsteps of the greatest activists in the fight for justice in all forms.' He speaks into the sacred space we have created. 'On the drive up I was thinking of what might be the best inspirational quote to spur you guys on to greatness today. I vacillated between Sartre and Nietzsche, Kant, Gandhi but my mind keep returning to Alice Walker, who is herself a true warrior for enlightenment. She said. "The most common way people give up their power is by thinking they don't have any." Never forget that you have the power to change, to make this sick, injured world a better place. Your resolve may be tested today, you may face opposition for what you know to be right, but never lose sight of the common goal - saving the planet. And until we achieve full sustainability, the Clan will be there fighting, shouting, raging against the dying of the light.' He raises his voice as he ends his rousing speech with the words of poet Dylan Thomas. We respond in a chorus of cheers. Eimear cries. A bit over the top if you ask me, but maybe she's just jealous of my and Aide's burgeoning connection. She's not blind, she must see it by now and realise that whatever they had is almost certainly extinct.

We all have the same items in our backpacks, one piece of cardboard with the paper bag logo of the retailer glued to one side, cut to size, on the other adhesive body tape. Posey, Eimear and I also have black masking tape to be applied where appropriate. One blanket for exit. No signs, no megaphones. Just us.

'Are you nervous?' Aide tugs my shirt as we get closer.

'No, excited,' I lie as we turn a corner and the queue comes into view, hundreds of people waiting until the doors open on the largest emporium of exploitation and corruption. My stomach falls at the reality of what we are about to do. With one last run through of the procedure we join the line and wait quietly. Sounds rumble down as feet start to shuffle towards the opening doors, the florescent lights and stark white walls beckoning us like some sort of warped afterlife. We cross the threshold together but immediately split in accordance with the plan. Aide and Seb in one direction, Po, Eimear and I in another. The noise of clinking metal hangers on metal rails, of shoppers calling for each other and generic pop shop music seeping through the speakers all mix together to form a crescendo in my already tense mind. I walk as if in a bubble, not aware of my own feet as they find their way into a changing room. I know Eimear and Po are in here somewhere too, but we spread out and I can't keep an eye on them, check if they are ready or chickening out, exactly what I am trying desperately not to do. My reflection surrounds me, I can't escape it. The only wall space that isn't mirrored is a thin strip of plasterboard where I've hung the cheap dresses I'm pretending to try on. I remove my leggings and t-shirt, stuffing them into my bag. My bra and knickers are next and I am fully exposed. Jesus am I really going to do this? Why am I doing this? For the cause Maeve, for the family. For him. For her. I pep talk myself and fasten the round piece of cardboard to my pubic bone. The tape pulls at my short pubic hairs and I immediately want to whip it off, but I don't. I just adjust it a little so it's not unbearable. Girls filter out into the common area, admiring and criticising each other's choices. I hope they can't hear sounds of ripping masking tape over the level of their excited voices. With the first strip I cover my right nipple, a second strip forms a black cross. I do the same on the left. Indecency laws are a little less strict here in UK territory than they are in the Republic. Aide had done his research. As long as the genitals and nipples are covered, there really is nothing the police can do to us. Sure, the security guards can man handle us and remove us from the premises, but we can't be arrested unless we damage property or harass members of the public. We will be breaking no actual law.

Shit, that was the easy part, now I have to actually walk out of here like this. I apply the last vital item, baby oil, squirting it all over my body. The more slippery we are the harder it will be for the guards to catch us. My phone vibrates. It's a group text, Po is ready, so is Eimear. Seb and Aide send a thumbs up. It's time, just me left to confirm, to give the green light. I send my reply.

Lets go.

The door opens to a stream of passing bodies, it takes a second for recognition to occur, for the eyes to process what they are witnessing. I don't make eye contact, I focus on the exit to the shop floor, I don't even look around for the other girls, afraid of finding opposition, a barrier to stop me. At the desk where the girls hand out numbered tags and hold onto your shopping bags, staff shout at me and call out for security, they don't touch me though. I run through the aisles, avoiding people who are in the main, already creating a path for the crazed, oiled up naked woman dragging a backpack behind her. The cardboard is chafing between my legs and I worry about its effectiveness at keeping me within the constraints of the law. In the centre of the shop there's an open space at the bottom of the escalators, there's an interactive floor map and an electronic stylist offering inane fashion tips. This is where Aide has instructed us to meet. I can see it ahead and just beyond it I see his pale flesh emerging through the crowds. I hold onto my cardboard modesty and stop running, planting my feet firmly as I face him over the divide. His eyes are wide, no doubt filled with the same adrenalin I am. His mouth opens in a smile at first, then widens to facilitate a shout.

'I'd rather be naked than wear fast fashion!'

I repeat his words. To my right, it echoes. Eimear, then Seb's voice across from her. Posey completes our circle and chorus. People are standing around us, holding up their phones, recording us, every inch of us, laughing, shouting, delighting in the unexpected performance during their Saturday morning shopping. Good, let them film us, if my bare ass helps to deliver the message then it will have served a much greater purpose than I'd ever imagined it could. We repeat the chant over and over until our time is up. They come for Aide and Seb first, naked men posing so much more of a societal threat than naked women of course. Thick men in black jackets grab at their greasy skin, struggling to make purchase. Aide resists and his cardboard barrier almost detaches. I keep my gaze fixed on it and fail to see the arms reaching for me. A female guard has me over powered and I have no choice but to let her drag me out of the store, still calling out our message. My captor's jurisdiction expires once we hit the footpath so she releases me.

'What's this all about you bloody head case?' Her heavy Belfast accent adds to the ire in her voice.

'You're working for a company that is killing the planet – don't you care? I start to preach at her while grappling in my bag for the dignity saving blanket.

'Maeve.' Aide is shoved out next to me. 'Leave it, come on.'

His command is urgent so I abandon my lecture and match his pace.

'What about the others?' I look around for them but they must be still inside.

'They will follow – just run.' He's already sprinting down the street as he shouts, his blanket flapping in the wind like a cape. My ginger, environmentalist Superman. I clutch my cape around my boobs and run. Keeping my eyes on him, I try not to think how I must look running through Belfast in runners, a blanket and a backpack. He has the car started when I catch up and jump into the passenger seat.

'Oh my God, I'm dying.' I press hard onto my chest.

'That's just the adrenaline,' he says calmly, barely out of breath.

I know it's more likely the full fat cow's milk flat whites I've been trying so hard to give up since I joined them coupled with my lack of physical exercise, but yeah let him think it's the adrenaline.

'Aren't you worried about the others, what if they get arrested?'

'That's exactly why we had to leg it, the shop will have called the police and if they got us on public nuisance we'd have to go to the station and get booked. It's all just a big waste of time and nothing comes of it but it's still a pain in the ass.'

'So they might have gotten the others?'

'Yeah, they might – we'll wait here for a few minutes but then we'll have to leave them.'

'Leave them?' Shit – would he have left me if I hadn't been manhandled at the same time he was?

'They're coming, open the back door, quick.' He revs the engine.

Three more blanketed bodies approach the car in a blur of vision steadily incorporating sound.

'Go, go.' Seb squeals as he dives head first into the back seat.

'Oh my fucking foot.' Po grunts as she scrambles in

behind him.

Aide looks behind to check his clearance before taking off. I notice he takes a second glance.

'Eimear where's your bag?'

'I dropped it.' Her response is barely audible over the screech of the tyres.

'Fuck.' He slaps the steering wheel with the palm of his hand.

'Sorry Aide.' She sounds like she's about to cry.

He's speeding and twisting our way out of the city and doesn't speak anymore, allowing an uneasy silence to fill the car.

'It's okay Eimear.' I twist around in my seat to look at my comrades. 'Most important thing is we all made it out in one piece and delivered the message – right?'

'Yeah … yeah Maeve's right.' Seb thumps the ceiling of the car. 'We fucking killed it in there, did you see all the cameras that were on us? This is going to go viral.'

'What was in your bag Eimear?' Posey asks firmly.

I watch Eimear's face drain of what little colour was in it to begin with.

'It's just clothes right?' I assure her. 'And the tape, same as ours.'

'I use that bag for work,' she whispers, not quite raising her head enough to make eye contact.

'So, you can have mine, I can get another one from college – no big deal.' See Aide, I have leadership qualities; I can put out these little fires that threaten to burn us.

'What else Eimear?' Posey continues.

'In the side pocket, I'm pretty sure my ID is in there.'

Chapter 14

The drive across the border is long and almost silent; peppered only with a phone call from the guy Seb is dating, which was news to me, Posey's complaints about motion sickness and the sad attempts from Eimear to establish communication with Aide. Each time she asks him something, anything from the possible ramifications of her carelessness to the innocuous inquiry as to whether he's listened to a fashion sustainability podcast she's recommended, he barely responds. And when he does, it's only to inform her that Ferdia will talk to her. I wonder if my role as both passenger seat occupant and Aide's partner means I should mediate or placate, do something to ease the rising tension in the people carrier. But I decide its best to do as he suggests, let Ferdia deal with everything, she is our leader after all. Instead I take the opportunity to compose my semi sincere apology to Shane. I need to be smart about his value. So much of my course is project work and marked as a team, if I can set myself up as his go to assignment buddy, he'll carry my lagging ass up to an above average grade at least. I find him on Instagram and repost the picture he had taken of us that day, then I open a private message.

Hey (wave hand emoji)

I hope you're not so mad at me that you ignore and block.

I'm really sorry about what happened in Sandymount, well the getting you involved part without telling you. That much I know was wrong. The actual event itself, I stand by. But that's not your thing and I get that. I hope we can still be friends?

College is kinda tough for me, I'm not settling in as well

as I thought I would. Guess I'm just secondary school smart and not actually in the same league as super brains like you (wink emoji)

Anyway, would love to grab a coffee on Monday, so say hello when you see me?

Mx

Just enticing enough without explicitly saying I have any intention of ever performing any sexual acts on you. But it will allow him the space to imagine it, no doubt. I'm listening to the podcast Eimear recommended when the notification almost deafens me through my ear buds. It's Shane.

Maeve – is this you? And a link to a YouTube video.

I click on it to see shaky camera phone footage of five naked bodies standing in a circle in the middle of a packed clothing store. I turn up the volume to hear our chant.

'I'd rather be naked than wear fast fashion.'

It's so perfectly timed it distracts me from the reality that my bare ass and breasts are on full display on YouTube. I've nothing to be ashamed of, my body is serving a much greater purpose than being a source of titillation. I mean, if it works for Shane, all the better but really I don't give a shit about being viewed sexually. The message is what matters, not the machine.

'We're up.' I break the silence in the car.

'Let me see.' Seb near jumps into the front seats as I hold my phone up for him. A second message pops up on screen.

What the fuck are you doing?

Seb hesitates in taking my phone. 'Oh do you want to reply to that first?'

'No, it can wait.'

'Okay great, I have to send this to Eoghan, he will lose his beautiful innocent little Irish Catholic mind.'

'Are we identifiable?' Aide asks without looking at me.

'No, I don't think so, the person filming tended to concentrate on places other than our faces.'

'Just don't share it on your personal accounts okay.' He says. 'We'll wait until Ferdia decides what will be the official release of the mission … okay Seb?'

'Huh?' He breaks his attention away from my phone. 'Oh yeah, just sending a private text to Eoghan, he won't share it, the poor child doesn't even know how.'

'Posey … Eimear?' Aide seeks their compliance. They confirm it. 'How did you find it Maeve?'

'A guy from college sent me the link.'

'How did he find it and connect it to you?' Now his clear blue eyes leave the road and rest on me. I realise I don't have an answer for him.

'I'm not sure actually, should I ask him?'

'Only if you can do it subtly.'

I open Shane's last message and type.

How did you find this?

The bubbles appear immediately.

I have a YouTube alert for anything connected to that activist group you mentioned. The person who uploaded the video tagged them. It's you isn't it? Are you okay Maeve … seriously?

The last line causes me to pause a second, maybe just a little unnerved by his concern. Why would he ever think I'm not okay? I'm doing exactly what I was born to do.

Thanks for asking Shane. I appreciate you being a friend and hope we can grab that coffee on Monday? I'm fine, trust me. (Flexing arm emoji. Smiley face. Coffee cup.)

Yes Maeve. Coffee Monday. Call me if you need anything or anyone in the meantime.

Bit dramatic for a Galway man Shane. I leave it at that. He won't be a problem for us.

'All okay?' Aide reaches across to squeeze my thigh.

'Yeah, he just had an alert for activism videos, it wasn't connected to me personally.' I smile a reassuring smile, hoping to allay whatever concerns are brewing inside him. The thought of disappointing him creates an uncomfortable heat in me. The last thing I want to do is damage my chances of picking up where we left off last weekend. He's been so preoccupied with the mission I know it's understandable why he's not had time for me, for us I mean. I'm not a needy girl anyway, I'm secure in the looks and touches he gives me. I know he wants this as much as I do. I can wait for sex. I can wait for the others to know we are more than just housemates and fellow warriors. But a kiss, just a kiss would be nice.

It's late when we arrive in Donnybrook and we are all tired and grumpy from the journey. Zamara calls out from the living room.

'Hey, come and tell me how it went' she shouts and Posey obliges. Eimear starts to follow her but Aide takes hold of her arm, halting her.

'Ferdia is waiting for you upstairs.' He says firmly. Eimear doesn't respond, just changes her course and heads for the stairs instead.

'Well I'm fucked, I'm going to bed,' Seb announces.

'Good idea, I'll join you.' Aide takes the stairs after them, without looking back to see what my intentions are.

'Oh … okay,' I say to myself, there's no one else listening. I stand there considering my options of joining a laughing Zamara and Posey in the living room or retiring to my single bed to await Eimear's return from whatever it is she is facing upstairs. I opt for the latter, passing the closed door of his room. What have I done wrong? Why hasn't he even kissed me since he went down on me, I mean, mixed messages. What the fuck? I rile myself up as I trudge the three flights up to my room.

Much later, I have no idea what time it is, just that the room is as dark as it gets, the creaking of the door and floorboards wake me. It's obvious that Eimear is trying her best to be quiet, to slip into her bed without disturbing me, but she fails. In my confused state of half sleep, I think I can hear her sobbing, but when I try to concentrate on the sound and determine if it's a dream or reality, I can't.

When I wake up late, Eimear is already gone. She always does early shifts in the coffee shop at the weekend, she must be wrecked after all the drama yesterday. Maybe I'll call down to the village and buy a coffee and try to grab a few minutes alone with her. I just want to check she's okay. I can't imagine how upset I'd be if I messed up the way she did, to have both Aide and Ferdia disappointed in me. It's my turn to cook for the house anyway so I could do with asking her advice, my vegan meal planning and execution still leaves a lot to be desired. I open the upstairs window to see everyone doing yoga in the garden. Why didn't they wake me to join in? Am I castigated as her roommate? No, it can't be that, they must have just figured I needed the lie in. I've been so busy this week. I decide against disturbing their bliss and quietly eat my granola and fruit in the kitchen, watching them. He looks beautiful today, a cotton hairband holds his hair back from his forehead, allowing the sun to fully illuminate his face. I watch his long, flexible body move gracefully, like a cat extending and bending, contracting and relaxing. My mind fills with images of what it can do to and with my body, what shapes and sounds and sensations we could create. It will happen Maeve, just be patient. I take two canvas shoppers from the press under the sink and leave the house unnoticed.

The coffee shop is one of a chain, but still has that cosy intimate feeling with mismatched comfortable furniture and soft instrumental music. I join a long queue and pass the time on my phone. Last night Aisling sent me a string of Snapchats and Instagram messages from her night with Cian. Like I really want to be a virtual third wheel on your date. Good luck to you and all that but keep it to yourself. She's trying desperately to smooth things over after our last communication but I really can't be bothered with keeping her secure and entertained right now. The video that Shane sent me has gotten some traction, almost 300 views, 42 shares, comments are mostly positive, support for the cause and our intentions. Of course there are the suggestions that we hit the gym or stop subjecting the public to our crusty, hairy hippie bodies. Are we hairy? Seb is, but the rest of us? I don't know what the standard is now to be honest.

'Hey, what can I get you?' The barista pushes his floppy dark hair behind his ear and fixes his thick rimmed glasses.

'Oh sorry,' I say, having not realised my position at the top of the line. 'Soya flat white please.' I was expecting Eimear to be on the machine. When I get his attention again I ask, 'is Eimear on a break?'

'No, she's not here.' His face suggests this is not a positive development.

'Not at all?' I tap the machine to pay.

'Yep, just me here on our busiest morning.' Frustration bubbles out the edges of his mouth.

'Okay, I'll just text her, thanks.'

'Good luck, I've been trying that all morning ... next there.' He snaps his head away from me and focuses on the next in line.

She definitely wasn't doing yoga with the others in the garden, she wasn't in the house and she's not at work. Where is she? There's still no reply from her after I've finished the food shop and return to the house.

'Oh Maeve, let me help you.' Zamara meets me in the hall and takes one of the bags from me, leading us to the kitchen.

She's talking about the mission and how she and Ferdia made the official announcement on our channels just an hour ago. I'm starting to question why they didn't wait until Eimear and I were here to go over everything, but my thoughts are stemmed when she opens the kitchen door and I see them. Locked in a tight embrace. Aide and Eimear.

'Oh, hey,' I splutter, the shopping suddenly too heavy to bear anymore so I set it on the floor.

'Oh dinner – thank you Maeve, you're such a great house-mate.' Eimear grins widely at me.

'Eh yeah – I called into the coffee shop to see you.' I watch as he continues to rub her back, in front of me, you do know I can see you?

'Oh yeah, sorry – I've left.' She says like it's nothing.

'Just like that – no notice?'

'No, I just decided making macchiatos and triple shot lattes was not a valuable use of my terrestrial time. I only have one life, in this body at least and I want to spend it doing the Clan's work.' Her wide eyes barely blink.

'We need her more,' Aide chips in now before enveloping her in another tight squeeze while looking at me.

'Well I certainly do.' I slap on a forced smile. 'I haven't a clue about what I'm about to cook – help me?'

She returns a beaming, seemingly genuine smile. 'Of course.'

'I'd offer to help too but I'm on gardening duty.' Aide makes gestures of apology and leave taking and soon the only sounds in the small kitchen are knives on wooden chopping boards.

'Is everything okay Eimear?' I venture after a while.

'Hmm?' she replies absently. 'Oh yes, everything is fine. Should I chop all the garlic?'

'May as well,' I say, chucking the diced onion into the sauce-pan. 'I mean after yesterday, the issue with your bag and having to speak to Ferdia.'

'Yes, I understand that Maeve – and everything is fine. How was Mathius this morning?'

'Who?'

'In the coffee shop, was he run off his feet?'

'Oh yeah him, he was. He seemed kinda pissed off that you weren't there.'

'Oh well, they'll find someone else and soon forget me.'

'When did you decide to quit?'

'Just last night.'

'I thought you liked it there and needed the money.'

'I do – I did. But we don't need money, not while we live here, that's why Ferdia is so wonderful, she provides what we need.'

'Oh shit, I think I added the wrong spice.' I hold the jar up for her to inspect.

'No, that's the right one.'

'Oh good – I can't afford any fuck ups, not on my first family dinner.'

'You don't need to worry about that Maeve, not for a long time,' she says quietly, her back to me as she takes a jar from the fridge. 'Here, try this.'

I taste a tiny bit of the red paste she offers me. 'Oh shit that's hot.'

'Just add a teaspoon – Aide loves it.' She smiles as she says his name and it makes me an uncomfortable blend of nauseous and furious.

'Yeah, he loves lots of thing.' I'm fast finding out.

'He's a very open spirit.'

'I lay down my knife and look her in the eye. 'Are you sure you two …'

She shakes her head before I finish my question. 'No, it's not like that.'

I believe her but I still think that she wants it to be like that. Maybe that's why she was crying last night, something happened between them, she made a move and he rejected her – for me. Oh. The injection of joy and self-satisfaction is tinged, just a little, with pity for her.

'Are you sure you're okay though? Last night, were you crying in bed?'

'Oh no, you must have been dreaming.' She smiles sweetly.

'Yeah, I thought that but it seemed real, you know you can tell me if something is wrong, it can just be between us.'

'Just leave it Maeve.' Now her knife is down and her eyes fixed on me. It's like looking at her for the first time, the real her. The mask of compliance and congeniality temporarily slipped. A steely, wretched expression on her cherubic face.

'Okay,' I say and return my attention to the celery.

Chapter 15

I buy the coffees, a contrite gesture to appease the obvious anger that still bubbles under his well-bred politeness.

'Thanks,' Shane says as he takes the cup from me and shifts over on the wooden bench.

'Not at all, thank you for talking to me after the whole ... you know.' I've already apologized, have to be careful not to give too much of my power away.

'Well to be honest Maeve, I'm still pretty pissed about what you did but I'm more worried about what you're doing or about to do.'

For Christ's sake, what price must I pay to get a little academic insurance? 'Don't be, everything is awesome in the house, perfect in fact. I love it and I love all of them.' I rub his arm in an attempt to assure and distract. 'How's everything with you? Anything exciting happen in the pub last weekend?'

'Awesome, perfect ... love.' He repeats my words. 'Don't you think it's all a bit much?' He takes a sip of his coffee, keeping his searching eyes fixed on me.

'Well maybe I'm not as good with words as you are Shane, which is why I'm hoping you'll agree to be my project partner – you know for the joint assignments. I think we would work great together.' I instruct my face to convey a heady mix of awe, vulnerability and sensuality – one of them have to work on him.

'Ahh,' he says into his cup.

'Hmm?' I try to sound unnerved.

'That's the reason for this free coffee then? Freeload on my work?'

'Well – I mean, I will do half of everything, we'll be a team.'

'I think you're already part of a team Maeve. You and all the other suburbanite Spahn Ranch wannabes.'

'The Clan has nothing to do with my college work.' I choose to ignore his Manson family insult, it is so unworthy of air and beyond his comprehension to even try to explain how we couldn't be further from the band of violent, murderous misfits.

'You do realise that whatever crazy shit they get you to do will follow you forever don't you?' He shifts on the bench to face me head on, as if his body is punctuating the importance of his lecture. 'You're studying media, please tell me you at least have a basic understanding of the prevalence and longevity of social media. These videos and images will follow you wherever you go – to job interviews, visa applications …'

'But my name isn't attached, none of our names are ever released. They can't be traced back to us.' Ferdia is the only one who sacrificed her identity for the cause, her members are name-less, just transitional faces, never the same ones in the same place, always moving and changing. That's why Eimear dropping her ID badge was a problem, I'd never be so careless on a job.

'I found you.' He cuts down my defence.

'Well, that's different, you knew where to look. You know me.'

'This is Ireland Maeve, you're going to meet a lot of people who know you. There's no such thing as anonymity here – that's all I'm saying. Be careful with your identity – it's the only thing you've really got.'

I let his words hang there in the campus yard for a moment, watching students pass by on their way to lectures, each one unique, special – identifiable.

'Okay, I hear you. I'll be more careful.' This time I don't think I'm fully lying to just get what I want from him.

'Okay then.' He stands up. 'I've got to get to Marketing, are you coming to class today or do you have more pressing business back at the ranch?'

'No, I'm coming.' I follow him.

'Okay, good. I think Conleth is giving us our assignment today so we can brainstorm some initial ideas together.'

Wait, so he's agreeing to be my partner? 'Oh yeah', definitely, sounds awesome.'

He shoots me a look that causes me to rephrase. 'Sounds great, thanks Shane.'

What's a little flagellation if you ultimately get what you came here for. My grades are secure, all I have to do is keep Shane sweet and he'll carry me through, he's not capable of submitting substandard work. This frees me up to devote even more time to the Clan, to what really matters.

It's later than usual when I arrive home, having had to appear eager and committed to the graphic design assignment our lecturer Richard had given us. I really couldn't care less about it, I know my real work only starts when I come through this door. It's quiet in the hallway, no sounds of cooking or chatter coming from the kitchen, which I've come to expect at this time of the evening. The living room door creaks open and Zamara appears.

'Oh Maeve, good you're home.' She opens the door wide to usher me in. 'We're having a family meeting.'

My instinctive smile upon entering the room drops as the scene inside reveals itself to me. It's darker in here than it should be, the heavy red velvet curtains are drawn, no candles are lit. They sit in hallowed silence.

'Hi,' I say as an almost inaudible whisper, unsure if my voice is welcome. Ferdia sits motionless in her chair and around Aide, Seb and Posey form a circle that Zamara joins and gestures for me to do the same, completing it. We all face towards the centre, at the focal point, standing there, rigid, silent, head bowed, eyes fixed on the floor at her feet. Eimear.

'Now that Maeve is here and the Clan is complete, we can begin.' Ferdia holds her hands in a sign of prayer.

'Zamara.' Ferdia looks to her. 'Please present the evidence.'

She reaches down the side of the sofa we are on and retrieves a brown paper bag. The logo on it is instantly recognisable, it's from the huge high street store we protested in. I recognise it instantly. She places the bag at Eimear's feet, who now lifts her head to look at us, one by one, but doesn't speak. She looks scared and I feel uncomfortable. I look to Aide, sitting directly across from me, maybe I can figure out how to act in this scenario by watching him. But he's still and silent, they all are, so I try to do the same. Then she speaks again.

'Eimear – can you explain to the family what this is doing in your bedroom?' Ferdia's voice is calm.

'No, it's not mine – I've never seen it before.' The crack in Eimear's throat is loud against the silence surrounding her.

'Lying will not favourably affect your case Eimear. Zamara, where did you find this bag?'

'Under Eimear's bed,' she replies dutifully.

'When?'

'This morning.'

'What is in it?'

'Clothing items Ferdia.'

'Eimear – enjoy a little shopping spree at the expense of child labour, global consumerism and environmental rape did you? A little treat for yourself after quitting your job?' There's a spark in Ferdia's eyes that's new to me, I daren't look at it too long for fear of being burnt by it.

'I swear I didn't, it's not mine.'

Ferdia halts her defence with the rise of a hand. 'I fully understand your situation Eimear.' Her voice softens again and my back relaxes. 'You had to leave the coffee shop, you're no longer earning a wage, but you still want to look nice, pretty, alluring to your housemates – correct?'

Eimear looks at Aide and it's so awkward I feel for her. 'Well, no.'

'Aide,' Ferdia says loudly. 'Do you want to fuck Eimear?'

My heart feels like it's stopped. I watch his face, then hers. He opens his mouth to speak but seeming unsure of his answer, looks to Ferdia, for guidance perhaps.

'Well maybe whatever is in that bag will help form your decision. Eimear why don't you show us what you bought?' Ferdia sits up in her chair, enthusiastically gesturing to the paper bag at Eimear's bare feet. She shakes her head.

'No. I don't want to.' She struggles not to cry.

'Put your hand into the bag and take out what is inside. Now.'

Eimear slowly follows Ferdia's order, her now glazed eyes find mine in her search for support. I look away.

'Oh, look at that.' Ferdia claps as Eimear lifts out a black satin robe from the bag. It trembles in her grip. 'Anything else in there, go on, show us what else you got for yourself.'

She bends again and returns with a black lace knicker and bra set.

'Oh very sexy Eimear. Aide – do you like?'

He remains still and silent.

'Hmm, seems he's not entirely convinced yet Eimear, maybe he – and indeed all of us – need a little visual stimulation. Why don't you try them on for us.'

'Please.' Eimear sobs openly now, clutching the items to her heaving chest.

'Do it,' Ferdia shouts and I grip onto my knees to steady myself. Seb and Posey stare at the floor. Zamara smiles at Ferdia, it looks like she's enjoying this. Aide's eyes fleet from Ferdia to Eimear to me, as if looking at what happening acknowledges yet absolves. Through quiet, painful gasps of breath, Eimear slips her dress off her shoulders, letting it fall to the floor before stepping out of it. Her plain white bra and floral underwear a direct contrast to the lingerie she's still holding.

'Oh dear – no wonder you needed a little help.' Ferdia laughs. Zamara follows. Ferdia looks at her and she stops.

'Maeve.' The sound of my name in her voice startles me. 'I'm sure you look better underneath your clothes, what do you think Aide?' She looks over to him but doesn't await a response from either of us. 'Strip,' she demands.

'Please Ferdia, I'm sorry. I'll do whatever you want,' Eimear cries.

'This, my dear, is what I want – so do it.'

And she does, she unhooks her bra and pushes her knickers down her legs, standing there completely physically and emotionally exposed. I can't look her in the face, it's too uncomfortable.

'Now, the moment we've all been waiting for.' Ferdia claps loudly. 'Let's see how these cheap corrupt pieces of filth transform you from the boring, plain country girl to the alluring sex goddess you truly know yourself to be. Please, go ahead.' She extends her hand and sits back in her chair.

Eimear slips into the black lace panties and manoeuvres herself into the bra. She stands there, still apart from the constant tremble of her body.

'Oh yes,' Ferdia says softly. 'Now, that's completely worth it. Don't you all agree? Eimear is now 100% fuckable – yes?'

No one replies.

'Well, Eimear darling, I truly hope you have aroused yourself because it would be a shame not to get something out of this. Zamara,' Ferdia diverts her attention. 'Take the vote.'

What's happening now, we're voting on whether or not she looks sexy – Jesus, okay yes she looks sexy – just make this stop.

'I vote her out,' Zamara says confidently and without hesitation.

Out. We're voting her out. This is a trial.

'Posey – what is your verdict?' Zamara asks.

'I vote she stays,' Posey speaks.

'Seb,' Zamara continues. 'What is your verdict?'

'I vote she stays.'

'Aide – what is your verdict?'

'I vote her out.' His voice sounds like it's not coming out of his body, having been silent for so long.

I feel Zamara's eyes on me now. 'So the final vote rests with you Maeve.'

'What about Ferdia?' I ask, not wanting this responsibility.

'Ferdia does not vote. She is evolved,' Zamara explains.

It's up to me, two to go, two to stay. I decide her fate. I don't want this, I really don't. But I also don't want to be the new girl who defies the leader and her second in command. I know what I have to do, she'd do the same to me. I have to protect my position in this family, in Ferdia's eyes, in Aide's. I have no choice.

'Maeve,' Zamara prompts my decision.

I look at Eimear, desperately trying to cover her exposed flesh as she stands there in judgement. Her eyes fix on mine and I feel a stab of discomfort, of shame perhaps, before I speak into the void.

'I vote her out.' Guilt. It's guilt.

Chapter 16

The room seems so big now. Her bed is still unmade, the blue and yellow herringbone blanket drapes onto the floor, as if in slow, imperceptible pursuit of her. I lift it up and place it in a heap. On the old, heavy chest of drawers beside where her head used to lie, various eyes watch me. The faded photographs of her real family, friends, pets judge me, find me guilty of betrayal. I turn the frames over one by one, slapping down their condemnation. Eimear was not my responsibility. Whatever happened to her, was the decision of the Clan. It is bigger than me, than her. The quietness all around me is unnerving so I play some music on my phone, sad slow playlist. I burn a white sage incense stick and light one of her Moroccan Rose candles. The space needs cleansing of whatever bad energy her departure has created. My attempts at serenity are so successful that it takes a couples of knocks at my door before I accept that someone is there. When I lower the music, the gentle tap is clear. I open the door to find him there, a new expression on his beautiful, symmetrical face.

'Aide, hi.' My voice is a breath.

'Hey – are you okay?' His asking this prompts me to adjust my smile to a lamenting frown.

'No – no, I don't think I am.'

'Yeah, that was … intense.' His body twists forward, as if ready to proceed. 'Can I come in?'

'Oh yeah.' I step aside.

'Only if it's okay, I understand if you'd rather be alone.'

'No, please come in.' I shut the door firmly after him. 'Take a seat.' I turn to see he has already done so, on Eimear's bed. My bed now.

He smiles and pats a hand on the blue and yellow blanket. I sit as close to him as possible without touching or revealing the reality that having him alone in my bedroom is the best outcome I could have imagined, no matter what price was paid.

'I just feel like I never really knew her at all,' he says to the open space, his eyes focused on something other than me.

'I know, it was such a shock.'

'I mean, it's like she was just pretending this whole time – does she not even believe in everything we've been doing, doesn't she care about any of it?' When he looks at me, I adopt a sympathetic mirror and accompany it with a gentle touch of his thigh. Initiate physical contact.

'I'm sure she did Aide, it was probably just one stupid mistake, don't let it get to you, it's not worth it.' These words leave my mouth instinctively having already spoken them less than an hour ago, almost verbatim, here in this room.

'Oh Maeve, what the hell just happened?' She had cried in my arms as I cradled her, here on the edge of this bed.

'I'm so sorry, can you forgive me? I just didn't know what to do for the best.' I had sought her absolution.

'It's not your fault, it wouldn't have made any difference even if you voted me to stay. Ferdia had made her mind up. She orchestrated the whole thing. I was out no matter what. You were right to protect your position here.'

Her understanding and compassion made me feel even worse. 'It's just a little mistake, Ferdia will get over it, she just needs some time.'

'But what she did to me – it was horrible,' she bawled, full on snot and streaming eyes.

I couldn't argue with that. It was horrific. I don't think I've ever seen someone humiliated like that before. But who am I to judge Ferdia's methods? This is her army, her house – we are all here at her good grace.

'Has she done stuff like that before?' I needed to know what is normal in this world.

'Not like that no, it's always different.' Eimear's voice was muffled as she pulled her suitcase out from under the bed.

'What – the punishment?'

'No,' she sighed as she flipped open the case. 'The banishment.'

Aide rubs my hand that rests on his leg. 'I'm so glad you're here Maeve. It's good to have someone here who understands me.' His eyes are watery and I wonder if he's about to cry. Did he like her that much?

'You can talk to me anytime, about anything,' I pause to formulate my next sentence wisely. 'So, what will happen now … to Eimear?'

I feel his leg tense under my hand.

'What do you mean, happen to her?'

'Will she ever be allowed back in – or even participate in our protests? She seemed really upset at the thought of abandoning her activism.'

'We voted her out Maeve. She's out,' he says firmly.

'Yeah but …'

'No buts, she is no longer a member of this family.'

'But what if she comes to one of our protests?'

'She won't.'

'How do you know?'

'Because she's seen how this works. Eimear knew that once she betrayed us, there was no coming back. You need to promise me something Maeve.' He shifts to move even closer to me and our faces are almost touching.

'Okay.'

'You can never talk to her again.'

I had repeated her word. 'Banishment. That's a bit extreme isn't it Eimear?'

'What else do you call sending someone away and never speaking to them or about them ever again?'

'You don't know what will happen, we'll still stay in touch.' I tried to salve my guilty conscience as she wheeled her packed case to the door.

'You won't be allowed to Maeve. I wasn't allowed with Hannah, you won't be allowed with me.'

Hannah. The passport. 'Who is Hannah?'

'No one, Hannah is no one.' Her usually cheerful and open face darkened before my eyes as she turned to face the landing. 'Bye Maeve, good luck.'

'Eimear – wait,' I whispered at the door, conscious that Ferdia was waiting downstairs to ensure her speedy exit. 'What about all your stuff – will I meet you somewhere with it?'

She shook her head. 'They are just things Maeve. Consider everything I had to be yours now.' She smiled a reluctant smile before commencing her solemn march down the stairs and out the front door before it slammed shut after her, rattling the bones of the entire house.

What was hers is mine now. 'I promise.' I say into the narrow void between our mouths.

'You are a true, loyal and courageous friend Maeve.' He brushes back my hair from my face. 'You do so much for others. What can I do for you?'

I barely think before speaking, for once not unsure that my wish will be granted. 'I don't want to be alone tonight.'

His eyes remain open as he brings his mouth to mine. I fight my instincts to close mine for fear of missing even a second of this glorious sight. His kiss is notably gentle, as if he's barely touching me at all. I want to pull him in closer, harder. But again, I resist. I want to gauge how he likes it first, I want him to enjoy this. I don't want him to change his mind, get up and walk out, never to mention it again, not like the last time. Whatever you like Aide, as long as you like me. When his tongue moves inside my mouth I feel it's okay to respond and match his speed and intensity, still slow and soft. I edge myself further up the bed, trying to angle my body for the optimum position for a throw down. Come on, throw me down, bury your head into my neck, breathe me in, rest your weight on top of me, let me feel how much you want me. He stops. His face comes into my full view again as he moves further away from me. What have I done wrong? Why is he stopping?

'What's wrong?' My voice sounds weak, both in content and construct.

'Nothing.' He smiles down at me and I relax a little under his gaze. 'Lie back,' he whispers.

I lay my head on the pillow and try to make my body form some manner of an alluring pose, legs open, one up one down? Closed and to the side? What are you supposed to do at this moment, invite him in or feign frigidity, make him work for it? That's not going to happen. He takes his shirt off and I watch intently as he tackles his jeans next. The pop of the button, the pull of the zip. I'm so mesmerised by the motion that there's a genuine yelp of shock when he grabs both of my ankles and drags me towards him. His hair falls over one eye as the other stares at me. His long slender hands remove my knickers. His focus stays on my face as he takes my left foot and kisses it, sending shivers through me. I pull it away but he tightens his grip.

'Be a good girl Maeve,' he squeezes it before sucking on my big toe. It's such an odd sensation that I can't be sure if I enjoy it or not. I still have my dress on, even if it's bundled up around my waist and he still has his open jeans on. As much as I'm up for whatever he's in to, I need to feel him on me or in me.

'Aide – I want to see you.' I sit up and reach for his waistband. His hand halts mine and firmly pushes it back down.

'Take off your dress,' he orders and I gladly comply.

I lie back, my breasts flattened against my chest, vulnerable and defenceless to his expectations and evaluations.

'Have you been fucked before Maeve?' he asks as he runs his fingers down the length of my legs, stopping where I most want them to be.

I nod my head and mouth a yes, even though my past experience is so pathetic I'm not even sure if I'm technically still a virgin.

'Would you like to be fucked by me Maeve?'

I'd have thought that was pretty self-evident, I'm lying naked in front of you, my legs wide open. But maybe he needs to hear me say it, a consent thing or maybe it turns him on, so I do.

He edges his jeans and underwear past his hips, releasing his hard penis as they fall. It's smaller than the few I've seen, but thicker and smoother and just an all-round good looking one. It has to be, it's his. He takes it in his hand and presses the tip against me, edging his way in. I try to take stock of what I'm feeling, to regulate my shallow breathing and isolate and identify the sensations and stimulations currently taking place inside me. I close my eyes to increase their potency. They all mingle together to form some sort of bliss. Not climactic explosion, not sensory intoxication, just bliss. I've often wondered what a heroin hit would feel like; this might be it or something close. I feel him move deeper inside me and I sit up, suddenly afraid.

'Aide wait.'

'What?' He slows his stride but doesn't stop.

'What about the condom?' I picture the lone one somewhere in my bag courtesy of The Dublin School of Media.

'Oh don't worry about that.' He continues.

'Why?' I know I should stop him but I don't.

'I never use them, I'll pull out, it's fine – don't worry, we're both clean. We're pure.'

I look into his darkened eyes, concentrated on the orgasm percolating inside of him, that I am responsible for, my body is giving him pleasure. I say nothing and move with him, bringing us both to the edges of two very different cliffs.

Chapter 17

For the first time since I've been part of the Clan, we are all going on an outing together. Of course there are six of us now, but it's still quite an achievement to get us all in the one place at the same time. Seb has been spending more and more time with Eoghan and Zamara is hardly ever at home in the evenings. I have no idea where she goes; we barely speak. Maybe today will be an opportunity for us to bond a little. It won't be as enjoyable as bonding with Aide but I'm still up for it. It's just past 10am when we leave the house, our bags packed with nutritious vegan lunches and a rain jacket. The sky is clear now but this is Ireland and the rain is never too far away.

'I hope you guys are ready for a bracing coastal hike?' Ferdia ushers us out the gate.

'I thought our day out was supposed to be a treat?' Seb whines as he adjusts the lace on his hardly used boots.

'I can think of no greater treat than spending the day immersed in the beauty and power of the natural world.' Ferdia leads the way towards the village.

'I can think of a better way to pass the time.' Aide says so only I can hear and it fills me with an addictive dose of satisfaction and anticipation. I give him a complicit smile. Soon, soon we can tell the others that we are together, properly, not like whatever it was he had with Eimear. This is real, mutual, transformative.

We follow her to Sandymount train station, where we each purchase a day return to Howth. I've not been to the Northside of the county yet and I wonder if it's anything like Cavan or Ballycastle even. Does this city sprawl all the way to the edges of the sea or is there a place for nature and animals and growth. I spot four free seats when we board the DART carriage and make a beeline for it. It's only when I'm seated that I realise no one has followed me. I look to Aide and beckon him down but he shakes his head and remains standing at the doors.

'Hey, why aren't we sitting down?' I ask them when I give in and get up.

'Oh no Maeve.' Ferdia lays a hand on my shoulder. 'We don't occupy a seat that could be spared for those more in need.'

'Oh.'

'It is just one simple way in which we practise our egalitarianism,' Zamara adds. 'We acknowledge that we are equal to others, yet we chose to demonstrate our altruism in whatever ways we can.'

'Oh right, of course.' I nod as if I completely understand what we are supposed to stand for now. Sometimes I feel like it changes, but maybe I'm just not keeping up. I need to spend more time with Ferdia. I can't let the Aide distraction harm my activism apprenticeship. I try to stay close to her as we alight the train and make our way through the village of Howth and towards the start of the coastal trail. It smells of fish and seaweed and is definitely nothing like Cavan. It's true that we have a lake for every day of the year but no static body of water can ever compare with the vitality of the sea, especially on a day like today when it crashes against the rocks and shoots spray up in playful dance. After the initial incline we stop to catch a breath and take in the views of the expansive blue of sea and sky separated by rocky outcrops and far away headlands.

'So this is Howth Maeve, how do you like it?' Ferdia reaches her arm around my waist and pulls me close to her side.

'It's the most beautiful place I've ever been,' I say without a bit of verbosity. I haven't been to that many places.

'I knew you would like it, you have a naturist soul,' she says into my ear and I don't disagree. 'You understand the balance of power between man and nature.'

Other ramblers approach us on the path so we step closer to the cliff edge to let them pass. The unsteadiness of my footing unnerves me but I try not to show it. I am at one with nature after all.

After walking for just under an hour, Ferdia takes a slight detour inland, leading us to a flat clearing of browned grass and rocks. She sits cross legged on the largest flat stone and closes her eyes to the sea in front of her. Zamara takes a seat facing her, her back to the scenic view. Aide follows and I quickly do the same, eager not to repeat my DART mistake. There is a soft drizzle falling now and it is welcome after the exertion. I'm a little hungry too, maybe we're having our lunches now but I'm not going to assume anything and decide to await instructions. They all close their eyes, cross their legs and adopt a silence. My stomach rumbles and creates a melody with the swirling cross winds around us. But these are the only sounds. We are silent. For the longest time. I peek to my side, Posey's eyes are shut, in front of me Aide's back is rigid. I try to manifest the serenity they are all obviously experiencing but all I can do is anticipate the moment this silence is broken. And then, it is.

'Breathe,' Ferdia almost sighs. 'Breathe in each other, in others who have been, breathe out those yet to come.'

The others make heavy breathing sounds so I do the same. Behind me I can sense there are people passing, slowing down on the trail to observe what we are doing. They don't speak until further down the path, their mumbled voices carrying in the breeze. My legs are a little sore now so I shift my position on the stone.

'Maeve,' Ferdia says without opening her eyes.

'Yes?'

'If you are not still, you are a disruptive force. Do you wish to be a disruptive force in our ceremony?'

'No,' I say, trying not to move as I speak.

'Everything we do, every movement, sound, intention is connected to the earth. We are linked together by an invisible thread. If you pull on a thread it can unravel, begin a slow but certain descent into destruction. Our obligation for our time on this planet is knowing what threads to pull and when to pull them.'

I open my eyes again to see that no one has moved. I shut them before I'm caught.

'We are made of dirt and stardust. We have come from the abyss of nothingness and there we will return. The only thing we can control is our legacy – what we have lived and ultimately died for. The earth has granted us leave to make a difference, to affect, to infect, to perfect. What will you do with your time? Wander blind? March with purpose? Lead others to the cliff that you yourself are not willing to fall over? Are you leaders in words only? Theoretical revolutionaries? Ineffectual intellectual pretenders to the thrones of the greats who have lived and died for their righteous convictions? Answer me.'

There is no inflection in her voice so I don't know if this is in fact a command.

'I said answer me,' she repeats louder now.

'No Ferdia,' everyone says in unison but I miss the cue.

'If our mother dies, do we die? Cut off at the source?' she continues. 'If there is no earth, there is no new life. We are the last bastion of hope for future generations. The mantle has fallen on our shoulders. Who among us will rise up and carry it? Who has the strength, the will and the humility to carry the cross and nail themselves to it in order to save all others to come?'

I had no idea Ferdia was religious, if I had have known that using Jesus metaphors was her thing I could have impressed her long ago with tales from my childhood where fish was always eaten on Fridays and the Angelus observed every evening.

'Jesus the prophet gave his life to save future generations, whatever he believed himself to be is irrelevant. Whether his instruction came from God, Mother Earth, extra-terrestrial begins – all one, all none – is not important; merely the intention. To preserve life, life itself must be lost. To live on we must die. Ashes to ashes, dust to dust. From the decaying remains grows forth the flesh and blood of tomorrow. Will you be the architects of tomorrow?'

'Yes Ferdia,' this time I answer with them.

'Will you be the symbols of the revolution?'

'Yes Ferdia.'

'Will you reject fear and pride in favour of glory and sacrifice?'

'Yes Ferdia.'

'Our time will come, my children. We must be ready – who among you is ready?'

Silence. I look around, no one else opens their eyes.

'Soon. The symbol is coming soon,' she continues. 'The earth will provide for us. We must be the symbol or we must find it. Let us meditate for guidance and strength to continue on our mission.'

I shut my eyes tight and bow my head, my body trembles from having sat in this unnatural position for so long, my ass is numb on the rock beneath it. I try my best to reflect an image of peace and inner wisdom while her words scramble around my mind. I know she wants us to do something big that we're not quite ready for. The wind howls around my head and magnifies our silence. We sit like this until the ever increasing rain becomes too much to bear. But it is only when we are all soaked through that she grants us permission to stand. My legs creak and almost give way as I attempt to use them again. We walk slowly and silently back along the trail, perhaps enraptured from our transcendental experience, perhaps afraid to speak in case we draw attention to our vulnerable humanity in the glorious utopia we know to be within our reach.

'What exactly was all that about?' I whisper to Zamara as we stumble down a rocky patch of the path, in a quest for information but also really just an attempt to be friendlier with her.

'What do you mean?' she replies without slowing down.

'Ferdia's speech – the whole are we ready thing, ready for what?'

Now she stops, her face inches from mine, halting me in my tracks. 'We do not question Ferdia.'

'Yeah, I know, I'm not … I just …'

'We do not question Ferdia.'

This time I don't offer any further ramblings and instead resolve to extract some information from Aide later. He might be more inclined to loosen his lips when we're naked.

I light the candles just after 11pm and spray my perfume on the bed sheets. Before putting on my thin strapped cotton nightdress I apply an all over layer of moisturiser, taking extra care on the areas I expect him to linger. Seb must notice his roommate's absence for hours every night this week, they must all be aware of what's happening between us, but no one mentions anything. Maybe it's out of some misplaced loyalty to Eimear. There's a physical reaction in my gut when I think of how he touched me last night, the effect he has on me. I am in withdrawal now, almost at the end of my drug reserve. I need another fix of him before the sickness truly takes hold.

When there's a gentle rap on my door I almost have it opened before realising it odd that he should knock, he usually just lets himself in.

'Oh, are we role playing strangers tonight?' I ask suggestively as my words land on their unintended recipient.

'Ferdia.' My heart races.

'May I come in? You aren't expecting someone else?' She smiles as her eyes search beyond me.

'No, of course not, please … come in.' I step aside.

'Oh how very atmospheric in here.' She stands at the disused fire place, touching all the objects on the mantelpiece. 'No pictures of family or friends?' She observes.

'No, not really my thing.'

'Aren't you lonely without them around you?'

'No, I feel the same when I'm actually with them so …'

'I can see that in you Maeve, you are a solitary spirit.'

I'm not sure that's true, especially as I'm expecting a man to enter my room any second now. My eyes fix on the door and I will him not to appear.

'Oh don't worry,' Ferdia draws my attention back to her. 'We won't be disturbed.'

I say nothing, afraid of confirming her suspicions. She sits next to me on the bed.

'Did you enjoy today Maeve?'

'Yes, it was very enlightening.' That's a general enough word to cover whatever it was I was supposed to have learned.

'I'm so glad you agree with my edict.' Her hand rests on my bare shoulder.

'Yes of course I do, we need to be ready for the revolution.'

Her head shakes slowly. 'We need to be the revolution. For any real change to happen, there are rituals that must be observed. The casualties must fall, the blood must be borne, the evils of war give birth to the glories of peace.'

I'm afraid I know what she's getting at, should I just say it? Let her tell me how ridiculous I sound?

'You want us to start a war – to be violent?'

Her laugh is reassuring and settles my over active imagination.

'Oh no Maeve, oh how terrible of me to lead you to think that way.'

'Oh good, I was worried.' My body releases the tension I'd built up.

'I'm sure you were, darling child, you are so full of innocence and purity – a blank page just waiting for the ink blot of influence.' She rubs my head and tangles my hair through her fingers. 'It would be such a waste to lose a canvas such as you.' Her face is closer now and it happens so instantaneously that I barely have time to register the reality of her kissing me. It's brief and unpassionate, more a loving parental kiss, a consoling seal of affection, approval.

'You can either be the symbol Maeve, or you can find the symbol.' Her eyes fix onto mine, her voice a little stronger now.

'What do you mean?' We do not question Ferdia. We do not question Ferdia.

'This room is way too big for just you.' She stands up and extends her arms to emphasise her point. 'You need a roommate – find one.'

'Sure okay – who?'

'Who?' she repeats with a widened smile. 'That is your choice Maeve – find the right person for us, for our mission, our destiny.'

'Ferdia,' I say, halting her exit, she turns back to look at me.

'Yes Maeve?'

'I won't let you down.'

She takes a long look around the room. 'Yes , you really do have the space looking lovely, you must be very happy here. It would be such a shame to jeopardise what you have here, who you have here.'

'I won't.'

'Good.' She opens the door. 'Oh by the way, your moisturiser, vanilla, he doesn't like vanilla.' The door closes behind her, leaving me alone in the once romantic ambience of my room, that has now transformed into something else entirely, an atmosphere of uneasy resolution.

Chapter 18

No one else came to my door that night. Or the night after. I know what I have to do. There is no one suitable in my college course, none of them have what it takes to become a member of our family. They're not worthy enough. They are either like Shane, judgemental and opinionated, or vacuous and fuelled solely on adulation and superficial success. I know I have to look further afield to find the right person to share my room. Some-one that doesn't bring baggage of any kind. Just like Ferdia had called me a blank canvas, I need a roommate with an open mind, heart and will. Someone who hasn't already been encumbered by the norms and prejudices of society.

Every morning when I walk the canal on my way to college, I see them, but I have always chosen not to look at them. Dotted along the scenic canal bank little domes of a pitiful city, plastic monuments to a failed human experiment. This morning I will look, I will look for something, someone in particular. For one of these unfortunate lost souls, I will become their saviour, the light amidst their darkness. I feel sorry for the ones I will not choose, they will never know how close they came to salvation. I take the homemade sandwich from my bag, ready to offer it when I find the right one. I wish I could feed all the others I pass, two elderly men still sleeping in their half erect tent, the young girl who shouts abuse at me, the old woman who appeals to me in a language I don't understand. I'm sorry, but you are just not what I am looking for. But she is. She is perfect.

She seems to notice that I'm slowing down as I approach her, she raises her head a second time, a look of suspicion on her face.

'Hey.' I raise a hand in peace.

She doesn't respond and just returns her focus to her belongings in her ripped bag.

'Would you like this?' I stand over her and offer the paper wrapped sandwich.

'Right, thanks.' She takes it.

'Are you here every night?' I crouch down next to her, only now becoming aware of the smell emitting from her, a blend of body odour and stale menstrual blood. Does she even have tampons or sanitary towels? I don't even have one to offer her, I don't use them anymore, Ferdia only allows organic cups or reusable pads in the house.

'Some nights, if it's not too cold.' Her accent is local, central Dublin as far as I can tell and makes me wonder where her family are.

'And if it is then where do you go?'

'To a shelter or sometimes I can crash on a friend's floor.' She opens the paper and lifts a slice of vegan bread cautiously. She takes a sniff of the contents. 'What is this?'

'It's chickpea mash with salad – it's good for you, try it.' I try not to sound offended by her ungrateful tone. Focus on your mission Maeve, you are her saviour.

She takes a bite and I watch as the soft filling is further masticated in her mouth. 'Good, yeah?' I ask encouragingly.

She declines to answer and rewraps the remains of the sandwich and tucks it into her bag.

'I'm Maeve.' I offer my hand now and after a second or two, she accepts it.

'Kaley.'

'Nice to meet you Kaley. I have to head into college now but I might see you tomorrow?'

'Alright – if I'm here.'

'Is there anything you'd like me to bring you – some

more food?'

'No – no thanks, you're grand.'

'Okay, well I'll think of something.' I was expecting a little more instant gratitude from my charity recipient. It might take a little longer than I'd planned to win her over but I know she's the one. I couldn't find anyone better for the Clan to help, a disadvantaged, disenfranchised, societal casualty of rising capitalism. She will be my gift, a living breathing talisman of our mission statement. She will be grateful to me once she is safe and warm in our bedroom in Donnybrook, once she has been embedded into the loving bosom of the Clan. She will be loyal and trusting and powerful. I might have to work on her embracing of the plant based lifestyle but baby steps.

My phone rings just before I reach the college gates, it's Aisling. It's weird that she's calling and not messaging, something must be wrong.

'Hey,' I answer.

'Maeve – are you okay?' Her voice is high and fast.

'Yeah, of course I am, why?'

'You're not messaging me back, I haven't heard from you in ages and neither have Maureen and Paudie.'

Jesus, what's this, an intervention? 'You're talking to my grandparents about me now?'

'Well of course you come up in conversation when I see them and Grainne stopped me in Hennessy's the other day to ask about you.'

'Fucking Grainne – you're actually giving me shit about her of all people it's not like she even tries to call me anyway.'

'She seemed really worried about you.'

'Why? What's to be worried about? I'm literally just living my life, what's the big deal?'

'Well maybe it's just because you're not where she thought you were.'

'What?'

'You know, the place she found for you.'

'Aisling – did you tell her I moved?'

'I assumed she knew, it just came out.'

'You told her about the Clan, about the activism?' It's taking all my patience not to scream at her.

'No – no just that you're in a house share now, that's all.'

'For fuck's sake Aisling, I'm not telling you anything ever again.'

'Jesus Maeve, what is your problem? Your family are just trying to look out for you, you're being a selfish bitch.'

'Well you're being a fucking traitor so I guess that means we're both done here.'

'Oh cop on, stop being so dramatic.'

'Have a nice life Aisling, go marry Cian Hanly and his lone brain cell and have lots of halfwit babies.'

'Fuck you Maeve.' The call ends.

'Same to you.' I say to no one.

Great, I wonder how long it will be until the biological mother militia rolls into town.

As expected there are texts and missed calls from Grainne when I come out of lectures. I know I have to deal with her sooner or later but later is always the preferred option. So I try to stem the tsunami with a sand bag.

Hi Grainne, I can't talk now, I'm working on a college project with my classmate Shane, it's due tomorrow. Can I talk to you then?

I have no intention of calling her but this will buy me 24 hours of peace at least.

Look Maeve, I really don't care where you're living as long as you're safe and not taking any more money off Mammy and Daddy, they are stretched thin as it is to support you up there. Don't take advantage of them.

Ah, so this is about money, not motherly concern. Good, that's much easier to handle.

Don't worry, where I'm living now is actually a little less rent than Sandra and Michael's. Plus we all chip in for food and bills so it's not costing anything extra.

Not true of course, but I'm not cutting off my financial umbilical cord just yet.

Right well, you might come home sometime to see me and the kids, they forget what you look like.

Yeah I will soon, just mad busy here and trying not to fall behind.

I turn my phone off after she reads it. I'm not wasting any more of my day on this, not when I have another distraction to deal with.

'There you are, I was waiting for you in the library,' I lie as I approach Shane in the AV room, where I know we had arranged to meet 30 minutes ago.

'Pretty sure we said here,' he mumbles as I sit next to him, a little closer than necessary. I wonder if he can pick up the scent of another man on me, like a dog. I've always believed that guys can tell when a girl has been having sex, it's like a secret code they have. In school it seemed that boys were only ever interested in a girl if other boys had green lit her, test driven and given the all clear to others. Sexual lemmings on a cliff of fraternity and insecurity. Maybe they just talked and told each who was up for it. Maybe I'm giving them too much biological credit. Just in case my theory is wanting, I reach across him, brushing my breast against his chest, to grab a pen from his case.

'Sorry, I forgot one.' I twirl it through my fingers. 'So what have we got so far?'

'Well, I was thinking we flip the brief of marketing a new book a little and instead of doing a literal translation of a book cover we do something that's completely graphic, no text at all.

The image alone has to speak for itself. What do you think?' He looks to be a little uncertain of his vision.

'I think it's brilliant, show me what you have in mind.'

He pulls up his sketches on his laptop and I can already smell the high grade. A single red balloon on a black background – Stephen King's *It*, a hooded woman in red – Margaret Atwood's *A Handmaid's Tale*, a small bird with a gun sight imposed over it – I need his assistance with this one – *To Kill A Mockingbird*, Harper Lee.

'I love it, what do you need me to do?'

'Well, we need to come up with our own book name and plot and a cover that instantly relates it, so I guess first thing first is to take some pictures and play around with images. Do you want to take the camera tonight and see what you can get?' He takes the camera bag from under the desk and hands it to me.

'So no limitations, anything I think could work?'

'Go for it, I'm sure you have a lot more interesting subject matter in your life outside of college than I do in my digs in Citywest.' He might be trying to take the piss but I don't care. He's right, I do.

It's dusk when I leave college and take the camera to the canal. The light is fading fast and my pictures are bleak and uninspiring. I aim at swans and leaves and pieces of litter willing them to tell me a story. It's only when I see her, in a different spot from this morning, that the picture comes into focus.

'Hello again.' I let the camera swing around my neck as I kneel down next to her.

'Oh, hi.' She glances at me quickly.

'How has your day been?'

'Great – I only got spat on once so you know, that's a good day.'

I can't read her face, is that a joke? Best not to laugh just in case.

'Are you going to sleep here tonight?' I don't see her tent.

'It's looking that way yeah.'

'If you got another offer would you consider it?' It's too soon Maeve, you'll scare her away. Your plan was to get to know her first, build her trust, befriend her.

'Depends on what it was, I'm not going into some place with junkies, better off here when it's not so cold.' She shifts a little towards me. 'Do you have any money on you though?' When she looks me straight in the eye I'm struck by how young she is, I can't tell if she's even an adult yet.

'No, sorry, I'm a broke student.'

Her eyes dart to the camera worth at least €300 hanging around my neck.

'This belongs to my college, I'm doing an assignment.'

'Oh, on homelessness.' She seems to be rolling her eyes at me.

'No, no, nothing like that, just an art thing.'

'So what is this then, what do you want from me?'

I'm losing my ground with her, she's losing her patience with me, I need to just come out and say it.

'Kaley – how would you like to come and stay with me tonight?'

Chapter 19

Her face doesn't form the picture of gratitude and joy that I'd been expecting. Instead I'm met with a furrowed brow and narrowed eyes, a half-open mouth.

'I'm serious, I have a spare bed in my room. It's yours if you want it.' I move an inch away from her, mindful of coming on too strong.

'Why – why would you do that? What's in it for you?'

'Can't I just help you out? I'd like to think someone would do the same for me if I ever found myself in your position.'

She eyes me silently for a while before turning her focus back towards the canal. 'Nah, you're alright thanks.'

Shit, I wasn't prepared for this outcome. Okay, think Maeve. She already suspects that you want something off her so why not prove her right. Maybe if she feels she understands the rules, she'll play the game willingly.

'Okay, I lied before.' I try to make my face contrite.

'I'm not interested,' she says a little more forcefully now as she stands up.

'No, wait please, hear me out.' I follow her along the path. 'I do need you for my college project, it's about homelessness and I think you could get me a really good grade. So there, you got me.'

She slows down, it's working.

'What would I have to do?' she asks without stopping.

'Just stay in my room for a night and tell me about your life out here – as much or as little as you like – and let me take your picture.' I hold up the camera for illustrative purposes.

'And that's it?'

'That's it.'

'Who else lives in the house? If anyone tries anything with me I have a knife.'

'Oh God no, you don't need to worry about anyone hurting you. We are all completely peace-loving and trustworthy. You'll be safe with us, I promise.'

'I'll get food?'

'Of course.'

'And a shower?'

'Yes.'

'And my own bed?'

'Yes, you'll be sharing the room with me but you'll have your own bed.'

She has led us to an overgrown section of the hedge where she pushes through the foliage to dig out her bag and rolled up tent.

'Alright, lead the way then.'

I extend my hand to shake on our agreement and she reluctantly reciprocates with a limp, cold hand, dirt caked around the fingernails.

'So what age are you Kaley?' I initiate small talk while we wait at traffic lights crossing the bridge.

'18, you?'

'Same. Where are you from?'

'Dublin.'

'Yeah I can tell that but which part?'

'Kevin Street.'

'How come you ended up out here?'

'Is this part of the project, are we doing it now?'

'Eh, yeah I suppose we are, unless you'd rather we wait until later? We can have a proper talk once you've eaten and had a shower?'

'Yeah, we'll do that,' she says as I stop outside a pharmacy.

'Hang on, I just need to grab something in here.' I dash in before she has the chance to respond or accompany. I don't want her to see what I'm buying, it might change her mind. I discreet my purchase in my bag and join her outside.

'Thanks for waiting.'

'Like a dog,' she says under her breath.

'What? No, don't be silly.'

'You worried I was going to knick something in there?' Her voice is high and barbed.

'No the thought never even crossed my mind.' I reach out to rest a reassuring hand on her shoulder but she baulks at my touch. If only she knew of my own recent chequered past in retail establishments.

'Yeah well I'm not like that, I don't rob stuff, just cos I'm having a rough time of it doesn't mean I'm a criminal or a waste of space you know.'

'Kaley, honestly, I don't think that – none of us in the house will think that. You'll like it here, we are non-judgemental and inclusive, no one will ever make you feel less than you are.' I try to channel Ferdia's grace and wisdom into my speech.

'Right well it's just for one night anyway.'

'Sure, whatever you say. We're just up here on the left, are you hungry?'

'What do you think?' She looks at me like I'm an idiot.

'Good, there's always something cooking here.' I open the gate and guide her in.

'Not that chickpea stuff?' She says as I locate my key in my bag.

'Oh no, not for dinner – it will be curry or tagine or pasta, depending who's on duty. Don't worry, you won't go hungry here.'

I watch her face lighten a little as the house presents itself before her.

'Welcome home.' I step aside to let her enter. She looks around.

'You live here?' Her voice echoes in the cavernous hallway.

'Yeah, but there's six of us. Hey anyone home?' I shout.

'In the kitchen,' a voice travels up the steps.

'Come on.' I beckon Kaley to follow me.

'Zamara, hi.' I'm a little disappointed that the first housemate I'm introducing Kaley to is the one that I know likes me the least.

'Oh hello.' She looks past me and straight at our visitor, resting her wooden spoon on top of the bubbling pot.

'Zamara, this is Kaley, she's going to be staying in my room tonight.'

'Hey.' Kaley raises a tentative hand in greeting.

'How fantastic, Kaley you are so welcome.' Zamara opens her arms and throws them around her, just like she did with me that first day in the garden. 'I hope you are hungry, here taste this.' She loads the wooden spoon with her vegetable curry and offers it to Kaley, who gingerly accepts the spicy mixture.

'Good?'

'Hmm, yeah.' Our guest politely nods her head.

'Maeve, why don't you take Kaley's things up to your room and make up the bed with fresh sheets,' Zamara directs me. 'Kaley can stay here and help me with dinner, okay Kaley?'

She looks at me as if seeking permission.

I smile reassuringly at her and take the weight from her shoulders, leaving her alone with Zamara. I can hear her laughing as I struggle up the stairs, dragging Kaley's worldly possessions behind me. Who does she think she is, ordering me around in front of my new roommate? I found Kaley, I've brought her home for Ferdia, just like she asked; not for Zamara to just take over. She's not my leader and she certainly isn't Kaley's.

I'm met with laughter as I come down the stairs, one of the voices I've not yet heard in this state. They stop it when I join them in the kitchen, Zamara grins at me as Kaley averts her eyes. Were they laughing about me?

'Maeve, why don't you set the table, Ferdia is almost home. I just called her to let her know about our guest. She's very excited to meet you Kaley.' Zamara extends a friendly arm and rubs her back.

'Why?' Kaley looks at me now, perhaps a little unnerved by Zamara's attention.

'Oh she just loves having dinner guests, any excuse to convert another vegan.' I laugh off her concern as we gather the cutlery.

'She'd better not take the piss,' Kaley says once we are out of Zamara's earshot.

'What? No, why would you think that?'

'Why are you being so nice to me, it's weird.' Her back appears to stiffen a little.

I lay down the last spoon and fork and put my hands on her forearms, holding her in place. 'Honestly Kaley, you don't have to worry, we just want to help you. All of us have been in the same position as you, not homeless no, but as the newcomer to the house. I know it can seem a little unreal that strangers who care about you actually exist, but we do. And after today, none of us will be strangers anymore. Okay?'

She looks at me a while before relaxing her shoulders. 'Okay.'

The front door opens and soon Ferdia appears at our side. Without speaking she envelopes Kaley in an embrace, gently caressing the back of her head. Kaley's eyes fix on mine throughout the encounter.

'We are truly blessed to have you in our home Kaley. What a gift the universe has provided for us.' She observes her from outstretched arms.

Excuse me, I think you'll find it was me and not the universe that provided her.

'You are cold,' Ferdia decrees. 'You must want to get some warmth into your bones, yes?'

Kaley nods. 'Yeah, suppose so.'

'Maeve.' Ferdia looks at me for the first time since arriving. 'Take Kaley to my bathroom and run her a bath and give her a fresh set of clothes.'

'From your wardrobe?' I've never even set foot in Ferdia's private bathroom let alone had a bath.

'Hmm ... no from yours of course.' She says as she walks away from us towards the kitchen. 'I just need to speak with Zamara, we will call you both down when the others arrive.'

'Okay.' I take my orders and lead Kaley upstairs.

'Is this your room?' She asks as we pass the first floor.

'No Zamara, Aide and Seb sleep here.'

'Where will I sleep?'

'Oh the top floor with me and then Posey is next door.'

'Jesus ... this place is massive.' She looks up the last flight of steps.

'This is Ferdia's floor, don't hang around here unless you're invited to, okay?'

'Why?'

'Because it's her house and just because she's good enough to let us stay here doesn't mean she doesn't want her privacy.'

'Okay ... shit this is the size of my old flat and four of us lived in there.' She takes in the high ceiling and opulence of Ferdia's chambers.

'This way.' I guide her to the ensuite and turn the antique brass taps on the claw foot bathtub. It smells of lemongrass in here.

Kaley touches all the bottles and boxes on the cabinet, opening each one to either sniff or spray.

'Be careful, please.' I add a little cold to the mix.

'Relax, I'm not going to steal nothing.'

'I didn't mean that, just try not to touch Ferdia's things.'

'Jesus Christ, this Ferdia one, either she's all generous or she's not. I can't make ye out at all.'

'How's that?' I stand back, inviting her to test the water.

'Grand, yeah.'

'Okay, I'll get some clothes and leave them on Ferdia's bed for you.'

'Maeve?' She says just as I cross the threshold.

'Yeah?'

'Is there really no catch to this?' Her eyes narrow as she speaks, concentrated on her search for clarity. I freeze for a moment, my response percolates its way up from my gut, past my stomach, my lungs, my heart until it settles in my throat.

'No, of course not.' I follow it with a smile. 'Just relax, you're safe here.'

Chapter 20

I lay awake most of that night, Kaley softly snored and made sporadic leaps in her sleep as if jolting herself out of a bad dream. It should have brought me comfort knowing that my act of kindness and selflessness had guaranteed her safety but the satisfaction didn't allay my restlessness. Aisling didn't help either, she's been trying to call and contact me on all of my accounts, to apologise no doubt. But she can wait. My new friend is my focus now. She had barely spoken at dinner, only providing monotone responses to the questions the others had politely put to her, revealing little to nothing of herself. I had been an open book when Ferdia brought me in, a sponge – weightless and ready for immersion. Kaley is stiffer, less porous. But even concrete is permeable.

'Oh, what are you doing up? My tiptoeing out to the bathroom must not have prevented her waking up. She's dressed and sitting on the single bed when I return from my shower.

'Heading out, what else would I be doing?' She shakes her head, her freshly washed light red hair brushes her shoulders.

'Oh, I just thought maybe you'd like to lie in and spend the day here, Ferdia would love to have you here.' I slip my knickers on underneath the towel as I try to persuade her.

'Nah, you're grand thanks. You want me to help with that college thing of yours now or what like?' She nods in the direction of my chest of drawers where the camera is perched. It takes me a second to remember my lie.

'Oh yeah – would you mind? That would be great.'

'Deal's a deal like, I don't want to owe you anything.'

'Okay great, fancy coming into college with me so we can

take some pictures on the way.' I apply some organic deodorant and moisturizer and throw on leggings and a long t-shirt. Best not delay too long and risk changing her mind. If I can get her to feel obliged to help with this fake project maybe I can convince her I need her to stay again tonight. That should be all it takes for the others to work their magic on her, to make her fall in love with them. The process seems to have already started with Zamara. She's standing at the bottom of the stairs when we walk down, holding out a flask and a Tupperware container.

'Good morning Kaley, how did you sleep?' She doesn't even look at me.

'Morning Zamara,' I say pointedly, she glances my way but quickly reverts to her chosen focus.

'Here, I've prepared some things for you. I know Maeve likes to sleep late and wouldn't have taken the time to do it.'

'What is it?' Kaley takes the items cautiously.

'Just some hot rooibos tea with lemon and ginger and some buckwheat pancakes with banana and sustainable peanut butter.'

'Thanks.' Kaley puts her breakfast into her bag.

'I hope to see you again Kaley, we all very much enjoyed having you here last night.' Zamara pulls her into a tight hug as I head for the front door.

'We'd better go Kaley. I have a lecture in an hour.' Zamara's going to scare her off, she's coming on too strong.

'I'll give your tubs back to Maeve.' Kaley waves awkwardly at Zamara as she holds onto the doorframe, watching us walk down the path.

'Is she gay?' Kaley asks once we are out the gate.

'Eh, I don't actually know to be honest.'

'She must be, she fancies me right? That's why she's being so nice, with the food and hugs and stuff.'

'Yeah, could be that – it must be that.' I allow her assumption to be supported, it could be true I suppose but either way, it's easier to explain.

'Thanks by the way.' Kaley speaks after a few minutes of walking in silence.

'Oh honestly it's nothing, you needed the bed so ...'

'Not just for that, for the things you put on the bed.'

The tampons I had bought on our way home yesterday. 'Oh that, well I thought maybe they were hard to come by out here and Mother Nature doesn't give a fuck if you're homeless or not, right?'

She laughs. Her face relaxes and I see a reflection of me, of Eimear, of Aisling, of all of us in it.

'Stop right there.' I raise my hand to stall her, readying the camera with the other.

'What will I do?' Self-consciousness threatens to overcome her expression.

'Not a thing.' I take the picture quickly, capturing what I could of her in the brief moment of levity. I kind of wish she was my college project, maybe she could be the star of Shane's book cover.

She walks with me all the way to the college gates, chatting about my life mostly, it's a more palatable past for early morning talks I'm guessing. I take one last photograph of her holding her breakfast in her hands.

'Wait, I need to eat these and give you back the tubs.' She lifts a limp piece of buckwheat pancake to her mouth.

'Don't worry about it, keep them.'

'I'll just bin them?'

'Oh no, don't do that. I'll get them off you again.' I notice Shane noticing us as he walks toward the main hall.

'You passing by the canal this evening?' She takes a drink from the flask and winces at the taste.

'Yeah, should be around 5pm, see you there?'

'Alright see you Maeve.' She smiles again only a little this time, before turning and walking away. She'll be coming home with me again tonight.

Shane is waiting for me at the door.

'Who is that, one of your housemates?'

'Not yet but she soon will be, why, do you fancy her?'

'What? No.' His face reddens. I like making Shane blush, it's a tool for me. I know I can use it to whittle what I want out of him. 'I'm just curious about the people you hang out with.'

'Well so you should be, they're pretty interesting.'

He looks at his phone after it vibrates, distracting him from me.

'Bit of early morning sexting there Shane, should I leave you to it?'

'Huh?' He gives me a confused look. 'No, sorry, it's just some girl who's been messaging me all morning on Instagram.'

'Jesus, I'm almost impressed, you've got a stalker. Show me.' I grab his phone out of his big country man hand.

'Maeve – give it to me.' He asks politely, resisting the urge to forcefully retrieve it, which is well within his physical power.

'What the fuck?' I stare at his screen, scrolling through the messages, not letting my finger rest and risk his screen lock activating. 'What the hell is this about?' My eyes leave her face so I can appeal to his.

'I have no idea, she just started direct messaging me, my account is public and you tagged me when you shared the picture I took the day we went to Sandymount, before you, you know.'

'Yeah – whatever, but why is she contacting you at all? That's totally psychotic.'

'It sounds like she's really worried about you, is she really your best friend?'

'Well, she used to be, sure as hell isn't now. How dare she go to you about me. Open this.' I thrust his phone at him so he can enter the passcode and I can read her treachery again.

Hi Shane. You don't know me and I hope you don't mind me contacting you. I saw you tagged in one of Maeve Daly's pics. She's the reason I'm messaging you. My name is Aisling Monaghan and I've been Maeve's best friend since Junior Infants and I'm really worried about her. We've had a huge fight and she won't talk to me, her family barely hear from her anymore either. I'm mostly concerned about the people she is living with, they just sound strange to me. Have you met them? Maybe they are grand, I hope you can put my mind to rest about them. Thanks a million. Aisling.

Then another one.

Please don't tell Maeve about this, I don't want to push her even further away. Thanks for understanding. A

And another.

I'm so sorry if I've put you in an awkward position Shane. I understand your loyalty is to Maeve. I have no idea how close you are, she hasn't mentioned you to me, only her new housemates. But I understand if you just ignore and delete these. A

'Why haven't you responded to them?' I ask him.

'I didn't know what to say – it was a bit of a surprise.'

'Tell me about it.' I hand the phone over. 'Reply.'

'What – why?'

'Because she won't stop until you do, trust me I know Aisling.'

'What will I write?'

'Tell her everything is fine, I'm working with you on our project, life is perfect and my housemates are all sound.'

'But I've not met them, all I know about them are their crazy videos. Maybe she saw them and that's why she's worried.'

'Just type it Shane – please.' I rub his forearm and give him an encouraging look.

'Okay, I don't want to be involved in your fight, so if this gets her off my back.'

'It will, she'll tire herself out if she's not getting any drama returned. Trust me.'

I read over his reply before he sends it.

Hi Aisling. Yeah I know Maeve, we're actually working on a college project together at the moment. It's going really well and she seems to be loving the course and where she is living. I don't know her housemates personally but I've not heard anything weird about them, so I wouldn't worry if I were you. Sometimes people just lose touch with home when they move away to college, it's totally normal. Take care. Shane.

Good. Rub it in that her clinging onto a past and to the people we used to be isn't normal. Me becoming the person I'm meant to be, that's normal.

'Now that that insanity is over with, look at the pics I took.'

He makes sounds of approval as we approach the classroom, it's empty but for another two person team from our course, working on their project. We sit and turn on our laptops, Shane opens his fancy photo editing software and I watch as he turns my portraits of Kaley into various iterations and dissections.

'I like her eyes, they are intense,' he says as he plays around with their colour.

'Yeah, there's a story behind them I'd imagine – she's not had the easiest life so far.' I think it's fair to assume this.

'Do you think she could be our inspiration for the story as well as the cover?'

'Yeah, I don't see why not. I'll be seeing her this evening so what do you need?' I figure if I offer up this conceptual insight he'll trudge along with all the actual work.

'I dunno, just take notes and then we'll brainstorm a narrative and see what single image could illustrate that. Can you take lots more pics of her?'

I'm not sure if that's a good idea, she might get pissed off at being made to feel like a performing seal. 'I can try.' I smile and nod appreciatively as he fills the space with his over inflated sense of artistic ability and originality.

The day is long and when I'm finally walking along the canal, it's a welcome reprieve. I don't worry too much when she's not at the exact same spot I found her last time. I'm sure it's natural to have to move about in this situation. I did tell her around 5pm didn't I? Maybe I said 6? I can wait until then anyway, I can walk it a couple of times until I see her. I get to the end and turn back, crossing over to the other side just in case I passed her. There are others there, in tents and sitting along the dock. I look at their faces closely, none of them are her. On the third trek I start to accept the fact that she's not coming. She's stood me up. A homeless girl has somewhere better to be than here with me. I sit on a bench, maybe she'll walk by if I just stay still. I use the time to block Aisling from all of my social media accounts. I still can't get over that she did that. Like what did she expect Shane to say, 'oh yes thank God you contacted me you random girl, let's team up and go save Maeve from her evil housemates who are giving her a free place to live, treating her like family and teaching her about what's important in life. You bring the cable ties and I'll get a roll of duct tape.' Well I hope she's happy now, she's totally destroyed any chance of us ever being friends again. And it's no loss to me. I have my new life, what does she have? I was the only interesting thing about Aisling Monaghan, I knew it, she knew it – maybe that's why she's trying so desperately to hold onto me. If only Kaley exhibited a percentage of that same interest. I wait until 6.15pm before continuing on my walk home. I hope something bad hasn't happened to her, what if she's in trouble. I don't even know her surname to call hospitals or shelters or wherever someone goes to check up on a homeless person. Visions of her impending doom ruminate in my mind all the way to the front door and are only dispersed by the sounds of enjoyment coming from inside. There's music playing loudly and the mix of voices indicates a full house. Are they having a party – without me? I push open the living room door and a cloud of smoke takes my breath away.

'Maeve – you're here.' Aide grins an intoxicating grin in my direction, his eyes struggling to focus. 'Here, have a hit.' He thrusts a joint at me.

I look past his offering to observe the others, all lounging happily in their chosen stupor, bottles and cans cover the entire surface of the coffee table. Cider. Who the hell drinks cider? A head of red hair emerges from the sofa in front of me.

'Ah hiya Maeve.' Kaley's glassed eyes meet mine, no longer our intense muse, our troubled heroine, but a drunk, relaxed, ordinary girl – just hanging out with her friends. 'Wanna swig?' She lifts her can so I may take it.

I shake my head.

'No, Maeve is more of a smoker than a drinker, aren't you?' Aide says before taking a long drag. He takes hold of my face with one hand, gently parting my lips with the pressure of his fingers on my cheeks. He presses his mouth on mine, releasing the smoke into my lungs. I choke and cough. They laugh. All of them, Seb, Posey, Zamara, Aide, Ferdia – Kaley. I can feel my face redden, from the smoke and the shame.

'Sit down Maeve – relax,' Ferdia decrees from her chair. 'Your negative energy is killing the collective high.'

Chapter 21

I smoke quickly and deeply trying to get myself up to their level. But even an hour later I feel on the outside of this newly formed circle. When there's an opportunity to sit next to Kaley, when Zamara and Posey leave her side, I take it.

'Hey, what happened earlier?' I say quietly so the others can't hear over their heated debate on fossil fuels.

'What do ya mean?' Kaley drains her can and eyes me suspiciously.

'Our arrangement to meet at 5pm on the canal.'

'Oh that, well when Zamara came to get me I thought that was out the window.'

'Zamara came to get you? When, why?' What is she playing at, trying to take the credit for my recruit?

'Around 3pm it was, the school kids were starting to walk past. Why does it matter anyway, I'm here now aren't I?'

I nod enthusiastically. 'Oh sure, of course. I was just confused. Main thing is you're here, are you going to stay?'

'For tonight anyway, then I'll see. I mean, so far Zamara's been pretty sound, bought me these cans and a chipper on the way home so I'm happy here, for now.'

'A chipper?' I didn't think Zamara would even know what they sold in chippers. Her idea of a battered sausage is a sausage that was suffering domestic violence.

'Yeah, snack box and onion rings. I had to eat it before we got home though coz I understand that ye are all vegetarians and I respect that like, not to bring meat into the house,' she says sagely.

'Oh right, that makes sense so.' I try to convince myself that it's not weird that Zamara is making these concessions for Kaley, none of which were ever made for me. Fried chicken, processed food, tins of cider for fucks sake. God I'm starving.

'Hey Pose.' I get her attention. 'Is there any dinner left?'

'Eh I think there's some dahl left and there's fresh pitta in the box,' she says before returning to her conversation.

'Great thanks.' Not as nice as Kaley's meal but I'm not supposed to like that sort of food, it's not conducive to the Clan's ideology. But the marijuana has kicked in and my only concern right now is to stuff my face with something, cold lentil stew will have to suffice.

I'm alone in the kitchen, leaning over the pot, scooping dahl with a pitta bread when she enters.

'Oh Maeve, you gave me a fright. I'd forgotten you were here.' Ferdia holds a hand to her bare neck as if to steady herself from shock.

'But I ... live ... here.' I laugh even if I don't actually find this funny, I can't stop, the giggles overtake me and I hold onto the counter to steady myself.

'Maybe you should lie down Maeve. This isn't really agreeing with you.' A caring hand rests on my back. 'Go on up to bed, we'll take care of Kaley. She's wonderful.'

I turn to look into her clear grey blue eyes, I want to see something in them but what I can't quite name.

'If you think I should.' Ferdia knows best.

'I do, go on Maeve.'

'I'll just tell Aide, in case he's looking for me.' I step towards the door.

'I'll make sure he's informed,' she says firmly. 'Go on now, be a good girl Maeve.'

I stumble to the stairs as she follows. She waits at the bottom as I make my way up. My head throbs as soon as it hits the pillow. The sound of their party travels through the floorboards and I'm part of it whether they want me to be or not.

After trying to sleep off my haze for what seems like hours, I give up. My mind is racing and not only from the drugs. I imagine them down there, laughing, planning ... without me, about me? I roll myself over to the edge of the bed and attempt to prop myself up. My head spins, my eyes hurt. But I'm half up now so just keep going. I swing my legs off the side and plant my feet on the old threadbare carpet. The paisley pattern swirls to create kaleidoscopic colours. I close my eyes and concentrate all my energy in standing. Holding onto the chest of drawers for support, I manage it, take a few deep breaths and move slowly one foot then the other until I'm at the door. Okay, I'm okay, it's worn off. Aide knows I can't smoke that strong stuff, why did he let me smoke so much of it. Maybe I told him I could handle it, that I liked it. The top step on the stairs creaks and it's the only sound I've heard that's louder than those coming from the living room. The next one is the pop of the door as I twist the knob and push. Smoke escapes with my entrance, music travels past and through me; loud, fast with a throbbing base. I've never heard them play that kind of music before. It reverberates within me and I feel a little motion sick despite the fact that I'm standing completely still, rooted to the spot, staring at them as they don't turn around, don't notice me.

'Hey,' I say against the oppressive noise. They don't respond.

'Guys,' I shout this time, Seb lifts his head.

'Oh Maeve, you're alive.'

'Do you want the music turned down so you can sleep?' Posey, next to him, asks.

'Oh no, no.' I wave a conciliatory hand. 'I'm up now, what are you guys doing?' I edge into their circle, tightly knit around the low coffee table, all eyes to the centre. I take the beanbag.

'Just getting to know our new housemate, what do you think we are doing?' Zamara smiles but I'm not confident in its intent.

Her arm reaches around Kaley, her hand rests on her waist, pulling her in closer. Kaley moves with it, they look intently at each other. I look away.

'Great, so Kaley is in?' My eyes scan the circle, trying to re-establish the power and respect I should have as her recruiter. 'So I've found the next member of the Clan, the symbol?'

Seb and Posey laugh, collapsing into each other as if the hysteria is too much for their bodies to bear. Aide takes a deep drag of his joint and smiles at me as he exhales before passing it to Ferdia at his side. I follow its journey to her lips and move my focus to her eyes, imploring them for communication.

'Maeve you need to relinquish control, let happen what is meant to happen,' she says in a low monotone voice. 'Do you understand me?'

I nod instantly, hoping my words can catch up quickly. 'Em … yeah, yeah.' I mumble.

'I don't think you do.' She takes another drag and instead of inhaling this time she turns to her right, takes Aide's face in both her hands and places her lips on his. Smoke travels between them as his eyes rest on mine. He inhales her, her lips stay on him, they move, their mouths open. They are kissing, properly, fully, deeply kissing. I watch, transfixed with impotent jealousy, rage. He's mine. He's mine. What the fuck are you doing? She's Ferdia. She's our leader. We are all hers. I do nothing. Nothing but watch as her hands move through his hair, his hands touch her breasts. She gets up from her chair and slides next to him, slowly positioning herself on top of him. Her back is to me but his eyes can still find mine and I try my best to appeal to them to stop. But he doesn't. Their hands fumble around each other's waists and then it's happening. I can tell by his face the exact moment he enters her. They're fucking. Right here in front of everyone. I look around the room for support, backup to make them stop. Seb is lying with his head on Posey's lap, she strokes his hair. They are deep in conversation and pay no attention to what's happening. Zamara and Kaley are in the initial stages of tentatively kissing, still negotiating the terms of their engagement. They don't care to notice that I'm drowning here, sinking deeper and deeper into the beanbag, desperately searching all around me for a life saver. This must be an hallucination. This isn't really happening Maeve, just get through it. I hold onto the edge of the coffee table just to feel something real, solid, unchangeable. It keeps me afloat. I look again into the flames, the fire in her eyes burns into me as she turns her head to smile at me, letting me know that the power building inside of her is hers to harness.

Chapter 22

It's cold out here, alone, the street not yet come to life. But I had to get here early before the people come, before the Gardaí come. They don't patrol the building at night, just in shifts during the day, symbolic keepers of the gate, protectors of our democracy. The chills I already feel all over my skin are intensified by the cold metal wrapping around my ankles. It clinks and catches on itself as I weave it around the black iron railings. The padlock shuts and I'm secure. A woman nears me, her eyes trying to focus in the early morning light, trying to make sense no doubt of the sight before her as she takes her routine route to work, coffee in hand. She stares as she passes while keeping her distance on the footpath. Her expression suggests at best disapproval, at worst, contempt. Count yourself lucky you're not passing here any later, I think. At least now I've still got my coat on. Slipping my hands inside it, I feed the second chain around my waist, the bracing impact of cold against my flesh shudders me. But I persist. A car is travelling up Molesworth Street, facing me. It stops at the junction and waits for its turn. I wait too. Once it passes I un-button the black wool coat that I had found under the stairs in the house. I hadn't asked permission to borrow it, no one could know why I needed it. This is my mission, mine alone. I couldn't risk any of the others hijacking it and taking the credit. There was no way I was going to sit back and watch as they tried to include Kaley, even make it her initiation. No, let them do that, they do everything else with her. I have to remind Ferdia what she saw in me that day on O'Connell Street, why she believed in me and my power to affect change. I am an activist, an anarchist, a catalyst.

And today everyone in Ireland will see me, all of me. They will hear what I have to say and where better to start than at the top, the seat of government. I let the coat fall and gasp as the full force of the crisp November air bites every inch of my naked body. I breathe deeply, gathering myself enough so I can bend to lift up the container at my shackled feet. I had tried to source real blood and despite the incessant slaughter of animals every day in this country, that stuff is hard to come by. My grandfather could have sorted me out with some, the only time he could have actually helped me would be in my pursuit to destroy his livelihood. Instead I had to concoct my own creation out of syrup, flour and water with plenty of red food colouring. I filled the container we usually use for soup. I pop the lid and let it fall to the ground. Closing my eyes I pour the contents over my head, it travels over my face and I can taste the sweetness. It's thick and I think I should have added more water. I aid its journey down my body with my hands, rubbing it over my breasts to cover them with something at least. More people are approaching now, from both ends of Kildare Street. I can feel eyes on me. Good. I grab hold of the railing of Leinster House with my outstretched hands and begin to shout.

BLOOD IS BLOOD
MEAT IS MURDER
CULL THE HERD
SAVE THE WORLD

The rhythm of my voice lulls me away from the reality happening around me. I concentrate on it and it drowns out the disapproving remarks and shocked exclamations of passing people. I don't look at them, instead I close my eyes, only opening them fleetingly to see the blood drip down my legs and over my feet, forming tributaries in the concrete. I follow a trickle as it slugs its way through an imperceptible valley before stopping suddenly at the rubber soul of an oppressive boot.

'Miss are you aware that what you are doing is a crime in this country?' A short, thick man with an even thicker accent stands uncomfortably close to my sticky naked body.

'Are you aware that what they do in there every day are crimes against this planet?' As much as I can, I gesture to the building behind me, where all the legislation of the land is made.

'Public nudity is an offence under the Criminal Law Sexual Offences Act 2017,' he says robotically.

'Only in cases where it is deemed to intend fear, distress or alarm or engage in sexual activity,' I recite my homework of the statute book. 'And I hardly think any of those are applicable do you?'

He sighs heavily. 'You'll have to come down to the station miss.' Pulling on his radio, he talks to someone else now. 'Yeah, I'll need you to come out to the Kildare Street gate. We'll need bolt cutters too, yeah, right so.' He looks back to me. 'What's your name and address?' A tiny notepad and pencil appear in his hands.

'I don't have to give you my name, I have the right to remain silent.' I stare straight ahead, trying to undermine whatever authority he thinks he has over me.

'I think you'll find that's in America miss, we have no such constitutional clause here that allows you to withhold personal information or answer my non-incriminating questions.'

Shit, I assumed that stuff was internationally standard. Distract. 'This is a peaceful protest, my nudity is not aggressive, so it is not illegal and therefore not an arresting offence.' I can see the exhaustion on his face as I speak.

'Even so, you're creating a public nuisance and will be removed and brought to the nearest Garda station.'

'BLOOD IS BLOOD … MEAT IS MURDER …'

I figure get in as many chants as I can before the cavalry arrive. Phones record me as their owners pass by invisibly. I try to connect with each one of the lenses, give them all the best possible footage for their social media channels, ensure the spread of the message; please Ferdia. She will be proud. Aide will be impressed, maybe even aroused by it, maybe enough so to want to come to my room again. An unforeseen consequence of Kaley's presence in my room; his absence. It must be that, I know he was just following Ferdia's orders the other night. That kiss was to teach me humility. As for the rest, I'm putting it down to my bad trip. It had to be. Kaley needs to see this too, to realise my standing in the Clan, remind her who brought her in, where her loyalties should lie. I don't see Zamara out here, naked on the street, covered in fake blood, chained and stuck to railings with a bolt cutter coming for her.

'Jesus Connors, it's not even 8am and you've got a live one already,' the Garda wielding the tool laughs at his awaiting colleague.

'Hold still now miss, we have to cut the chains and we don't want to nip ya,' Connors says.

'Are you threatening me? Police brutality!' I shout.

'Calm down, calm down.' The second one, who is tall, thin and much younger, raises a conciliatory hand. 'Now, I'm not going to touch you, just reach down to cut the chain at your feet, okay?'

I nod reluctantly. I know I couldn't stay here chained up forever, this was an inevitable part of the mission.

'Good, now nice and easy.' He cuts it with one snip. 'Now, I'm going to go around the other side to cut the one around your waist, okay?' His eyes are trusting and I allow myself to give in fully, truthfully a little relieved that I'm going to be able to move soon. My body is stiff and trembling from the cold. I feel a massive relief as the weight drops from my hips and instinctively I fall to my haunches. Garda Connors drapes my coat over my shoulders.

'You're alright, gather yourself there and we'll head down to the station.'

Garda Connors and his colleague who introduces himself as Garda Remi direct me into the back seat of the car, cautiously touching the draped coat that separates them from standard arresting procedure and alleged sexual assault of a person in custody.

'What's next?' I ask when they stop talking to each other in police speech.

'We just need to process you down at the station,' Remi says.

'Am I being arrested?'

'Well yes miss that would be what's happening at the moment.' Connors isn't as nice as Remi.

'Yeah but am I going to jail right now, do I get my single phone call?'

'You're a fan of the TV shows I see.' Connors glances at me via the rear view mirror.

'Well, isn't that what happens?'

'No.'

Another thing that not's like the movies so. I stay quiet for the rest of the journey, wondering if news of my mission has made its way to the Clan yet. Surely all those watching phones have done their work by now. They'll be celebrating me in Donnybrook, preparing a feast in my honour. I will be rewarded again, like the times before when I pleased Aide, he pleased me. The anticipation warms my goosebumped skin.

Inside the Pearse Street Station, a female garda takes me into a room and gives me face wipes. I attempt to remove the blood from my face and look somewhat sane when my arresting officers enter the room.

Cop Connors sits and speaks. 'You are not obliged to say anything unless you wish to do so but whatever you say will be taken down in writing and may be given in evidence.'

'Finally,' I mutter. 'Something that's like the movies.'

'What's your name miss?' Nice guy Remi takes the seat next to Connors.

'Do I have to give it?'

'I'm afraid you do, yes.'

'Don't I get to have a lawyer present?'

'We're not charging you with anything yet, this is still just part of the arresting procedure.' He smiles and maybe because he's kind of hot, I trust him.

'It's Maeve.'

'Maeve?'

'Daly.'

'Okay Maeve and what's your permanent address?' He writes on a form.

Of course Belmont Crescent is on the tip of my tongue but I stop it from rolling off. If I send them there they could arrest the others for previous protests or disruptions of the peace or whatever it is they have me in here for. I can't risk exposing them and subverting the cause. Look what happened to Eimear and all she did was lose her ID on a mission.

'What happens if I don't give my address?'

'Well if you decide to so do, that changes your situation from a fixed charge offence to a summary offence for which there is a maximum penalty of a Class C fine,' Connors says without looking at me.

'Really Maeve.' Remi really does have kind eyes. 'It's in your best interest to cooperate with us.'

I'll just give my home address, Nana wouldn't open my mail anyway if they send something there. She's uncommonly respectful of privacy for an Irish granny.

'It's Mountain View, Virginia Road, Ballycastle, Co. Cavan.'

'And do you have any identification on you?'

I give Remi an incredulous look before scanning my body. 'Eh, no I didn't exactly bring my handbag.'

'Okay, then we'll just need to confirm this with a phone call, your home number please?'

Fuck.

Chapter 23

I've been alone, waiting in this holding room for so long that when another voice nears I assumed I'd be pleased. And I would be if it was any other voice, anyone other than her.

'She's in here? Again, I'm so sorry about this, believe me this is not how she was reared, we don't know what's gotten into her.'

Her voice penetrates the heavy door of the windowless room and suddenly this place doesn't seem so bad, maybe I could live here? Light comes in with her and she stands still in its projected path.

'Get your things,' Grainne orders.

'I don't have any things.' I stare at the floor.

'Then get up and get out.' She steps aside to clear the way out.

My limbs are caked in dried syrup and it cracks as I rise, my thighs stick together when I try to walk so I spread my legs wider and waddle to the door like a deranged duck.

'What the hell are you doing?' she hisses.

'It's the blood,' I mumble.

'Yeah well just be grateful it's not real, that could soon change believe me.' She lets the door slam shut behind us. 'Go on.' She directs me to the exit.

'But I have to get my charge.'

'I've paid the fine – just get out.'

'So it's just a fine?' I was expecting a charge sheet and a court date. I don't know whether to be relived or disappointed.

'Count yourself lucky this time Maeve. Get in the car.' She beeps her keys and the lights on her beige SUV flash.

'No, it's grand thanks I can walk from here.'

'Like that?' She nods at my appearance and cowboy posture. 'I'll get the bus then.'

Grainne opens the back door of her car and throws her over-stuffed handbag onto the seat. Tastefully clear varnished fingers push her fringe away from her face as she lets out a deep sigh. She keeps her eyes closed as she starts to speak.

'Maeve, if you think for one second that I've driven up here to Dublin in rush hour traffic to literally bail you out of jail just to let you off on your merry way you really have lost your mind. Get in the bloody car before I go back into that station and withdraw my payment.'

'Okay, but just drop me home then.' I pull at the hem of the coat as I sit in the passenger seat, conscious of staining her cream leather interior.

'Oh I'll drop you home alright.' She gets in and clicks the central locking.

'You actually going to kidnap me now Grainne? Bit dramatic even for you.'

'You're hardly in a position to judge dramatics Maeve. Do you have any idea what you put us through with your little stunt this morning? Can you imagine Mam getting a phone call from the Gardaí? I'm just surprised the auld lad didn't keel over from a heart attack on the spot.' She starts the car and edges her way into Dublin city traffic.

'It's got nothing to do with them, I am my own person and I decide what I believe in, what I live for. You couldn't possibly understand passion like that, what it feels like to care about something bigger than yourself – to be willing to die if that's what's needed.'

'And thank Christ for that, one lunatic in the family is enough.'

'Well can you at least stop by the house so I can get my things?' I plead as she crosses to the north side of the city, homeward bound.

'Absolutely not, you're never going back to that place.'

'Oh yes I am,' I calmly resolute.

'We'll see about that. This is exactly what we were afraid would happen, after that internet thing.'

I ignore her bait. 'What about my phone, my bank card, my laptop? I won't be able to do my college work.'

'Don't even pretend you care about your college work Maeve, it's a complete waste of Mammy and Daddy's money keeping you up here. For the amount of time you spend in college you can easily commute from Cavan.'

My frustration rises as she continues to lecture me. 'How do you know how much time I spend there, I'm in college every day, I'm actually doing really well.'

'Really?' She deadpans.

'Yes.'

'Hmm, that's not what I heard.'

What the hell could she have heard? Aisling.

'Oh what's Aisling been saying then?' I unstick my legs from each other in an attempt to get comfortable for the journey ahead.

'That all you talk about are those criminals, and that's before you stopped talking to her at all. She sent me some of their videos too, honestly Maeve do you have the sense you were born with?'

Her phone rings and interrupts her big speech. She activates the speaker.

'Hi Mam.'

'Is she okay, did you get her?' My grandmother's wavering voice fills the car. The fear in it stabs at me and for the first time in all of this, I feel a little of what Grainne so desperately wants me to feel, shame.

'Hi Nana.' I can hear her exhale at the sound of my voice.

'Thank Jesus Maeve, you're okay – did they hurt you in there?'

'No.'

'Did those people make you do that, tell me the truth now love, I won't be mad.'

'What? No, I wanted to do it – it's what I believe in.'

'See Mam,' Grainne chips in.

'Leave her Grainne,' her mother commands. 'Maeve is very easily led, you know that, she's not a very good judge of character, she's too trusting. When I think of what could have happened to her had you not read her messages to that dirty old bastard.'

This again. I never did find out if he actually was a pervert. Grainne just made that decision for me after months of building a bond with him. He could have been real for all they knew. We could have just met up for a milkshake that Saturday. But they did what they always do, control me.

'Don't worry love, just get home and we'll sort everything out, you don't need to go back to that house, don't worry about the deposit you paid or anything like that, me and Grandad will take care of it.'

I stay quiet, afraid to say anything that might be used against me at a later date.

Grainne talks along the N3, through Meath and into Cavan and I respond with just enough enthusiasm and cooperation to stop her from imploding. She probably thinks she's succeeded in getting through to me, by the time we reach Ballycastle she's probably already congratulating herself on another successful perfect mother mission. The truth is she's the one who needs getting through to, but she'll never be enlightened enough to realise that. I pity her. But I also need her. I need the loan of her laptop. There's no way I can be cut off from the Clan, not now, not when I've done such a great thing for them. They will want to thank me and I want to be thanked. I'll try to act acquiescent to her advice. It's too soon to ask though, I need to act remorseful a little longer.

The car doesn't make it into our driveway, its path is blocked by two other cars in front. There's usually just grandad's dirty old Jeep.

'What's going on?' I say more to myself than to her.

'Come on.' She switches off the engine and exits the car with a bang of her door.

'Who's here?' I ask but she ignores me, just guiding me towards the back door.

She pushes it open and I instantly hear the sound of voices hush. That awful stomach sinking feeling you get when you walk into a room and people stop talking. That but times a thousand. Great, this is unbelievable. Sitting around my kitchen table, all heads turned towards me, my grandparents, Declan and my now confirmed former best friend Aisling Monaghan.

'What is this, a fucking intervention?' I roll my eyes at the absurdity of their collegiate intensity.

'Sit down Maeve,' my grandfather growls.

I look to my grandmother for back up. She usually offers it when he's being thick, but not this time. This time her eyes fix on the wall, on the picture of the Sacred Heart illuminated by a red electric candle. I take my seat beneath it and steady myself for my flogging.

My grandfather's index finger extends across the table to point at me before he speaks.

'You're not going back to that Dublin place.'

'I think you'll find that I am.' I laugh.

'Maeve … stop.' My grandmother looks at me now, I can't tell if it's disgust or despair in her eyes.

'Nana … come on, this is a bit dramatic isn't it? I didn't even get charged.'

My grandfather's fist bangs the table and all the bodies around it jump.

'Enough! No granddaughter of mine is going around getting

charged or arrested or whatever the hell it is you think you're doing.' He leans in closer to me. 'And look at the state of you, coming home like that.' He's referring to my coat and red dye streaked appearance.

'That's Grainne's fault, she wouldn't let me go home to get my things.'

'See what I mean Mam?' Grainne shoots from the benches.

'This is serious Maeve, you were on the news, what do you think people will be saying about us?' Maureen Daly shudders at the thought of local curtain twitching while I focus on the main point of what she just said.

'Was I? When – what channel?' I have the good sense to at least try hiding my excitement.

'The proper channel, the 1 o'clock news,' she says like it's a bad thing. 'Thank God they didn't name you.'

Damn. I don't want another activist taking credit for my work. 'Could you see my face though?'

'Well I knew you, not sure if others would, the blood was sort of disguising you.' She waves a hand over her face to illustrate.

'Jesus Christ Maeve,' Aisling plucks up the courage to verbally announce herself. 'Is that all you care about – getting famous from it?'

My head snaps in her direction and my eyes narrow on her pious pallid face. 'Famous? What a pedestrian concept Aisling … I want attention, but not for me, for a cause greater than anything you could ever comprehend.'

'This the vegan thing is it?' Declan – why is he even here? Surely there's a llama that needs worming.

'Yes Declan – the vegan thing, you know the whole planet is burning thing – that thing.' I snap.

'You're taking this too far Maeve.' Aisling's all business. 'No one is saying you can't believe in your cause but we can't sit back and watch you get arrested for them, throwing away your future – that stuff sticks with you for life. Think about your career prospects.'

Sweet Jesus, she's become middle aged in the space of three months.

'I am Aisling – this is my future.'

'Well I'm not paying another fucking cent for it.' Paudie pushes himself away from the table.

'Sit down Paudie.' Nana tries to coax him back.

'No, Maureen. I said I'd be calm and hear her out but I'm not listening to another word of this shite. She gives up this Clan nonsense or she's on her own – let them pay for her rent and food and put clothes on her back.'

'We can't just leave her in the lurch like that Paudie, she needs to get her education.'

'Education? A first class degree in how to be a fucking eejit is what she's getting as far as I can see. No more – you stay home and get the bus to college or you go and don't come back.' He bellows at me, I can feel the heat of his breath on my face.

'Fine,' I say.

'No, love.' My grandmother reaches a hand across the table.

'Oh please, here we go.' Grainne rolls her eyes.

'No, it's fine,' I affirm. 'I agree to his terms, I choose option two.'

'But Maeve love, you can't.' Nana's a lot softer now.

'I can Nana. The Clan are my family now, they will look after me.'

'Grand so, good luck to ya.' My grandfather lifts his arms before walking across the kitchen, towards the back door. But before he can make his customary dramatic exit, there's a knock from the other side.

'Who's that?' My grandmother looks around the table. No answer comes. 'Paudie are you expecting someone?'

'He has a right to be a part of this,' my grandfather says quietly as he reaches for the door.

I can feel Grainne tense next to me. Her sudden rise from her chair makes us all jump a little. 'Mam, he didn't?' She implores my grandmother's confused face for something.

The white PVC door opens to reveal his large imposing figure. He steps into the kitchen, our kitchen, into my world that he until now, has not existed in. My father.

Chapter 24

Mark Hennessy glances around the room, noting us but not looking long enough to class as a greeting.

'Thanks for coming.' My grandfather performs a pathetic little bow of his head to Ballycastle's most treasured and profitable son.

'Well I didn't have much choice did I, this is already all over the town.' His voice is strained, as if holding in anger. I've never seen him this close up, not long enough to really study him, to wonder what traits we share. None I hope.

Grainne stands still next to me like a rock or a tree, petrified, or maybe like some creature that plays dead until its predator has given up and left.

'Take a seat Mark.' Paudie pulls an extra chair towards the table.

'No, no it's alright Paudie, I'll stand, this won't take long.'

'How could you Daddy?' Grainne finally moves to face her father, standing next to mine, in solidarity.

'Now's not the time for all that Grainne, he's still the girl's father, he deserves to know what she's dragging us all into.'

'Deserves?' Grainne raises her voice and it makes my Nana recoil, her hands reach for her head. 'He's the one that deserves to be in prison, not Maeve.'

'You can't say things like that Grainne,' Grandad shouts. 'Mark could have you up for slander for the terrible things you've said about him over the years, but he's never done a thing about it because he's a good upstanding man in the community and it would serve you right to remember that.'

Grainne sits back down but it's like she has no choice, like her legs won't support her a second longer. She breathes deeply before speaking again. 'Mam, can you please make him leave?'

I watch my Nana look at her daughter and then to her husband. Declan and Aisling are still, willing themselves invisible no doubt, caught unwittingly in a Daly family vortex. 'I can't make him do anything Grainne, he's here now so let's get this over with.'

'Some things never fucking change, you didn't stand up for me then and you're not doing it now.'

'Grainne, can we not just be adult about this for once?' Mark Hennessy stands against our sink, his thick arms barely meeting across his broad chest, his hard belly hangs over this straining belt buckle.

'Adult?' Grainne snaps at him. 'Not exactly your thing now is it Mark?

'Stop that now.' My grandfather bangs his fist on the counter, rattling the cups drying on the draining board. 'Mark is here to help and if you only knew how lucky you are you'd shut that mouth of yours'

I look at him while my mother and grandfather argue but not once, not even a fleeting glance, does my father look at me.

'There is no circumstance under which I would want help from you or count myself lucky for ever having anything to do with you.'

'Look Grainne.' Mark raises a hand to steady her assault. 'I'm not here to dredge up the past, what happened happened, there was a pair of us in it.'

'I was a fucking child,' Grainne screams and only now does Declan reach for her, to offer comfort or protection. She rejects it, choosing to stand alone in this.

'Paudie, I'm not interested in being accused of this again, if that's the way you want it I'll just cancel our arrangement and leave it at that. The child is over 18 now anyway so really my obligation is over.'

'Ah now, hang on Mark, don't act on hysterics, you know how Grainne gets.'

'The child has a name,' Grainne hisses.

'Well as long as her name is not associated with my name, we've got no issue here.'

'So that's why you're here, afraid that Maeve's stunt will tarnish your grand empire of embalming fluid and chicken fillet rolls?'

'I have a family to think about, so yes, that's why I'm here. What do you think people would say if they put two and two together, it's already the worst kept secret in the town. I can't have this sort of insane carry on connected to the Hennessy name. I'd lose all the respect I have in this town.'

'You don't think picking up 15 year old schoolgirls for sex in the back of your car might do that?' Grainne says calmly.

'Ah to hell with this. I've tried to talk to her Paudie, I'm done, you're on your own from now on.'

'Hang on now Mark, we can work something out, just enough to get her through college.' My grandfather follows my father towards the door.

'What's he talking about Mam?' Grainne asks my grandmother, whose eyes are fixed to the table top.

'Mam?'

'I don't know Grainne.'

'You do fucking so.'

'I'm sorry, it was hard, we had to.' Maureen raises her hand in defeat.

'You didn't, please tell me you didn't.'

What the hell did they do? Whatever it is, this shitshow is certainly taking the heat off me. The ticking bomb will create just enough debris that I can escape amongst.

'When you left Maeve with us we needed help, Mark offered to help, we had no choice.'

My mother slumps back in her seat, cradling her head in her hands.

'Now look what you've done.' My grandfather bellows at her as Mark slams the door shut behind him. 'He won't give us another penny for her now.'

'You took his money – after what he did to me?' Her eyes are glazed when she lifts her head to her parents.

'You went to England, we needed to feed the child you left behind,' Paudie barks.

'I left because of him. Because I couldn't bear to be in the same place as him, when you two wouldn't help me stand up to him.'

'Well we reared your child didn't we, you didn't ask us how we were doing it.' Grandad leans on the table to face her.

'I was sending money back, if I had have known you went to him I would have come back for her.' She reaches her hand to mine and I let her hold it. 'I would have come back for you Maeve, I swear. I never wanted you do have anything to do with that man.'

'I think it's time I brought my wife home.' Declan finally takes a stand. 'Come on love.' He places a protective arm around her, guiding her away from her family.

'I'll be going too,' Aisling's voice croaks after being out of use for so long. I bet she's sorry she stuck her nose into my business, that will teach her.

'Grainne … hang on.' I follow her to the door and she stops, looking at me expectantly. 'Can I borrow your laptop later, I really need it for a college assignment.'

Her eyes cast down before she replies, steadily and without feeling. 'Sure, Declan will drop it over once the kids are in bed.'

'Great, thanks,' I say to her back. Now I just need to figure out how to get some cash for the bus fare out of here.

Chapter 25

The 16 inch TV in my room glows blue from the corner and I sit on the edge of my bed and await the news headlines. Breaking news of some train derailment in Cork, hundreds of people injured, at least two dead. Great, this is going to push out my story. The Clan won't get to see me on the 6 o'clock news. Why does shit like this always happen to me? Why can't I be lucky for once? A knock on the door pulls my attention away from the telly.

'Yeah?'

'It's me.'

'Come in.'

My grandmother opens the door tentatively, as if not confident of the reception she might receive. 'I have Grainne's laptop for you.'

I jump up to take it from her. 'Oh great thanks – passwords?'

'She put them on a sticky note inside.'

I place it on my desk and push the power button.

'Are you having any dinner?' she asks from the doorway.

I am starving. 'Well I would like to eat but not if it means having to listen to him rant and rave.' I enter Grainne's password. The kids' names. How original.

'I'll bring it up to you. Last thing I want is to referee the pair of you.'

'Ah thanks. I knew you'd understand and be on my side.' I turn around to flash an adoring granddaughter smile at Maureen but her face is stony.

'Get one thing straight Maeve, I neither understand nor support whatever is going on with you and those ... people. But

I'm your grandmother and I'm still going to feed you.' She closes the door behind her before I have the chance to respond.

Fair enough. I just hope she remembers I'm vegan now.

Oh sweet internet connection, like a river after a drought. What to check first ... YouTube. The Clan's official channel, most recent videos. It's still the one from our Belfast mission. That's weird. They mustn't have had time to edit my footage from to-day or maybe the camera phones weren't good enough quality or maybe the people who recorded me haven't shared them online yet. But there was the 1 o'clock news footage, they could have used that. I check their Facebook. Nothing. Instagram, Twitter, no new posts. They haven't seen it, that's the only explanation. I can't believe I've done this amazing thing that made the national news and my leader hasn't seen it. They must all be missing me by now, I'd be long home from college if I'd been there and I would have been texting them all throughout the day. My phone must be on fire at this stage. I log into my Gmail and await the flood of new emails from them. There are four new messages in bold. First one is a marketing email from the college social club. Delete. Next one is from a rainforest relief fund I signed up to sponsor. Delete. Then another marketing email leaving me with one last hope ... it's from Shane fucking Brennan.

You missed class again today Maeve and now you're ignoring my calls. Thanks a lot for fucking up this assign-ment for me. I've asked Richard to remove you from it and grade me on my own. College might just be an excuse for you to get to Dublin and take over the world or whatever but I actually want a career out of this so leave me out of your drama in future.

Well now, Mr. Brennan, look who just showed up to play. He's quite passionate in his contempt. I like that. I can work with that. I hit reply.

Shane, I am so sorry I let you down. You have no idea what

I've been through today, the truth is I'm in big trouble and I really need your help. Actually I think you're the only one who can help me.

Send. Just enough bait on the hook to reel him in. He won't be able to resist the bolstering of his ego. I open a fresh message to all the Clan members.

Guys I'm in Cavan, family kidnapped me following my epic Leinster House protest. I made the news. Please tell me you all saw it - you'll be so proud of me. I was covered in fake blood, naked and screaming. You've all probably been trying to call me but my phone is in the house and I'm stranded here in the sticks with just email, so contact me here and please come rescue me? Aide can you come? We could have some fun on the way back up.

Love you guys. Long live the revolution!

Before I even send I see a response in from Shane. He's so easy.

You'd better be in serious trouble Maeve. What is it?

He just can't help himself.

I don't know if you saw the news earlier but I was protesting at Leinster House and got arrested. My mother came to get me in the station and now they won't let me leave, they won't let me go back to Dublin, to college, they say I have to support myself and get a job here in Ballycastle. I'm hiding as I write this on my mam's laptop, which I had to take when no one was looking. I'm afraid my grandfather will catch me and I don't want to make him even angrier. He was so mad before but I know it's only because he loves me, he doesn't mean to hurt me. Oh Shane, can you help me?

Candy. Baby.

What do you need? Instant reply.

Thank you Shane. I knew I could rely on you. Can you lodge €50 in my bank account so I can get the bus back to

Dublin. If I can just get away from them I know I'll be okay. My bank details are attached.

I know my new family will come for me but just in case they don't get my email, I need a little insurance. I stare at the screen and bite the hanging skin at the edge of my fingernail. Come on Shane. You know you want to do it. Be the hero of the story.

Okay, it will be in your account tomorrow. Let me know when you get it. X

Yes. Thank you Mr. Brennan. That X though. He's letting me know there's a price tag on his coming to my rescue. I will be billed for this in the future and I know the preferred currency. This is going to cost me at least one blow job.

I refresh my email again. Nothing comes through. The Wifi must be slow. Shane's got through though. They must be all having dinner, that's it; no one checks their phones during family dinner. They will reply later. I eat my own meal, courtesy of Maureen, in front of the screen, sometimes imagining I see the print turn bold. When I return from the toilet it's the same, when I check the news at 9 o'clock – just in case – it's still the same. I get into bed, taking the laptop with me, placing it next to me so I can stop it from screen saving. I refresh it again. And again.

The cows wake me first at 5am, then soon after it's my grandfather shouting around the house. My grandmother attempts to quieten him.

'Take it handy Paudie, Maeve is asleep.'

'I don't give a shite what she is, let her get up and get out,' he bellows.

Oh don't worry, that's exactly what I intend to do. I just can't get my cash until the bank opens at 10am so no need to get up just yet. The laptop is boiling hot after being plugged in all night. I unplug and enter the password. I hit refresh. Two new emails. My heart jumps and sinks in quick succession. A job alert and a rental property in Crumlin. A sickening feeling percolates in my stomach. Are they upset with me? What have I done wrong? Have I disappointed the Clan, betrayed the mission? Why can't Aide email me at least, just to check I'm okay – I'm still his girl-friend aren't I. I don't care if he kissed Ferdia. I'd kiss Ferdia if she asked me to, we all would. It's not about sexual attraction, it's loyalty, reverence. Eimear's face appears in my mind. When she left none of us were permitted to contact her, Aide had told me that himself. Is this what's happening to me? Stop, you're being paranoid Maeve. You've done nothing wrong, not like Eimear did and I've no doubt that Hannah girl before her. I attempt to still my mind by distracting it with the live news stream online. Let the death and destruction happening around me remind me why I am doing all this in the first place.

I wait for my grandfather to finish his 9am cup of tea and return to the yard before I venture downstairs. I'm dressed and have my old school ID card in my pocket. They know me in the bank and will accept that.

'You're up.' My grandmother states the obvious.

'I'm just getting some breakfast and then I'll be gone,' I say while looking in the fridge for something edible.

'Gone where? Sure you've no money Maeve. Give it a few days and he'll calm down. He didn't mean for you to leave for good.' She puts instant coffee into two mugs.

'I'm not commuting to college Nana. I'm going back to live with the Clan. It's not up for discussion.' I settle for a banana.

'What'll you do for money? I don't know if Paudie will be able to fix things with Mark and I'm not sure we can manage without him.'

'It's okay, they will cover my rent for me.' She doesn't need to know that I've never actually paid any.

'Right well, sounds like you have it all figured out so.'

'Yep.' I take the hot black coffee from her hands.

'I know I can't stop you but I'll tell your grandfather that

I tried.'

'Why – he won't care.' I sip it.

'He will.'

'Nana – I don't suppose you have a €20 on you, just for a single ticket on the bus?' No harm having a little back up.

She rummages in her purse and digs out a fiver and loose coin. 'Six, seven, nine, fifty, seventy five. That's all I have, €9.75.'

I take it. 'Thanks.'

'Will you call me, let me know you're safe at least,' she says as I turn my back to her.

'Course I will. Bye Nana.' I pull the door shut with a bang and walk the gravel path to the main road.

It's not long before one of our neighbours, Tom Fitzpatrick, pulls up to offer me a lift. He asks questions along the way and I fill him full of shit. He drops me off at the bank and I'm first in line when they open. Shane comes through. I withdraw his cash and take it to the bus stop at the other end of the village. I'm the only one waiting and it always amazes me how more people aren't clambering to get out of here. I sit at the window when the bus arrives and imagine the conversations ahead of me in Donnybrook. It has to be a hero's return, it just has to be. The alternative is too unbearable.

Chapter 26

Home. I'm home. Where I belong. The sense of contentment I feel peaks when I turn my key in the lock of the heavy white door. But when it opens to present an empty hallway, it takes a slight decline. Okay, so no welcome party but how were they supposed to know when I'd be home? I walk the creaking stairs and when I pass Ferdia's room I can hear life inside. I continue to the next floor and push open my bedroom door, it's not shut, just ajar. My heart jumps a little when I step inside and see two bodies on the bed, my bed.

'Oh sorry.' I fight my natural instinct to excuse myself and leave. This is my room after all.

'Oh, hi Maeve.' Zamara turns her head towards me and smiles, or it is a smirk?

Next to her, Kaley sits propped up on pillows. Their legs are intertwined and even though both are fully clothed, there's an obvious sexual connection between them.

'What are you doing home?' Kaley asks, looking a little confused.

'What do you mean, I live here.' I'm reluctant to sit on the single bed, as if doing so is some sort of acceptance of my stature now.

'You said she left.' She turns to Zamara, who shrugs her shoulders in response.

'Did I? Oh you must have taken me up wrong.' She dismisses it with a rub of her thigh.

'So you're not gone?' Kaley looks at me.

'No, I was on a mission. Didn't you see it?'

Zamara whispers something into Kaley's ear and they both laugh. I stand there at the foot of the bed, unsure of my next move. They continue to whisper and giggle, their eyes fleeting to and from me.

'Is Ferdia home?' I'm going straight to the source, I've had enough of this, they're not important anyway.

'In her room.' Zamara states without looking at me.

'Fine.'

'Oh Maeve,' Kaley halts my exit.

'Yeah?'

'Shut the door after you.'

I do it and it's followed by a burst of laughter. I'm surprised at Zamara, I thought her activism was more important to her than sex, but turns out she's weak.

I knock on Ferdia's door and hear the slight shuffle of activity before she answers.

'Enter.'

She's sitting up in bed, the thin straps of her silk nightdress falling off her shoulders.

'Hi Ferdia.' I stand and await further instruction.

'Maeve. Come closer.'

At the edge of her bedside, she beckons me to sit.

'You look tired,' she says softly.

'I am Ferdia, I've been in battle.' I match her tone.

'You have?'

'Yes – didn't you see it?' How can they have missed it?

'Your battle Maeve? No I don't believe I did.'

'But it was on the news, I was arrested at Leinster House, I was covered in blood Ferdia. My mother came to get me and my grandparents tried to keep me captive. I emailed you all for help. None of you saw it?' My tone is altered now, no longer able to hide the emotion in my voice; it peppers it like rain hitting a tin roof.

'Oh that.' She gives a slight nod of comprehension.

As I try to process her underwhelmed response, my attention is pulled to my left, a sound coming from her bathroom. Before I have time to question it, he emerges, naked and smiling.

'Maeve, hi.' Aide's penis is right there, hanging flaccidly in my line of sight, I move my gaze upwards as he reaches down to kiss me, a friendly greeting on the lips.

I'm rigid, unable to determine the correct reaction to this. My naked boyfriend is in the bedroom of another woman, casually kissing me like it's the most natural thing in the world. I stop staring at him only to look at her. She's smiling at him, she adjusts her position in her bed and lifts her sheet to welcome him in. His long slender fingers take it from her and his pale, hard body slides in next to her. His face turns towards hers and they kiss, only not like the one we just shared. Her hand reaches down his chest and disappears under the sheet. He gives her audible indications of pleasure. I hadn't imagined it that night, it wasn't the drugs. They were having sex.

'What are you doing?' I finally find my words in my throat.

'Like today?' Aide replies.

'No not like fucking today – like right now – you're cheating on me?' I can feel the sting of tears forming but will them at bay.

'Cheating?' He laughs softly. 'No Maeve, we don't use words like that here.'

'Do you use words like asshole?'

'Sure we do, when we are talking about people who destroy the planet or perpetrate injustices or harm animals or each other, not for committing acts of love.'

'But you're harming me. You're hurting me.' A tear escapes and travels down my cheek. Ferdia reaches across his chest and grabs a tissue from her night stand. She presents it to me and I thank her. I thank her.

'That's your choice Maeve,' he continues. 'We all choose how we react to each situation. You are choosing to be upset right now. If you can accept that you can change it.'

'I can?' I want to change it, I don't like how this feels.

'Of course you can, you are in charge of your emotions. You can't control the actions of others and when we try to, we only hurt each other. You can see that can't you, people are not meant to belong to one another. They are meant only to love, to make each other feel good. Don't you want to feel good too Maeve?' His hand moves across the bed sheet and rests on my knee. His touch stills me and I want it. That much I know; my body wants him. It will never not want him. But under what terms am I currently negotiating? Is he asking me to join them, to have sex with him in front of Ferdia … with Ferdia? I can't think clearly.

'I need to get out of here.' I say almost to myself as I stand as best as my weakened legs will allow.

'Maeve, wait don't go, not in so much negativity, let's just meditate it out,' Aide says as I struggle to navigate my path to the exit. I notice he doesn't get out of bed to stop me though.

'Let her go,' Ferdia decrees. Her firm solemn directive sends a chill down my spine. It freezes me in my tracks.

'It's okay, she'll get there.' Aide reassures her, about what I'm not aware.

'No she won't – she's without.'

'She can do it.' His voice is so small in the space it shares with hers.

'She's not who we thought she was. She's a fake, a fraud, a little girl playing dress up, an activist without action.'

My face burns from the intensity of her fire but I keep my face to it anyway.

'How can you say that?' In my head I'm screaming but I know it does not translate with such force.

'Because it's the truth.' She holds her stare.

'I've done everything you've asked of me, I lay in the street for you, I vandalised a shop, I ran naked through a city, I brought a new member in for you, I even voted out my friend for you.'

'I did not ask you to do that,' she interrupts me. 'That was your own free will, as was everything else you did.'

'Why won't you talk about what happened yesterday? The only thing that actually was of my own free will.'

'What happened yesterday?' She pours infuriating fuel on me.

'My protest!' I shout, the ferocity of my outburst worries me for her reaction.

'Oh … that … your little stunt.'

'What …' I'm trembling and crying now. 'I did it for you, it's all for you.'

'It was amateur!' She shouts, louder than I did, it winds me. I gasp for air.

'Just leave Maeve, you're not ready.' She almost whispers now, the contrast making me doubt that she ever got that loud.

'Give her another chance Ferdia.' Aide rubs her back as she sits up in bed, cradling her knees.

'She'll never be ready, she's taking up a space in my house. We can't waste any more time.'

She wants me out of the house, out of the Clan, no, no this can't be happening.

'I'm sorry Ferdia, I'm sorry.' I rush to the bed and drop to my knees, my head bowed for her mercy.

'It's not your fault Maeve.' Her hand is on my head, her fingers brush through my hair, lovingly. I calm. 'You're just weak.'

'No, no please. I can be better, teach me how.' I lift my head in appeal to her. My eyes are clouded with tears but I can still see the compassion in hers. She is good. She is light.

'I had so much hope for you Maeve. I'm sorry for my error in judgement. Go home to your family, where you really belong.' She smiles so sweetly at me.

I wipe the tears from my eyes and swallow whatever is left of my petulance, my insolence, my misinformed, misdirected rage. 'I will prove it to you. Whatever it is you saw in me, I will be it. Just let me be it, please.'

She turns her head towards the window, the sunlight dapples on her face, she sighs and lifts her hands to cup her cheeks. She inhales deeply and then lets the air out in long, loud breaths. I look to Aide for an indication of what this might mean for my fate but his head is bowed and still.

'Okay Maeve,' she finally speaks, the relief escapes my body in a pitiful yelp.

'Thank you, thank you Ferdia. I won't let you down, I promise.'

'This is your final chance Maeve, one opportunity to truly prove to me that you're committed to our cause. I am planning a true act of martyrdom, a symbolic purge and primal scream into the void. I need to know that you're in, truly and fully in.'

'Yes Ferdia.' I hold her gaze and rest my hands on hers. 'I am in.'

Chapter 27

We eat our dinner behind a closed door. Sitting around the kitchen table, occasionally catching each other's eye between mouthfuls but never verbalising the questions in our stares. Four of us, the support crew, the roadies, the backing singers to whatever showstopper our headline act are planning in the front room. They locked the door. No one in this house ever locks a door, it goes against our ethos of equality and freedom. But when each of us tried to enter their sanctum, we were all turned away. Seb, Posey, Kaley and finally me. Although that was hardly a surprise after this morning in Ferdia's room, I should just be grateful I'm still here no matter what the conditions, even if it means I'm not in her trusted inner circle. At least I'm not alone on the periphery. I still have a family, my brother and sisters. We will be better, work harder, be more obedient. We will win her favour and trust again. Whatever it is she, Aide and Zamara are planning, we will obey.

'So how is work guys?' I look to Seb and then to Posey, desperate to mask the anxious atmosphere with some inconsequential conversation.

'Oh good, good,' Posey takes the bait. 'I managed to convince my manager to stop stocking plastic cups in the water cooler so you know, little wins.'

'Oh good, well done.' I give her accomplishment more enthusiasm than it warrants.

'And you Seb?' I pray for something more to work with.

'I suppose you could say it's good. I got a raise,' he says, dejected.

'You don't seem too pleased about it, capitalist guilt?' I tap his shoulder but he doesn't respond in jest, remaining sullen. 'You okay Seb?' I change the pressure of my hand from jostling to comforting.

'Oh just a bit sad I suppose. I had to finish things with Eoghan.'

'Oh no.' I make the requisite sounds of sympathy. 'What happened?'

'He wasn't right for us,' he says as Posey's hand reaches across the table to find his.

'What do you mean?' I've never really thought about it but are he and Posey a couple? One with certain rules of engagement obviously.

'You did the right thing Seb,' she consoles.

'Are you two a couple or what?' Kaley says what I'm afraid to.

Posey laughs. 'No silly, we don't mean us *us* – we mean all of us, the whole family. Isn't that right Seb.'

He nods his head. 'Eoghan wasn't right for the Clan.'

What does that mean? He wasn't an activist? Okay then don't ask him to join the group. Why does he have to dump him? I want to ask all these questions but I'm cautious I know I'm not in good standing right now. My ground is less than steady. Instead I look at Kaley and try to telepathically transfer my thoughts from my head to her mouth. She looks at me as if expecting me to do the same. After a moment of patience, she gives in.

'Just don't let him join then, why'd you have to dump him?'

'Kaley – it's not our place to ask these questions.' Posey reaches her other hand across the table to rest on Kaley. This time it's not comforting, it's cautionary.

'But sure he was his fella, why can't I ask him?' Kaley seems to be getting frustrated.

'Because we don't question Ferdia's decisions. You should understand that and accept it if you will be staying here.' Posey's smile attempts to neutralise her sternness.

'That's mental,' Kaley says under her breath and glances at me before returning her attention to her food.

There is still a part of me that agrees with her, that wants to speak up and out against the control unfairly wielded. But the greater part of me, the part I'm allowing to take control, commands my silence, my complicity. If Ferdia ordered it, it must have been for a good reason. She knows what's best for us. I will not doubt her. Not again. The silence is shattered by a loud knock on the front door, it travels down the hallway to disturb our collective discomfort.

'Should one of us get it?' I ask, unsure if we should even pass the front room.

'No, let one of them take care of whoever it is,' Seb says quietly.

We listen without making it obvious, none of us speaking. Seconds later Aide appears at our door.

'Maeve – someone is here to see you.'

Aide's narrow body moves to reveal the large mass making its way down the steps and through the threshold of the building's 1970s kitchen extension. The vision of them there, side by side, is jarring to me. They should never occupy the same space, like a Disney prince and a Pixar creature have stumbled upon some undiscovered animated realm together.

'Shane,' I say his name as if to cement his presence here is real and not a frightful figment of my imagination.

'Hi.' His deep voice lowers the base of the room.

'What are you doing here?' A little more realised to the situation now, I stand.

'I was worried about you, you weren't contacting me back … so here I am,' he says without embarrassment or apology, his confidence almost impressive.

'Aide,' Ferdia calls him from the front room, he turns to her voice.

'Maeve, if you and your friend can discuss whatever issues

you have quietly we would appreciate it. Ferdia doesn't need any further distractions today.' His voice is cold, his eyes … icy.

'No … no.' I usher the others to remain seated when they attempt to leave us. 'No need to get up, Shane and I will go.' I take hold of his lower arm and attempt to pivot his body in the direction of the exit.

Seb, Posey and Kaley sit back down, no one speaks. Shane, a slave to his pastoral upbringing bids them a good evening. They are the only words uttered as we make our way to the front door, my hand still firmly gripping his arm. I see her in the corner of my eye as we pass the living room, watching me. She waits until I deposit him on the preferred side of the door before she takes her gaze off me and shuts the living room door, resuming whatever it is that's going on inside.

'What's going on?' Shane asks as we walk down the footpath.

'Nothing … why?' I need to gather myself, I cannot display anger or frustration at his unbid visit. That is not beneficial to me right now.

'Inside, why are they all so sheepish?'

'Oh … they're just shy to outsiders, we don't get many visitors, especially unexpected ones.' I shut the gate and look back at the bay window of the living room. A curtain twitches, then settles back into place.

'Well I'm sorry about that but you left me no choice. I was really worried Maeve.' He places his big manly hands on my shoulders and roots me to the footpath. He must feel me tremble because he pulls me in close, steadying me in his arms.

'Come here, you're shaking.'

I allow him to think he's comforting me. There's currency in helplessness.

'It's just been so hard,' I mumble into his chest, my mouth pressed hard against him. He smells of cheap, chemically charged antiperspirant.

'I know,' he says reassuringly into my hair. 'You're okay now, can we go somewhere to talk?' He extends me on his arm's length and lowers his face to mine with a misplaced confidence that he is providing comfort, support, even stimulation to me. I nod.

'Yes, I'd like that, we can walk to Herbert Park?'

He places his arms around me and gives me a firm squeeze. 'Come on so, I'm all yours.'

I know that. All I have to figure out now is what to do with you.

He buys me a coffee at the van in the park and we sit on a bench, just like that first day in college. We take cautious sips and watch the ducks glide past for a moment before one of us ventures into a conversation. It's him.

'So are we going to talk about what you said in your email?' I can hear the trepidation in his voice.

'Which part?' I know exactly which part. Now I have to abort or commit.

'Come on Maeve, you practically accused your grandfather of you know … hitting you.' He looks at me over the rim of his coffee cup defence barrier. 'I mean, did I take it up wrong, am I being overly dramatic here?'

I let him think on that for a while, no harm in unsettling his confidence. I need more time. 'How did you find me anyway?' I ask as if the thought just occurred to me.

'What … the house you mean?'

'Yeah – did I ever tell you the address?'

'Ah please, I'm an aspiring investigative journalist remember? Hardly a challenge to find you in the suburbs.'

'Oh, that's interesting, tell me how you went about it?' He won't be able to resist reliving his process.

'Stop it.' He holds my gaze. 'You're not getting out of answering my question.'

Crap. Bloody investigative journalist is right.

'It's not that easy to talk about Shane.' Obligatory bashful downward glance to the ground.

'I know but you've started now.' His hand finds mine and gives it a reassuring squeeze. He's a fan of the squeeze. I can only assume that translates to his sexual performance, all force, no finesse. Not like Aide. I wish his elegant fingers were resting on mine at this moment, not these turgid sausages lying there, sweating on me. Suck it up Maeve. You might need him again.

'It's not so bad anymore, not since I got old enough to hit him back.' I surprise myself with how easy the lie drips from my mouth.

'Bastard,' Shane mutters. 'Go on.' Another squeeze.

'My grandfather just doesn't like women to have a voice of their own, thoughts and opinions you know that sort of man.'

'Oh I know them, I just thought they'd all died out by now.'

'Well Cavan must be a bit late catching up to the rest of the world.'

'So your involvement with the activists, that must have driven him mad altogether.' Shane compliments my story beautifully. He's a terrific audience, I don't give him enough credit for his usefulness.

'Exactly, getting arrested didn't go down very well in Paudie Daly's book so he let his right fist do the talking for him.' I turn my head away from him, both to hide any tell-tale signs of deception on my face and also to convey the pain of relived trauma.

'Tell me you're not going back there.'

'I don't plan to, no.'

'Good – and these people you live with, they're looking after you?' I can sense his distrust of them underlying his seemingly supportive questions.

'Honestly Shane, if it wasn't for them I'd probably be dead by now. They saved my life.' It would be great if I could cry now. I think of something sad; veal farming, fox hunting, great orca whales in captivity. Yes, this is good, I can feel it working.

'I can't say I agree with the stuff they make you do Maeve, that shit will get you in serious trouble one of these days, but I am glad that you have them looking out for you.' He opens out my hand and intertwines his thick fingers with mine. On cue, my tear falls.

'Now do you understand why they mean so much to me?'

'I do, a lot of it makes sense now, I'm sorry if I gave you a hard time about them. They might be crazy but their hearts are obviously in the right place. Don't get me wrong, I'm not exactly saying I want to come over and hang out with you all and discuss world domination one hemp plant at a time, but I get what you see in them now.'

'You do?' I'm interested to hear his journalistic assessment.

'Well yeah, if you've come from a home where you never felt secure and these people are offering you that; belonging, community, and unconditional acceptance: I get it.'

I almost buy his utopia. I wish it were true but I know my fraternity is not without caveat. I know there are conditions of my membership. And knowing that is the only reason I'm sitting here with him. He is my security deposit, my break glass in case of emergency. If I fail them, if this next mission exposes my ineptitudes and ends Ferdia's grace with me, I will need somewhere to go. Someone to go to.

'Thank you Shane.'

'For what?'

'For being there for me, for the money, which I'll pay back by the way.'

'Stop it, no you won't.'

'You're a good person Shane, I'm sorry for being such a mental case before, forgive me?' I shift my body towards his and hold his gaze with my nicely glazed over eyes.

'There's nothing to forgive Maeve. I just want to be here for you in whatever way you'll let me.'

Okay, there it is. I can take my chances on his platonic promises or I can secure his commitment with a physical, bonding contract. I close my eyes and go for it. Don't think too hard Maeve, it's just lips and a tongue. Imagine it's Aide, imagine it's his beautiful, inviting mouth.

Chapter 28

That moment between dream and reality, that second of infinite possibilities, is as achingly beautiful as it is painful. It's his mouth beckoning me back into the world. I close my eyes to it, wise to the tricks of my necrotic, cannibalistic brain. I'm shook, my body jolted into wakening and there it is again, his sweet, intoxicating mouth. It forms shapes of words and I concentrate whatever wits I have to understand them. When my eyes focus into his, they smile. Its real, he's real. He's come back to my bed. Kissing Shane had set off some cosmic Newton's Cradle, pushing him back on the right path, the path to me. I sit up in the single bed.

'Aide.' His name leaves my mouth and he presses a finger to my lips to stifle it.

'Come, Maeve, it's time.' His smile widens, the white of his eyes strikingly bright in the moonlit room.

'What, for what?' Still not fully awake I struggle to gauge what he wants from me. It's not what I want from him, that is becoming clearer.

Sounds from across the room draw my attention from him. A figure stands in the darkness, at the double bed, rising Kaley from it. The same softly hushed tones, it's Zamara leading her from her dreams.

'What time is it Aide, what's happening?' I allow him rouse me from the bed and start to shuffle into my clothes. I can hear Kaley doing the same.

'Is it tonight?' she asks Zamara as she slips into her runners.

'Yes,' Zamara confirms. She moves to the door, waiting in the golden light of the hallway for us to join her.

'Where are we going?' I ask Kaley quietly when they are out of earshot, maybe she is more favoured than me and has been trusted with the information.

'It's the mission, isn't it?' she says.

'But where though?'

'How should I know, you're the one that brought me here, you tell me.' She walks down the stairs in front of me, Zamara and Aide leading her.

They start to sing. A song I haven't heard before, a soft melody, like a lullaby. It reaches a crescendo when we pass Ferdia's door, her voice adding depth and strength. The lyrics are about flowers, trees, birds, life ... love. Seb and Posey are waiting at the bottom of the stairs, they are singing too. Everyone but Kaley and me. I don't want to be classed with her, she's my recruit, my inferior. I am a graduated, decorated disciple of Ferdia Cusack. I have earned my place. I start to hum loudly, trying to match their tune, occasionally catching a word in time. We sing our way out onto the street, the 2am winter night air cutting us like a thousand tiny knives. Everything glows gently in the street light, there are no sounds but our voices and our feet on the footpath. It's as if the whole world is still and we are the only true living feeling things. And I feel the cold, I want to ask if we should go back and get our coats but I don't cause a problem. We shuffle along until an artificial beep cuts through our song. The sound of a car unlocking. Ferdia opens the side door of the people carrier.

'Get in.'

I'm first in so I take the back seat, Aide gets in next to me, which makes me more favourable to this journey. In front Kaley is at the window, Zamara next to her in the middle and Seb pulls the door shut behind him. Posey takes the passenger seat next to Ferdia.

'Do you know where we're going?' I whisper to Aide as Ferdia starts the hybrid engine.

His hand moves to my thigh and travels down the crevice before resting between my legs. 'Just enjoy the ride Maeve.' He smiles and kisses me on my lips, softly, featherlike, teasingly.

'I'm just nervous, I want to do everything right. I know what tonight means to me, to my future here with you.' My concern lands on his ears only, the others preoccupied in song.

'All you will have to do Maeve is whatever Ferdia tells you. Then your destiny will be affirmed.'

'Is that what you did – just whatever Ferdia told you?' I still need to hear him say it, that she wanted him, that he had no choice, that if he could he would still be with me.

'Of course I did,' he says, his face fills with childlike simplicity.

'So what does that mean for us?'

'How do you mean?' His hand rubs my thigh, demonstrating his concern.

'Can we be together?' I know that I will take him in whatever form I can, a timeshare with Ferdia if that's all that's on offer.

His head dips to one side, he looks at me with uncomplicated clarity. 'Well that depends on Ferdia, whether she wills it or not.'

'Hey you two stop whispering back there and join the party.' Seb's huge hand reaches behind to smack Aide across the back of his bowed head.

The intrusion immediately pulls his focus from me and into their revelry. His voice rises in song and matches their intensity, instantly, like zero to sixty, the flick of a switch. I take short, shallow breaths to steady myself, make the transition from heartbroken, pathetic, weak female to something infinitely greater, more powerful, fortifying. Let her go Maeve, leave that parochial, emotional dependent girl behind. Become who you always knew you were, who they can see in you, someone bigger than just one person, an anarchist, a catalyst, a symbol. I open my mouth wide and scream, even higher than their voices in song. As I reach my climax, they join me, a chorus of primal praise.

'Yes!' Ferdia calls from the driver seat. 'Yes, my children, feel the power you possess and release it righteously.'

Posey turns the volume up on the radio, a heavy base thumps through the car, she turns to look at us.

'Are you all ready for the most important night of our lives?' she calls.

We affirm in unison, Kaley turning to look at me as she does so. I give her a subtle nod of confirmation that yes, this is good, we are good, what we are doing, whatever it is, will be the right thing. In Ferdia we trust. The car is filled with exalted voices as it travels away from city lights. Soon only our high beams illuminate the way ahead. We pass the odd motorist out at this time of the morning but mostly the roads are ours, maybe even the world is. I can tell we are steadily inclining, gaining higher ground.

'Are we driving into the mountains?' I say in a moment of rare silence.

'We are going wherever the earth is taking us Maeve.' Ferdia's voice is still in song.

'What will we be doing up there?' Kaley shifts in her seat to ask me.

'Ferdia will reveal the mission to us when the time is right.' I tow the party line with her. I am not risking my favour just to make her feel more comfortable. I fill the silence that follows with song, eager to drown out any further questions from my protégée.

Deeper and deeper into the darkness, the blanket of stars lays out before us and I feel like we could touch them, taste them, ingest what we are all made up of; stardust. The altitude dilutes any anxiety I had, my head is light and my fortitude resolved. I will do what she asks. The car comes to a stop. Nowhere, we are nowhere. The black night is outside, but nothing else, nothing but the watching, whistling trees.

'We have arrived,' Ferdia says after switching off the car. She takes a deep breath before turning around. 'Take nothing with you but courage.'

Doors open and people start to scurry out, feet squelch in the dampness of the mountain soil. Aide offers his hand to steady my exit.

'But won't we need our phones?' I ask him, concerned about the legacy of our mission. How will the world come to know of our animal liberation or hunters sabotage if we do not record it? I assume that is what we are doing here, in the Dublin mountains at 3am, to rescue wildlife, destroying man's attempts to trap them, to preserve life. Her face appears behind his shoulder, glowing in the moonlight.

'You won't need your phone tonight,' Ferdia smiles, her eyes like phosphorescent pools in the abyss.

'Come with me.' She extends her hand to me and I take it. She leads me away from the car and into the trees. She hums a gentle tune, I try to join in. The others follow behind us, twigs break underfoot. The clearing falls away until there is nothing but trees and sky. We walk further into the night.

Chapter 29

When I was four and Grainne was nineteen, she had brought me into Mullaghmeen Forest for a picnic. I remember holding her hand as she led our way through the overgrown grass and remnants of fallen trees. I had liked her then, loved her even. She was all the best parts of grown up and child; reliable and responsible yet knew how to build a pillow fort and play hand clapping games. I fell that day, off a massive oak that had fallen and settled at a 45 degree angle to the earth. I'd dangled from its furthest branch before making my inevitable descent to the waiting ground. The fear in Grainne's face was frightening to me, I'd not seen her look so vulnerable before, so like me. But then she took a box of plasters out of her backpack and stuck some on my grazed chest, legs and arms. My tears subsided even if the pain and shock took a little while longer. She was in control again, she knew what she was doing, I was safe. Now I know that was the day she stopped playing with me, she left after that. My grandmother would tell me stories of her exciting life in London until I forgot about her after a while. I was nine when I saw her again. She left her own childhood behind that day in the forest. I can see it so clearly now as Ferdia's hand guides me just like hers did. I feel the same assurance that everything will be okay, that my hand is in another of clear and steadfast resolution. Our feet come to a sudden stop.

'Here – we will begin here.' Ferdia turns to speak to all of us following her. 'Gather some dry wood and start a fire.'

In the surrounding darkness all I can see are the eyes and some of the clothing of my friends, only the pieces of them bright enough to reflect the moon.

'Yes Ferdia,' Aide responds and I edge closer to his voice.

'I will go with you,' I say, afraid to wander too far on my own into the woods. I notice Kaley and Zamara also team up as do Seb and Posey. Ferdia stays behind, our lighthouse in the harbour.

The forest floor is damp and we forage under trees for anything dry enough to burn. My body starts to tremble from the cold setting in. I must make audible signs of my discomfort and Aide holds out something to me.

'Here.' It's his black woollen hat.

'Oh thank you.' I take it and put it on. 'If I'd have known we'd be up here in the mountains I'd have brought my own.' I say as an apology and a condemnation for him not warning me of the details of this mission.

'You will not have to worry about the cold for much longer Maeve,' he says without emotion, as he stands rigidly before me, his arms full of firewood.

I nod my head in the darkness and carefully trace his footsteps back to the gathering site. It beckons us with the flicker of virgin flames as it struggles to take the oxygen out of the air whilst defeating the moisture. A burst of orange glow appears amongst the moss and twigs as we near it. Ferdia is already sitting in front of it.

'Leave them there with the rest,' she orders us and we dump our offerings on the pile of kindling under the tree.

'Maeve, Kaley,' Ferdia calls us without looking away from the flame. 'Sit across from me.'

Aide steps away from me, Zamara leaves Kaley. They both take their places either side of Ferdia. It's only now that I notice Zamara has been carrying a bag. Typical, she always gets special treatment, she probably has a blanket and food in there. Kaley's eyes are wide in the moonlight as she looks to me for guidance.

I do all that I know how to, I do as Ferdia asks. I sit cross legged directly across from her, the burgeoning fire glowing between us. Kaley sits down next to me, so close our knees touch. Seb sits at my other side, Posey at Kaley's. Our circle is complete.

'My children,' Ferdia speaks after a long silence. 'Have you been pleased with me?'

We look to each other, perhaps cautious to speak first. Her eyes open in expectation of a response so we give it.

'Yea Ferdia,' we say together.

'Have I ever led you into danger or away from righteousness?'

'No Ferdia.'

'You have all pleased me greatly, you have pleased the Earth. You have helped to stem the tide of deprivation and chaos. Your actions, your rebellion, have preserved life. You are the givers of life, the custodians of creation. Nothing you can ever do can be wrong. Even the greatest sin is justified if the sinner is just. And we are just.' She smiles broadly now, her face floods with warmth; both from within and from the campfire. It relaxes my slowly thawing body, everything is okay. This is a celebration, a thank you, a reward.

'I want you all to turn to the brother or sister to your left and thank them for their sacrifice to the earth. Reach out your hands and mouths to each other my children.' I extend my hand to find Kaley and we smile before kissing, a quick and unpassionate kiss on the lips. The action travels through the circle, Kaley kisses Posey, who kisses Zamara, Ferdia, Aide and to Seb before landing back to me. It's followed by giggles, nervous laughter on my part at least. Images of a campfire orgy pop into my head. I'm not so sure that's something I want to do. Is that what we are here for?

Ferdia raises a hand and everything stops. 'Even the darkness of night must give way to the light of the morning. We do not have time to waste. The mission is upon us, our wait is almost over.' She turns to give Zamara an unspoken instruction. The bag is brought forward, she opens it and removes a small camera and tripod, which she assembles and places in front of Ferdia, its lens aimed directly at me.

I look to the others, their eyes are fixed on the fire, all except Kaley. Her eyes are fixed on me, searching for answers I cannot give. Another item is taken from Zamara's bag, something wrapped in a scarf, a beautiful silk scarf of reds, purples and blues. She places it down reverently next to the tripod. A light shines on me, it's coming from the camera. My eyes adjust to it in the haze of the fire.

'Maeve, Kaley.' Ferdia takes the intricate scarf in her hands, its hidden contents rigid and not without weight. 'Do you accept your fate as our chosen ones?'

I can sense Kaley is trying to get my attention but I keep my focus on Ferdia, on the camera. It's our initiation, of course it is. I've made it to the real level of membership, the fur coat was just step one. I don't understand why Kaley is graduating at the same time as me but that's something I can point out later.

'Yes, Ferdia,' I say confidently. Kaley's succeeding voice is weak and unconvincing.

'And as our chosen ones do you accept this final and unwavering mission?'

'Yes, Ferdia.'

'Good.' She smiles as she carefully unwraps the silk scarf, revealing something that catches the light, reflective, shining, metal. They make sounds, clinking, grazing. The scarf falls to the soil leaving them to absorb the light, two large, pointed knives.

'What are they for?' Kaley seeks an answer from the circle but all eyes evade hers.

'We have waited a long time for the right person to join our family.' Ferdia speaks as she twists the knives through the flames, playing with them. 'So many have come close, Posey, you tried so hard with Hannah but she was weak, selfish. Seb, I know you cared for him but Eoghan was never going to be the one, he thought himself too important in this world. Zamara, my most trusted ally, you worked so hard to find a symbol – I do know that.' She reaches a hand out to pat her knee reassuringly. 'Aide, my beautiful, dutiful Aide, Eimear was perfect, you chose perfectly. Her failure was not yours.' She turns her head to him and kisses him before once again facing me. 'Perhaps it was only right that I should be the one to find her – our one true symbol of the resistance, Maeve.'

Instinctively I smile, a nervous, uncertain smile.

'And that she should then bring in her own martyr – well that is just a manifestation of the virtue and sanctity of our quest.'

'A martyr?' Kaley says loudly as her body shifts next to me. 'What the fuck - I know what that means – I'm no fucking martyr.'

'Silence!' Ferdia screams and it disturbs the sleeping birds above us.

I grab hold of Kaley's hand in an attempt to steady her, calm her.

'Just wait, hear her out,' I whisper to her. I know Ferdia, she talks in riddles, all will become clear soon. She doesn't want us to die, of course she doesn't mean that.

Ferdia stretches out her hand, each one wielding a knife. Zamara takes one, Aide the other. They in turn pass them to Posey and Seb. Their hands extend to Kaley and I.

'No fucking way, I'm not taking that,' Kaley shouts.

I take the knife from Seb's hand.

'Are you for real?' Kaley pushes against me. 'Are you seriously taking that?'

'All will become clear Kaley, trust in Ferdia,' I say to convince both of us.

'Trust in Ferdia me bollocks – what do you expect us to do with these?' She takes the knife from Posey and stands up, pointing it at Ferdia.

'I expect you to do what is right – to finally make something useful out of your pathetic, wasted existence.'

'This is a joke right – yiz are all taking the piss out of the new girl, right?' She tries to lighten the tension around the fire. 'Zamara, come on, you're messing right?'

Zamara's eyes rest on her for a while before she speaks.

'No, this is what you are here for – why do you think we have been looking after you?'

'So what, I have to cut myself just so I can have a place to sleep, is that is?' Kaley waves the knife as she speaks.

'No, no of course not.' Ferdia looks at her and smiles. 'You have to die, so any of us can have a place to sleep.'

Chapter 30

I wait for their laughter, for their breaking of this eerie, lingering silence, but all I can hear is the sound of a distant owl, the rustling of leaves, Kaley's breathing, a shallow gasping.

'You're all fucking crazy, I'm getting out of here.' She throws her knife into the fire. Posey jumps up to grab hold of her. I edge my body away from their scuffle. Ferdia, Aide, Zamara and Seb remain seated and still, their eyes fixed forward.

'Get off me you mad bitch.' Kaley kicks against Posey's hold, which seems stronger than I would have imagined. It's as if she's fuelled by the same force that has turned her eyes dark.

'Why are you fighting your destiny,' she shouts as she manages to drag Kaley to the ground. She holds her face down into the mud. 'You should be honoured to be chosen for this sacrifice that will save so many. How can you be so selfish?'

Kaley's face twists against the ground, she looks at me, her eyes are wet. 'Maeve,' she cries and I see the frightened little girl she is. 'Please, help me Maeve.'

I'm frozen, I do nothing but watch as a shrieking Posey sticks her hand into the smouldering edges of the fire. It makes fast probing motions into the charred firewood, searching for something. On the third attempt she screams in pain as she retrieves the blade, the red hot metal must be scorching her skin. How can she hold it, why is she holding it? It's only when Kaley screams merge with hers that I realise what's happening. She's pressing the molten metal against her neck, digging it in between her jaw and shoulder blade, branding her. Kaley's eyes shut tightly and I am relieved that they no longer look to me for help. I've never heard such screaming. It doesn't sound human. Until this moment I thought the worst sound I ever heard were the cries of calves snatched from their mothers by my grandfather. I didn't think people could make sounds like that. It is punctuated only by Posey's rising laughter and then one sharp, firm command from our leader.

'Enough!' Ferdia shouts.

Posey's head turns to her master's voice sharply. She throws the blade to one side and rolls off Kaley, who twitches where she lies.

'This is not what I wanted. This is not what we planned.'

'Sorry Ferdia.' Posey sits down, contrite.

'I thought you all understood, that you were all enlightened to our purpose. But you're just children, stupid, selfish, useless children.'

'Tell us what we should do,' Aide speaks but his head remains bowed.

'I'm sick of telling you all what to do, when will you start to think for yourselves? When will my work be done? I'm tired, I'm so tired of all of you.'

'Don't say that Ferdia.' Zamara leans closer to her. 'We only want to serve you, tell us what you want.'

'You know what I want, what the planet needs. I want a willing martyr for the cause, not a murder victim. Violence, murder – these are weaknesses of mankind. Sacrifice, the giving of oneself back to the earth, that is divine, the ultimate protest against the diseased world we were born in to. A message to the rest of the sleeping masses that we do not have to accept it, that we can stop the spinning, sinful world just for a second and simply, get off.'

We all watch her intensely as she speaks, all but Kaley, who takes the opportunity to crawl further away from the fire. I am the only one who notices her slow, painful retreat. I move my body slightly closer to Posey in an attempt to shield Ferdia's eyes from her. But my movement attracts Aide's attention, he looks up now and points through the smoke.

'Stop her, she can't leave.'

I remain still as Seb steps across me, Posey rushes to stand. Kaley screams as they grab her, dragging her to her feet and back to the circle.

'Should we tie her up?' Seb asks.

'I can cut her ankles to stop her from running away?' Posey stoops down to find the knife in the dirt.

Tears mix with mud on Kaley's face, her eyes are searching for something to save her, no longer for someone. She has lost whatever little faith she had in me. I am one of them as far as she is concerned. I finally belong to the Clan. I have made it.

'Stop,' I shout, startling myself with my volume. 'Stop, let her go ... I'll do it.'

Silence follows, peppered by crackling firewood and yielding cries.

'You will?' Aide looks at me with some kind of admiration or respect or wonder. I cannot be sure, all I know is that it's the way I have always wished he would look at me. I just never imagined this is what it would take to achieve it.

'Do not play games Maeve. I am too disappointed in you as it is.' Ferdia dismisses me again but I hold my nerve and repeat my offer.

'I will do it.'

'You will?'

'Yes.'

'You will die for us – for all of humanity?'

'Yes.'

'Willingly – explaining to everyone why you have chosen to make the ultimate sacrifice?'

'Yes.' I hear the word leave my mouth repeatedly as if it's coming from another source. I am not in my body anymore, I am just another watching bird, sitting safely in the tree above me. I cannot be harmed, I cannot truly die. My life, my legacy will live on. My time on this planet will have stood for something. I will have mattered. Is there really anything more I could achieve than this, even if I lived to be 100 years old? Martyrs are immortal. Time is an illusion and life only a blink of an eye, a flap of a wing. Die now or die later. Either way there is no other way out.

'Maeve.' Kaley sounds frightened, but she needn't be, not now.

'It's okay Kaley.' I smile at her. 'I want to.'

'Let her go,' Ferdia commands Seb and Posey and they release their grip.

'Maeve, come on, come with me,' she screams at me but I remain still, calm. I shake my head.

'You go, my place is here.'

'They're going to kill you!'

'Just go Kaley.' My face hardens and my voice rises as I look at her. I will her to run, just fucking run Kaley. She looks around one last time, as if searching for a way out for me, but there isn't one – just for her. So she takes it.

The sound of her feet running through the debris of the forest floor quiets us around the fire. We all take deep breaths, close our eyes, centre ourselves. A calmness sets in. In the peacefulness of the early morning, the camera whirs into action, the light shines on me.

'Let us begin.' Ferdia presses the record button and I look into the red light, travelling through the smoke to find its target.

'Wait, wait.' I hold my hands up in humble protest. 'What's going to happen … exactly?'

Ferdia stops recording and makes sounds of frustration. 'I knew you weren't the one.'

'It's not that,' I assure her. 'I'm just scared, that's all. I don't know how to do it so it doesn't hurt.' I've seen the movies and read the books, I know a slash vertically along the inner wrist is the most effective way to bleed out. I always told myself it would be the way I'd do it, leave a dramatic bloody corpse for my scorned loved ones to find, but one with minimal visible trauma. I'd just never imagined the pain before. I try to reason it against a paper cut or a split knee. Sometimes the smallest cuts are the most painful. Maybe these gapping wounds will only sting at first impact and then dull thanks to the adrenaline flooding through my veins, flushing out of my veins.

'Do you think death should be painless Maeve?' Ferdia asks. 'Do you think yourself so special that you should not suffer? It's the suffering that makes you special.'

I shake my head. I can feel my heart pounding, my mouth is dry and it quivers. I try not to let the tears betray my weakness, my selfishness.

'Well then, what other excuses do you have to resist your fate?' She nods to Seb who presents the knife to me reverently.

My trembling hand takes it. The closeness of the fire has warmed the blade. I press my finger into the tip, instantly drawing blood. A prelude to a cascade.

'Embrace the abyss Maeve,' Ferdia says sweetly to me. I smile at her, I feel her love, her energy. She believes in me, in my power to affect change; to leave the world a better place than when I entered it.

'I'm ready.' I close my eyes only to open them again to her lens, ready to immortalise my ascension.

'My name is Maeve Daly, daughter of Grainne Daly from Ballycastle, Cavan. Father known but undeclared. I hereby denounce that label of my birth and embrace my true identity as a child of the earth, a devotee of the Clan.' I take my eyes from the red light briefly to look at my family around me. They are all watching me, smiling, loving me. Aide loves me. Seb and Posey reach out their hands to rest them on my knees, reassuringly they guide me on.

'My life on this planet has only been for one purpose, to agitate the society that is slowing killing us, poisoning the air we breathe, the water we drink, salting our earth so nothing will ever grow to feed our children. My life, though short, now has meaning - my death. I will give up my future for yours, I will die so you may all live. Take this as your wake up call, your call to action, your last chance of redemption.' My words please them and therefore, me. I feel a peace come cover me as I lift the blade to my wrist. It shines in the fading embers of the fire. My hand shakes but I fight against it. Why is my body letting me down, portraying my fear. I am better than that, my mind is stronger. I take a long deep breath and press the edge of the knife into my skin. My eyes narrow to avoid a bright invasion of light, a reflection from the metal shining directly into my face. It is not the fire, it is artificial light. It's coming from the trees, floating through the night. It comes for me, followed by feet, screams.

'Stop,' someone shouts. 'Stop her.' Kaley appears in the spotlight of her companion's torch.

Chapter 31

There's something else in his hands, hanging from his hooked elbow. It's large even in his broad silhouette. Kaley reaches for the torch, shining it at each of us. The man next to her lifts the other object, it makes a loud clicking noise and extends its full length in our direction. It's a shotgun.

'It's her.' Kaley lights up Ferdia's unmoved face in bright blue light. 'She's the crazy bitch who's trying to kill us.'

The blade hovers in my hold, like I'm stuck in freeze frame. I stay still as the others rise to their feet, in defence of her. They rush to her attacker. He steadies his stance in the earth.

'Stay back, get the hell back or I'll shoot every one of ye,' he speaks, an aged, worn voice. In a better light, he could be my grandfather.

Posey drops to scramble in the dirt, finding a stone to hurl at him. It impacts his shoulder and he flinches, the gun shifts its focus to me. I remain where I am.

'And who might you be?' Ferdia asks calmly, as if he's someone who has called around for tea. Her voice attracts the barrel of the gun. Aide, Zamara, Seb and Posey form a human shield between it and Ferdia. They are on springs, just ready to pounce when the moment requires it.

'This girl says you tried to kill her.'

'And how does that answer my question?' Ferdia looks him up and down. 'You are a farmer? No, a hunter perhaps?'

The man shifts in his heavy wellington boots. 'What business is that of yours?'

'What business is that of mine?' Ferdia laughs. 'You are the one pointing a gun at me, surely I am the one in the rightful position to ask what business it is of yours what we are doing here.'

'I've called the Guards; they'll be on their way, any minute now.' The man doesn't seem as assured as a man with a weapon should be.

'Let them come. We have nothing to hide.' She turns her focus back across the dying fire, just the two of us around it now, 'Maeve, the world is ready whenever you are.' She switches the camera back on and gives me a gentle nod of permission. I unfreeze and continue on my mission. The knife pierces my skin and I wince.

'Stop her, she's making her do it.' Kaley grabs hold of the man, pushing him closer to Ferdia. They perform a dance that neither of them are leading. The others move closer, their feet joining in the steps, all of them are dancing now. Their bodies create the music, their voices mix together and I cannot tell who is screaming, shouting, calling for help. I can only hear her clearly. She turns the camera away from me and finds them. Her face floods with excitement.

'Oh yes, this is even better,' She says to everyone and no one. 'Go on, kill us, shoot us with your big shotgun, give the animals you stalk and slaughter the night off and graduate to humans, become the murderous creature you truly are.'

'Get off the gun!' the man shouts as he hits Zamara with it, she falls with a thud. I think she's unconscious. The others step over her to wrestle for control. Ferdia watches, smiling. Kaley bites Posey's neck, they are no longer dancing, they're trying to kill each other. Are we all meant to die here? Do I carry on cutting, my small wound trickles but it will never be enough to drain the life out of me.

The birds hear it before we do. A thunderous rumbling of the trees and sky. They flee from its source, from the barrel of the gun. They seek refuge in the covering darkness, but it's too late for me. I don't have time to move away from its trajectory. Their eyes are on me, all shocked to stillness, confirming what I already instantly knew. I've been shot. My stomach is open. My hands clasp the hole in my body. I can see them, Ferdia is laughing, her camera records me. Aide is pacing, speaking in panicked tones, pulling at his hair. I can't make out what he's saying. They spin and blur in and out of focus. I'm dying, am I dying? Am I speaking? I think I am, I think I'm asking for help but I can't be sure. I must be because Kaley comes to me. Her face fills my vision, she smiles and her lips move. I know she's speaking and it comforts me. The man who shot me stands behind her. He looks so white, like he is the one who is dying. I don't see anyone else around me, but I can hear them, screaming, shouting, fighting amongst each other, with Ferdia maybe. Someone tells her to get up, to go, but she won't. She stays there, across the smoke, smiling, watching me bleed.

Blood is warmer than I realised. I suppose I've never really given it that much thought before. But now, it is all I can think of as it gushes through my clasped hands, oozing like lava from the source of intense, unfathomable heat. Its warmth contrasts the bitter damp air that's circling around us and through the watching trees and it is almost pleasant. Somewhere back there, in my rational mind, I know that's not the response I should be having to this situation. I know I should be screaming, calling for help, fighting to save the life I've been complicit in taking. It is so dark up here on the mountain, the blanket of city lights are too far away from our site to offer any assistance in illumination. Our fire is dying. I know that the ashes are grey, the soil is brown and the blood is red. But colour does not exist without the light to see it. They all mix together at my feet, creating a new substance, a new reality. Maybe this is how it was all supposed to end. Maybe this is my silent, irrevocable revolution. Yes. Because what are words without actions? What is light without shade? What is life without death?

Chapter 32

'Why are you here Maeve?' Her voice echoes in the windowless, grey room.

I look at my mother sitting next to me, hoping she'll speak for me, just like she did the last time we tried this. But Grainne fixes her stare at the heavy door behind Detective Neary's head, its glossy brown hair falling behind her shoulder as she sits back to await my response.

'To answer your questions.' I give her the obvious reply.

'Honestly?' She folds her arms across her white shirt.

'Yes. I told you everything I remember.' The Gardaí at my hospital bed pushing me; tell us what happened, who shot you, who helped you, who stemmed your wound and stopped you from bleeding to death? Why Maeve, why did you almost die? Why did you not die?

'She's already been through this over and over again.' Grainne cannot stay silent for long, usually a negative trait of hers but today I'm glad of it. 'She was having some sort of dawn celebration ceremony with those ... people, when that mad man startled them and just starting waving his gun around – isn't that right Maeve?' She places a steading hand on my knee.

'Yes, that's what happened. He tried to kill us. My friends stopped him.' I remember that night, how Ferdia revelled in the idea of our attack at the hands of a murderous hunter. I know this is the story she wants me to tell, even if she has not come to tell me herself.

'Mmm.' Detective Neary sits forward. 'Mr. Oliver Hodgers is claiming accidental discharge of his weapon.'

'Well he would say that wouldn't he,' Grainne snaps.

'The only thing that puzzles me Maeve,' she looks to the ceiling before fixing her hardened stare on me, 'is that Mr Hodgers is also claiming that during the assault on him that lead to the accidental discharge of his weapon, your friends …' She looks down at her notes. 'Aiden Dunleavy, Przemysława Sajdak and Sebastian Gutierrez aimed the gun directly at you. Why would they do that?'

They wouldn't. She's lying. Trying to come between us. I say nothing. Grainne does though.

'Of course he's going to try shift the blame for what he did to my daughter, an innocent 18 year old girl who will probably need a colostomy bag by the time she's 30, thanks to his carelessness.'

Neary ignores her. 'We know a bit about guns, being in the Garda Síochána.' She smiles at me and I don't know whether to be assured or unnerved by it. 'Of course, we don't carry them as Gardaí, but we still have to train in ballistics, handling, marksmanship. And then when you get to rise up the ranks …' she fingers her lanyard smugly, 'you get to carry one, along with the responsibility that comes with being in control of an object that can so easily take someone's life.'

'I really don't see what this has to do with anything.' Grainne is silenced by a sideways glance from Neary. She continues.

'Mr Hodgers is a licenced culler, do you know what that means Maeve?'

I shake my head, suddenly very aware of the rising pain in my side. I've spent too long sitting in this hard back chair, it's been too long since my last pain medication. I feel weak, like I could faint, why won't she stop talking, why won't she just let me sleep.

'He's licenced by the state to kill wild deer, to keep the numbers down so the population doesn't overwhelm the natural habitat of the mountains.'

'So he's a legal murderer, am I supposed to be impressed?' I say to her grinning face.

'Maeve,' Grainne loudly whispers a caution.

'Well yes Maeve, you're exactly right. He's a killer, he can stop a wild deer in her tracks from 300 yards. So what I just can't get my head around is how you're not dead.'

'Because my friends stopped him, they saved my life.'

'Very noble of them.' Neary smiles and I confirm my suspicions that she is in fact a massive cunt.

'And have you heard from them, have they been to visit you since your discharge from intensive care, these friends of yours?'

'Kaley has,' Grainne told me she came by the hospital but I didn't want to see her.

'Oh we know Kaley has, Kaley has been most cooperative with our investigation.'

'I'm alive aren't I, I don't see why you can't just leave us alone. I'll change my statement to say it was an accident if that's what it will take. Why do you need to investigate something I don't want to press charges on?'

'Oh no, not your shooting Maeve, we are writing that up as an accident. Mr Hodgers will be fined and cautioned and lose his gun licence.'

My mind is cloudy anyway, groggy after weeks in and out of consciousness, confined to a hospital bed, detached from reality. I cannot trust my confusion. 'What do you mean then?'

Her face looms closer to mine across the table, the grin widening as she speaks. 'The investigation into Ferdia Cusack.'

'Why are you here Maeve?' Her warm voice is absorbed by the surrounding wood panelling and soft leather chairs.

I look around the room of framed degree walls and hard backed book shelves. Possibility and opportunity seeps out of everything. 'To make a difference,' I say to her open, optimistic face.

'Well you are certainly in the right place.' Professor Coffey slides the weighty course prospectus across the solid mahogany desk. I lean forward to finger the first few pages of Activism and Public Policy at The National University of Ireland, Galway.

'We were very impressed with your previous experience in protest organisation and demonstrations.' Prof. Coffey pushes an errand strand of chestnut brown hair behind her ear, adjusting her black rimmed glasses as she does so.

'Thank you, I have always been very passionate about social justice and climate change. I believe it's our duty to stand up and shout, even if no one listens, for however long it takes.'

'Rage against the machine.' She smiles a kindred smile.

'Or the dying of the light.' I assume quoting Dylan Thomas will impress her. It worked on me when Aide did it.

'We are very excited to see what great things you can achieve with the right guidance and education behind you Maeve. Tell me more about the group you were part of, the Clan, what was it like?' She slides her laptop to one side, giving me her full attention.

'It was … reformative.'

'And the leader, Ferdia Cusack, tell me about her.'

The sound of her name, the pull of her. She floods my brain and I'm back in that room, six months ago.

My face must betray something I cannot control. It makes Neary happy and I hate it. You will not make me doubt her, forsake her. I am smarter than that. I know all the tricks you people play.

'Aren't you curious?' Neary narrows her eyes at my apparent indifference.

'There is nothing you can do to destroy Ferdia. She is not like the rest of us.'

I can feel Grainne's eyes on me as I speak.

'Well whatever she is, she's facing accusations of attempted murder, gross bodily harm and violent disorder under the

Criminal Justice Public Order Act,' Neary states.

'That's impossible – she did nothing wrong, you have nothing on her.'

'We have the sworn statement of Kaley McCann, who affirms that Przemysława aka Posey Sajdak assaulted her with a hot knife at the instruction of Ferdia Cusack, that the same Ferdia Cusack instructed you to in fact, take your own life for and I quote "the cause".'

'What?' Grainne's voice is small in the cavernous room. 'Maeve, that's not true?'

I keep my eyes on Neary. I keep my resolve. 'Whatever I did, I did with my own free will. Ferdia Cusack did not make me do anything I didn't want to do.'

'So you wanted to die – out there that night? It didn't matter if it was at your own hand or the bullet from Mr Hodgers' gun?'

'I wanted to make the ultimate sacrifice for the greater good, for my family.'

'No, no Maeve – we would never want that, we would never want you to harm yourself.' Grainne grabs hold of my arm.

I turn my head to her sharply. 'Not you people, my real family – the Clan. They love me, they get me. I could never expect you to understand what we were trying to achieve out there.' My disdain travels across the table to Neary.

'"Maeve Daly is just a small town, unworldly girl who thought she was an activist",' Neary reads from her open folder. '"She came to my house at Belmont Crescent, Donnybrook on a number of occasions in the company of my housemate Aiden Dunleavy – who was casually fucking her".' She looks up at me. 'Shall I go on?'

'You're making this up, Ferdia would never say that about me. I'm her chosen one.'

'"Maeve Daly invited herself along to our dawn worshiping ceremony. She became increasingly unhinged as the night went on, her erratic behaviour resulting in the threatening of Mr Hodgers and his subsequent self-defence discharge of his weapon. My housemates attempted to avert his gun and save Ms Daly. My housemate Zamara Bangura was knocked unconscious in defence of Ms Daly, she suffered a mild concussion. As I tended to her, I noted that Kaley McCann and Mr Hodgers were nursing Ms Daly's wound until emergency services arrived at approximately 5.05 on the morning of 12th November. I swear this is my true and full account of events. Signed Ferdia Cusack".' When she looks up at me I wonder if she can see the tears forming in my eyes. I hate that she can see my weakness.

'Do you have anything to add to your statement Maeve?' Neary flips over the folder and takes out a piece of paper from a plastic sleeve. She slides it across to me and I recognise my handwriting.

'What does she need to say to make all of this just go away?' Grainne stiffens in her seat. 'We just want this whole sorry mess to be over with and for Maeve to get on with her life.'

'She needs to tell the truth.' Neary hands me a pen.

'I did. I have nothing else to add.'

'So Ms McCann is lying?'

I shrug my shoulders. 'If you say so.'

'You do realise that you're not special to her Maeve, she will go on to the next lost misguided kid. There are thousands more like you out there, just waiting for her poison to fill them up.'

'I think we need a solicitor if you are going to continue questioning my daughter in this manner.' Grainne asserts herself. Neary keeps her gaze on me.

'If you don't stop her, she'll keep going until she gets what she wants, until she gets her martyr. Is that what you want?'

I push my statement back across the table and lay my hands on my knees. 'I have nothing to say about Ferdia Cusack.'

'I have nothing to say about Ferdia Cusack.'

Prof. Coffey's face adjusts to my unexpected response. 'Oh I'm sorry, I didn't mean to pry.'

'No, not at all, it's not that.' I attempt to soften my words with a smile. 'It's just that I don't believe that any one person could or should become the focus of an act of activism. You understand what I mean?'

Whether she does or not, she appears to. 'Of course and you are right. One of us cannot achieve real change alone, it takes an army.'

'My thoughts exactly Professor Coffey. Which is why I hope to meet lots of fellow activists here in Galway.'

'Fantastic Maeve – well whatever you need, just ask. I can start by emailing you some links to all the groups currently active on campus and who knows, maybe in time you might even start your own.' She rises from her chair and I follow.

'Yes, maybe.' Can she see the real me?

'Welcome to NUIG,' she says as she opens the door for me. 'I think it will be a very, what's the word you used … reformative … experience for you.'

'So do I.' I shake her hand before the heavy door closes between us.

'Interview terminated at 16.46pm. Detective Clare Neary exiting the room.' She presses the button on the machine and pushes her chair away from the desk. 'Off the record and as a mother,' she addresses Grainne. 'I'd suggest you get Maeve into psychiatric treatment unless you want to be back here in this room or worse still, coming in to identify her.' She leaves the room echoing from the weight of her words.

Grainne cries into her hands, I can feel her body pulsate as it attempts to control the release of her emotions. 'Tell me what to do Maeve. Tell me how to be your mother.'

'I don't know,' I answer.

'Will you at least try to figure it out because I can't do this, I can't live with the thought of you hating me that much that you would kill yourself just to hurt me.'

'Oh my God Grainne,' I shout as I turn my body to face her. 'It wasn't about you, I didn't think about you for one second, it was about her, it was all about her. It was about love, not hate.' My tears rush to the surface as the force of my repressed truths hit my mother.

'Maeve.' Grainne attempts to reach for me but I avoid her touch. 'The only reason you loved this Ferdia woman to the point of ending up in here, is because you can't love me. I'm sorry, I'm so sorry that you can't. I know it's my fault but I love you Maeve, whether you're ready to believe it or not.'

I turn my face away from her, instantly repelled by her declaration of love. Too little too late.

'I know I've fucked this up for a long time and I've made a lot of mistakes. What happened to me, having you the way I did, it messed me up a lot, he messed me up. Maeve look at me.' She grabs my shoulders forcefully until I concede and turn towards her. 'I'm your mother, I'm not going anywhere, ever. I'm getting you the help you need, okay. You're a good person Maeve, you have so much good in you.' She pulls me to her and I allow her to hold me. My stiff body begins to unfold onto her, I can feel the rigid steel of my resolve bend. For the first time in my life, I let my mother comfort me.

Chapter 33

When I dream about my new life, I do it in technicolour. Seamless, swirling mutations of the endless possibilities of my potential. Some nights red is the dominant colour, thick and deep and flowing unbounded, equally frightening and freeing in its uncertainty. Other nights it's blue, a calming sea that hugs me as I float to the next island that will sustain me, nurture and nourish me. But sometimes I don't make it to the island, sometimes I drown and wake to the fearful darkness, gasping for breath. It's in those moments, those jarring first seconds of reality, that I long for a purple dream. I want to reach my hand into my brain and mix it all up like paint until there is no red or blue, only purple, only the result of their combination. I can live in this purple kingdom.

It climbs up the walls here. Fibrous tentacles clinging to the stone for survival. I am enveloped in the slowly reddening September leaves of the ivy surrounding me on all four sides of the University's Quadrangle. I am awake here, I can breathe. I feel like the past six months have been some kind of suspended reality, like I was being kept alive in a hyperbaric chamber, my mind switched off so it could give my body a chance to catch up. It healed as best it could, Grainne brought me to the best doctors she could find, for both my external and internal injuries. I could never quite understand what she and the psychiatrist were on about but I let them talk, to make sense of it all, to try to fix it. Fix me. I gave her what she needed and in fairness, she tried to give me what I needed too. But no matter how hard I tried to go back, to rewind and restart, I couldn't shake the feeling that it was just too late. I get it now, I saw with my own eyes how my mother was wronged, by my asshole of a father, by hers. My therapist, Aine, spent session after session guiding me to this conclusion and I get it. But realising that she was also a victim doesn't make me any less of one either. But she's trying and I'm trying and I promised her I'd call the moment I left the meeting with the Course Director.

'Hi Mam.' I call her that sometimes, when I feel like being nice.

'Well, how did it go.' I can hear the anxiety in her voice, letting me move across the country took months of convincing.

'Really good, I think I'm going to like it here, Professor Coffey seems lovely and the campus is amazing.'

'And how was your first night in the flat, don't worry if you don't like it, I only signed a six month lease so we can move you whenever you want, no problem. I don't want you staying anywhere you're not happy.'

Grainne and I had agreed that my own space might be the best idea this time around. 'No, it's grand, honestly. Smaller than it looked in the pictures but it's quiet and the area seems safe enough.' I give her the assurance she needs to allow me to get properly settled in.

'Okay, well you know, just to say the word. Declan and the boys say hi.'

I can hear them in the background. 'Yeah tell the boys I'll see them in a couple of weeks, and Nana too if you're speaking to her.'

A second of silence. 'Yeah, yeah, will do.'

I had been the link between the two houses during my stay with Grainne. She's still not completely ready to be just Paudie and Maureen's daughter again. I don't judge for her it, how can I?

'What are you doing now love?' She changes the subject.

'Oh just walking into town, there's something I need to do in there.'

'I'll let you go so. Well done today Maeve, I'm really proud of you, you've been through a lot and well, well it just needs to be said that's all.' Her voices falters and I don't force her to go on.

'Thanks Mam, I'll call you tomorrow.' I hang up and see on my screen that he's replied to the message I sent him last night.

Hi Maeve, it's really good to hear from you. I'm glad things are going well. Crazy how you've ended up in Galway, yeah absolutely I'd be up for a catch up when I'm home.

I stop at the Cathedral gates to compose my reply.

I'll look forward to it. Winky face emoji. I never got the chance to thank you for everything you did for me and to say sorry for what I did. I just want a fresh start here, you know what I mean?

He replies instantly. Some things in this life are consistent. Shane Brennan being one of them.

I do Maeve. Sure, chat soon. Thumbs up emoji

That's a little distant for him, but it's naïve to expect a fawning string of love hearts just yet. I know he's just trying to exert his pride and I'll give him the space to believe it's working. He'll be there when I need him, whenever that might be. It will be nothing like what I had with Aide, but Shane's affection will be useful. Truth is I kind of like the idea of being the addiction rather than the addict.

The afternoon sun reflects on the River Corrib, blinding me as I cross Salmon Weir bridge. I put my sunglasses on and take a baseball cap out of my backpack. I bought it yesterday from a high street chain. It cost €3. I wondered how many gallons of water it had taken to produce it, how many underpaid fingers had stitched it. I wondered these things but I still bought it because I needed it. I put it on, pulling my hair out through the back and follow the footfall towards Eyre Square.

The smell of freshly ground coffee lures me into a chained coffee shop and I order a flat white. They don't ask me what kind of milk I want, so I let them assume it's cow's. There's no one behind me in the queue to hear me ask for another kind anyway. The rich creaminess coats my mouth and travels a warm silky trail down my throat. The hit of caffeine quickens my pace to the Square. People have already gathered and I place myself behind them. I don't want to be seen today. I am happier, safer here on the periphery. Even if I want to move, I'm not sure my body is capable of it, not now, not that she is close. I can sense her even before it starts, the alluring, commanding sound of her voice.

'You are all looking at me.' The familiar mantra fills the air. 'Because I am the one up here on a wooden box, holding a microphone. Did you all just come here to look up?'

I watch the crowd as she speaks, their faces slowly changing from expressions of suspicion to recognition and ultimately, admiration. That is the power she harnesses, it takes all the strength I have not to join them in their responses, in their adulation. My fear still overpowers my courage. But I will be stronger, one day. I have to be. It's my destiny. I don't see any of them with her, not even Zamara. Surely she hasn't left her master's side. Maybe Ferdia has banished them all, maybe she's starting with a clean slate too, the names and faces of her followers too criminally connected to her after that night in the mountains. But not even the bullet could save me from her, I would never have willingly walked away. But I'm different to the others, I know that now. I had saved Eimear that night, maybe being betrayed by me was the ice water that shocked her awake. She was never going to be the chosen one, she was stupid and weak and I did her a favour. I could never see what Aide saw in her. I knew soon after I'd bought that cheap mass produced lingerie set, from the very high street brand we had just protested, that I could not use it to seduce him. He wouldn't have touched me in it. I thought under Eimear's bed was the safest hiding place for it until I could sneak it out of the house. I didn't expect Ferdia to find it but she was already looking for something to hang her on after her fuck up in Belfast. It just happened to be my knickers and bra set in the end.

'People will try to tell you that you can't make a difference …' Ferdia approaches the rising crescendo of her performance. I study her crowd, their complicit captivation. 'That one person can't possibly make a difference. And do you know what I tell them?'

She awaits their awed silence. My mouth prepares to form the words I know are coming. Together we give her audience their much anticipated climax.

'Maybe you haven't met my friends'

The resulting chants rise with each repetition, 'WE ARE YOUR FRIENDS'.

I watch the familiar flush of joy on her face, safe from my distance.

I am a camera with its shutter open, quite passive, recording not thinking.

Someday all this will have to be developed, carefully printed, fixed.

My time will come to lead, when they will all see me for who I truly am, the chosen one. I know I'm not ready, I need to learn how to harness her power and not be overwhelmed by it again. Revolutions don't happen overnight and leaders are slowly created like a faultless pearl formed in the grit and abrasion of sand.

From now on, I'm going to be the change I want to see in the world.

Acknowledgements

There have been a lot of people who have helped me since I first took a notion in the Ilac Centre library in 2011 to write a book. The first person was my new housemate Deborah, who, probably because she didn't yet know how easily influenced I am, simply said, 'why don't you then?' So I did. And I've been doing so ever since. Deb, thanks for being there from day one. Your friendship means the world to me.

That first book brought the amazing Vanessa Fox O'Loughlin into my life. If you pick up a copy of an Irish authoured book, you're highly likely to find her name in the acknowledgements; she is quite simply the life force of the community. Also known as the bestselling crime writer Sam Blake, Vanessa has coached, critiqued, comforted and supported me through the past decade and a thank you just doesn't suffice. But here it is anyway, thank you Vanessa, for everything.

Having the support of another writer, that is in the place you aspire to be, is priceless. So thank you Noelle Harrison for being that shining beacon for me. I always felt I could ask your advice and be met with grace, kindness and understanding. Your spirit is as beautiful as your books.

Writing without readers is as satisfying as a one hand clap. We need them to hear and feel our own thoughts. Throughout my previous books, these first readers have given their time, enthusiasm and valued input into my work. Thank you Rosie Curran, Sarah Foley, Hanna Spencer and Paul Forde. For *The Good Activist*, thank you to Gill Billane for staying back late with me after work, for reading each iteration hot off the printer, for your palpable love of books and storytelling. Readers like you are enough to keep any writer going through the fog of self-doubt.

To Aoife and Adrian Grant of Merdog Books, thank you for believing in this story. I knew from our first Zoom meeting that you were the right publishers to entrust *The Good Activist* to. I will be forever grateful for your faith, guidance and commitment to independent Irish publishing.

And lastly thank you to my parents. To my mother Paula, for being a living breathing book character who inspired me to explore and navigate that world existing inside my head. To my father Tommy, for being the grounding rock to which all our dreams were moored.

merdogbooks.com